THE VIRGIN SERIES

By

KATE RICHARDS

Featuring...

The Virgin and the Playboy
The Virgin and the Best Man
Virgin Under Ground
Two Men and a Virgin
Two Men

ಆ

Decadent Publishing Company
www.decadentpublishing.com

This book is a work of fiction. Names, characters, places, and incidents are the products of the author's imagination or used fictitiously. Any resemblance to actual events, locales or persons, living or dead, is entirely coincidental.

Published by Decadent Publishing Company
Look for us online at:
www.decadentpublishing.com

Printed in the United States of America

THE VIRGIN AND THE PLAYBOY

"The characters were very real and delightful."
Author Diane Alberts

Chapter One

*J*ulia drew a deep breath and looked around the lobby. This was not only her first trip to Las Vegas, it was going to be her first time—well, her *first time*. She had managed to make it all the way through college without losing her virginity, and she was sick to death of waiting around for that perfect guy, that prince charming, to give her innocence to as though it were a wrapped present. Finally time to join the rest of the world and take advantage of the sexual revolution. Her heart threatening to hammer its way out of her chest, she clutched the strap of her overnight bag with a sweaty palm and headed toward the registration desk.

Finding 1NightStand online had been like a dream come true. She could fly to Las Vegas, spend one night with a complete stranger, lose that troublesome membrane and come back caught up with everyone else. Ready to have ordinary dates and hop from bed to bed at will, as all her girlfriends seemed to do. Decision made, she contacted Madame Evangeline and provided the required information and her American Express card number. All the arrangements were made. Julia Hooper, virgin at large, was about to give up what had become most inconvenient and embarrassing—her hymen.

ভ

In the room only fifteen minutes, Mark had already paced back and forth so many times he could see a pattern of his steps in the freshly vacuumed carpet. He couldn't even believe he was here, about to spend the night with a woman he'd never met. What if she was a dog? Okay, that sounded bad, but still...

His buddies had been merciless in their insistence he try out 1NightStand. It was his own fault—his bragging about dating a different woman every week was probably over the top. When he didn't want to sign up, the guys dared him. He hadn't ever been able to refuse a challenge, and they all knew it, damn them. But he figured once the beer wore off, they would see how ridiculous the whole idea was and let him off the hook.

Not.

If anything, they were more persistent the next day, excited and planning the whole thing. He could barely stop them from coming to Las Vegas with him. Finally, his oath to cancel the whole thing had made them back off and promise to wait back in Los Angeles for his return.

After some more persuading from the guys, he'd decided to go ahead and meet the girl. If she looked like Frankenstein, he would just have to make the best of it and try not to gag. He faced a lot of pressure being the playboy in the group, the single dude who dated all the hot women. Those guys hung on his stories, and he liked seeing the envy in their eyes. It wasn't his fault they'd all let themselves get tied down. Although he was fond of their wives—lovely, sweet women who fed him home-cooked meals and tried to set him up with their friends—he couldn't imagine picking only one woman from the hundreds crowding the clubs. At least not for longer than a week or two.

So, with his usual strut, he'd boarded the plane and wound up in a luxury hotel room on the penthouse floor of a Las Vegas casino. Pacing back and forth, he stared at the door. Any minute now, she would be here. Dear God, what had he been thinking?

CB

Julia approached the desk and waited while the desk clerk finished checking in an older couple wearing matching Hawaiian shirts.

"May I help you?"

She scanned the young man's face—was he aware of the nature of her visit?

"Yes, I need Sam Adams's room number please." Julia's voice cracked, her nerves raw.

"Oh, you must be Miss Ross? Betsy Ross?" He looked down at his monitor, and back up at her, his expression pleasant, non-judgmental, she decided. "Mr. Adams is expecting you in Penthouse 4."

Why had the first flag maker's name seemed like a good pseudonym to give for the check-in? Her cheeks flooded with heat. That's what she got for watching *Notting Hill* the night she made the reservation. Using a famous historical figure's name for anonymity, as Julia Roberts had in the film, had sounded dramatic and fun...and apparently her date had felt the same. What had Madame Eve said his name really was? Oh, right. Mark.

"Thank you." She accepted the card key the clerk handed her and turned to look for the bank of elevators. She saw one way at the other end of the casino and another set nearer to where she stood. Which one?

A tall man passing by stopped beside her, smiling. "Are you lost?"

"I'm afraid I am," she said, her cheeks flushing under his dark-eyed regard. Was this good-looking guy her date? It would be too good to be true.

"I'm with the hotel," he said, his pleasant expression giving nothing away. "What can we do to make your stay more enjoyable?"

"Direct me to the penthouse elevator?"

He took her arm and turned her to face the closer set of elevators. "Right over there. You'll need to use your card key to get to the penthouse floor."

"Thanks," she began, but he had already given her arm a little squeeze and turned away. Wow, if all the men at the hotel looked like him, she might go there again, just for the view. She watched him walk away, stopping to chat with several other patrons as he went. That was no hotel uniform he was wearing. It was tailored to fit his very cute rear end, and she stared until he went around a corner and disappeared from view. The elevators were past a row of slot machines, and she paused to put a dollar in one, for luck. She pushed the button and came up with three sevens. Fifty dollars! That was more than she had bargained for. She tucked the printed-out winning slip in her purse and faced the elevator just a few feet away.

Her lucky win giving her more confidence, she pressed the button. The doors opened and she moved to board, but back in the corner was a couple wrapped in each other's arms. The strawberry-blonde woman looked like she was about to rip her partner's clothes off, and Julia's eyes went wide. She moved back and let the doors close. After a moment, another elevator opened and she stepped in, slipping her card in the slot to send the car to the penthouse level. She used the time to draw a few deep breaths and try to calm her racing heart. The passionate lovers in the other elevator had reminded her of what she was letting herself in for.

The numbers above the door lit up in turn as the glass box rose, giving her a view of the busy casino floor below. There was still time to back out, wasn't there? The bell pinged at her floor—should she get off? Or maybe stay on the elevator, and go back to the lobby. The doors began to close again, and she reached out and held them open—if not now, when?

Overnight bag slung over one shoulder; she stepped into the penthouse hallway. There were only a few doors visible from the where she stood, and a sign on the opposite wall told her that suites 1-5 were to the left, so she took a deep breath, squared her shoulders, and marched off to meet her fate.

Chapter Two

$\mathcal{M}$ark was surprised to hear a knock at the door. His one-night-stand should have her own key, so he opened the door expecting to see housekeeping, or maybe room service with the drinks he had ordered. Instead, he faced a very petite, very determined looking young woman with a hand raised as if to knock again. He took in her alluring, feminine figure, wavy brown hair around a pink-cheeked face, and wide blue eyes gazing curiously back at him.

"I take it you're not housekeeping, then?"

A pucker formed between her straight brows. "No, did you want me to be?" She jutted her chin toward him and dropped the hand that still hung in midair.

"Absolutely not," he said, looking up and down the hallway. "I had asked for some extra towels..." He trailed off, and a moment of silence stretched out while they looked at each other. When she didn't say anything, he smiled and said, "I'm Mark and you're?"

"Julia." She spoke so quietly he had to lean in to hear her.

She certainly didn't act like someone who was brazen enough to book a one-night-stand with a stranger. "Just to be sure—Madame Evangeline sent you?"

She looked up and met his eyes. "Yes. May I come in?"

"Of course, please." He stepped back to let her pass,

following her with his eyes as she dropped her bag on a suitcase rack by the door and walked to the windows. She looked out, facing away from him. "Didn't you get a card key, too?"

Standing between the parted draperies, she held it up for him to see. "Yep. I just felt funny using it when you were already here."

He joined her and looked over her shoulder out the window. She froze when he stood so close behind her. That was a surprise.

The Strip lay below in all its flashing, neon glory. A faintly floral fragrance from her soft-looking hair drew his attention back to the room and the very desirable woman in front of him. Nice. He lifted a hand to touch it and then stopped, surprising himself with his hesitation. "I love the lights here."

When she turned around to face him, Mark understood why he'd held back. Julia was utterly different than the women he spent his weekends with. And it wasn't just the soft curves of her no-doubt natural breasts, or the minimal makeup on her lovely face. The slight tremble in her full, lower lip as she stood under his scrutiny. The whole package together took his breath away, and for once in his wild, playboy life, he had no idea what to say. Or how to begin.

ᘓ

Julia was stunned. She had never imagined that the guy Madame would send her would be so magazine-cover drool-worthy. He had tall, dark and handsome written all over him in letters two inches high. He was either lightly tanned or his natural skin color was a pale gold a couple of shades lighter than his amber eyes and much lighter than his hair, which was deep mahogany. Was there a crayon that color? Maybe in the sixty-four pack.

Her gaze drifted lower; she should probably be thinking about the six-pack right in front of her. Even lower, her blush crept into her cheeks again as she took in the tented front of his very nicely fitted slacks. Had pants always been so...eye catching? She hadn't even had sex one time, and yet, she was focusing on the below-the-waist assets of every man in Las Vegas! Doubts assailed her, and she forced her eyes closed. It truly was too late to back out now; if she did, she'd never try it again. The image of herself as a withered spinster, left on the shelf, never having had the guts to lie with any man imprinted itself on her closed lids and made her shudder.

Her eyes slowly came back up and up, across the broad chest and the proud chin, the full lips and to his golden eyes. The guy in the lobby was nice-looking, but she'd hit the jackpot with the hunk in front of her. Madam knew her business. She couldn't have found a sexier man if she'd built him from a kit. A virgin's dream.

"What are you thinking?"

"I—that is, I'm thinking that you're very good looking." She blew out a breath. *Smooth.*

"Thank you." His low, rumbling voice sent fingers of excitement right to her core. What did he think of her? She was curvier than was fashionable, but a compliment of some kind would be nice.

A long moment of silence drew out while they stood facing each other. Less than a foot apart physically, it seemed an uncrossable barrier stood between them. Finally, Julia couldn't stand it anymore and lifted on tiptoe to brush a soft kiss across his lips. It certainly broke the ice. He wrapped his arms around her and pulled her hips tight to his, bending to take the kiss to the next level. Julia wasn't new to kissing—she had dated, after all. And she had enough experience to know that the guy was amazingly gifted. She looped her arms around his neck and surrendered the last of her doubts.

His lips were firm and insistent. When she parted her own, he took advantage of the opening to plunder her mouth. Her world contracted to just that kiss, his nip at her lower lip, the teasing tip of his tongue stroking hers until her knees threatened to give out from the dizzying sensations. He held her firmly against him, and his hands slid down to cup her ass, strong fingers digging through her silky skirt and lifting her slightly so she was back on tiptoe, and even more off balance.

Mark pulled back, let her drop to her feet again, and looked down at her, amber eyes darkened to a deep gold and smoky with desire. Before she could wonder what he might have planned next, a knock sounded on the door followed by a voice announcing, "Room service."

When he released her, Julia grasped with both hands for the windowsill behind her and watched him go to the door to let in the waiter with a tray of drinks and a platter with a silver cover. Mark dealt with the man, his voice as cool and even as if they'd been sitting across the room from one another discussing the weather. Julia was dismayed until she saw his shoulders shake as he drew a deep breath before turning back to her. He had great self-control, but he wasn't, thank God, unaffected by their kiss.

When he turned back toward her, he was pulling his shirt over his head. The cocky smile that was revealed as he tossed the garment into a corner belied her earlier impression. But before she could carry the thought any further, he dropped his hands to his leather belt. Julia felt like a mouse playing staredown with a snake. Transfixed. Still silent, he loosened the silver-colored buckle, pulling it out through the loops, and then began to unbutton his jeans. Moving to the bed, he sat to pull off his black leather boots, stopped, and tilted his head to the side, one boot held in his hand.

"Aren't you going to undress?"

"Oh, yes, of course." She smiled and tried to look confident, but the warmth of moments before chilled. When she had signed up for this evening, she hadn't exactly been forthright. In filling out the paperwork, she had implied that her level of sexual experience was "moderate". She was afraid the service would turn her down, that maybe a virgin was unqualified for a one-night-stand under their policies.

Mark had no idea what he was dealing with, but even with

her inexperience, she'd expected more seduction than this. Narrowing her eyes, she glared at him. Whether he knew it or not, it was her first time and she was *not* going to be rushed. If he didn't have the sense to make this encounter special, she'd have to provide guidance

She pasted what she hoped was a sensual smile on her face. What had he asked? Oh, yes. Would she take off her clothes. Years of fantasies surfaced, thousands of romance novels devoured, imagining her own moment of truth. "I was hoping you'd do it for me." She fluttered her eyelashes, cliché? Whatever. The gleam in his eye told her he was interested in her plan.

She turned away from him to show the row of buttons that ran all the way down her indigo blue sundress to the knee length hem. "Please? I can't reach them all."

⚃

Mark's mouth dried. He stood quickly and took a step toward her, stumbling over the boot he still wore. Hopping on one foot, he managed to yank it off and dropped it to the floor, never halting his forward motion.

He'd unbuttoned a few dresses before, although he couldn't remember much about them at the moment. He placed a hand on each of her hips and turned her to face him. Reaching behind her, he slipped open one after another of the tiny, fabric covered buttons. His eyes focused on her tempting, ivory throat, and he bent to press his lips against the pulse that beat there, inhaling her light, floral perfume and the underlying, spicy scent that could only be Julia.

When he'd opened the buttons to her waist, he stepped back and slipped the dress off her shoulders, revealing her white lace bra with its front hook, then her smooth, white abdomen. So feminine, he rested a hand on the softness of her slight roundness there, her skin silken and the curve doing things to his breathing that he would never have expected.

Week after week, he went out with hot women from the club scene. They were all beautiful, and not one had anything but an absolutely flat abdomen, earned through starvation and a strict workout routine. Setting her slightly away from him, he took in what he had revealed with hungry eyes. Nothing about those nearly-identical women had ever made him feel... Had ever made him feel anything except an unremarkable lust.

He pulled her close again, reached around her and opened the buttons to below her hips. With a swish, the dress slid off and fell to the floor. She followed its fall with her eyes, and when they came back up, she shuddered, just seeing him looking at her. Could she see his hunger? Her hands were still at her sides, and her eyes met his, as she stood there in her bra and very tiny white lace panties. Her breasts curved above the tops of the bra cups. Were her nipples pink or deeper, maybe coral-hued—he wanted to find out. *Now.*

He stepped back and finished unbuttoning his jeans, pushing them to the floor and stepping out of them. He wore the skintight boxer-briefs that so many women seemed to find sexy. *Does she?* They were standing only a few feet apart, but again his finesse had deserted him.

He was never hesitant in the bedroom? He slept with different women every week. Inches separated them, and he reached for her, but something in her face stopped him. Her eyes were wide and her full, lower lip trembled slightly. As did her hand, when she raised it to her cheek.

"Are you cold?" he asked. "The air conditioning is set pretty low, let me raise it."

"No." She moved her hand away from her face and rested it on his arm. "I'm not cold." Her face was tilted up toward him, and he bent to capture her lips, savoring their softness, and her intoxicating scent as he moved to close the distance between them. He reached to unhook the front of her bra and looked down between their bodies as her breasts spilled out. Satisfying his curiosity.

"Lovely." He slid his hands underneath them and cupped

them in his palms. Their soft fullness caught him off guard, and he stroked their undersides with his thumbs. Most of the club girls had implants because very low body fat didn't usually equal big boobs. But Julia's silken handfuls were one hundred percent natural. Her nipples were a deep rose color that made his mouth water. Returning his gaze to her face, he saw her eyes were drooping. So sensual, so erotic. His cock pushed against his shorts, straining the fabric.

He stepped back and took her hand, tugging her toward the bed and pulling her down to sit with him on its edge. He kissed her again, softly, lifted her legs onto the mattress and piled fluffy pillows under her head.

"Julia? Are you comfortable?"

"Hmmm?" Her gaze me his, but her lids were lowered halfway and her breathing was an audible pant. "Oh, yes, very comfortable." She lifted a hand and rested it on his arm, trailing her fingernails over his wrist.

He sat on the bed, taking in his one-nighter.

She looked like a renaissance painting, all lovely colors blended together. Her brown hair with its coppery highlights that made it reflect light in a golden haze, her creamy skin. Against the hotel's indigo comforter, her eyes looked even bluer and her skin even paler. She was more vivid and more elegant than anything he'd ever seen before. And for one night, she was his.

He filled his hands with her breasts, loving their softness against his palms. He'd never realized how much he disliked hard, silicone boobs until now. Julia was a real girl.

಄

Julia was a girl veering between turn-on and terror. Every touch of Mark's hand sent new sensations racing through her body. She had indeed been bare-breasted before with a man. But there was something about the way Mark touched her and looked at her that made her heart pound and her mouth dry.

Probably it was because she planned to sleep with him. No-holds barred—she wanted it all. And she hadn't told Madame because she didn't want some guy who was looking for a virgin to add to his woman collection. No, she wanted an exciting evening of being treated like a woman, finally.

She rested her head among the fluffy down pillows and allowed him to take the lead. He crawled up beside her, gracefully, like a jungle cat, and lay beside her, nude. She could see his underwear on the floor by the bed. She craned her neck to try to see what she'd gotten herself in for, but the angle was wrong. *In just a few minutes, I'll be done with this virginity nonsense.* She closed her eyes tightly, fear overwhelming the desire, waiting for his next move.

"Look at me," he said, and she opened them again. "Blue like the Caribbean."

She was caught in his own amber gaze, taking in how long his lashes were and the stubble she could see on his cheek. Her fingers strayed up to touch the roughness, and she rubbed her palm across his face, liking the tingle the little hairs gave her. She wondered how it would feel against her lips, and raised her head to find out.

His rough cheek felt great, and she rubbed her lips back and forth, savoring the sensation. Why had she never taken the time to explore anyone she had been with before? She would have lost her virginity years ago. Or maybe it was just Mark. His scent drew her, something wild and spicy, cinnamon and sandalwood, and male.

He turned his head and kissed her again. Lips slightly parted, they breathed each other's breath, slow, sweet, intoxicating. The tip of his tongue stroked her lip and she sighed before timidly reaching out with her own to touch his, tangling in a complicated, erotic dance. Julia squirmed, feeling vulnerable when he parted her legs and pinned her beneath his muscular thigh.

He reached for her breasts again and began to stroke them, speaking softly. "Julia, you have the softest skin, and your nipples are so hard. I want to lick them, bite them, make you scream."

Her squirming increased. Moisture pooled between her thighs, and as he went on, she began to feel a wet spot on the bed beneath her. "Shall I do that, beautiful Julia? Do you want me to bite your nipples? Will you beg me to?"

"Oh, yes. I want you to." She thrust her chest toward him, his words wiping away her fears in a wash of desire.

"What do you want me to do? Tell me." He moved his mouth to her earlobe, nipping it with sharp teeth. "Is this it? Shall I use my teeth on your nipples too?"

"Yes, yes," she said, shuddering.

"Yes what?"

"Nip me, bite me, lick my breasts, please. I want your mouth on me."

"Where?" He gave a tug on her lobe and she felt an electric shock all the way to her toes.

"Everywhere, lick me everywhere."

He released his hold and licked slowly down her neck, making her want to squeal. "All you had to do was ask."

She opened her mouth to respond to his cocky remark, but closed it when he blew cool air on her stiffened nipples. Her blood rushed through her veins, and she felt so alive she almost forgot that she wasn't the wanton woman she was showing him.

True to his word, he laved her nipples with his hot tongue, one at a time, while pinching the other with his fingertips. She tangled her fingers in his hair, her head tossed back on the pillow and eyes squeezed very tight. He was licking slowly, taking long seconds to make each circle around her nipples, and the sweet agony of waiting for each part of her areola to be touched by that rough tongue was almost more than she could stand. Suddenly, he pulled back and looked up at her from under lowered lashes, searing her with his gaze, before dropping his head back and sucking her nipple into his mouth, biting down, just enough for the pain and pleasure to mingle and she cried out.

"Mark, God, where did you learn to do that?"

The preposterousness of her question struck her just as he chuckled. The vibration of his lips while her nipple was held tightly in his teeth sent her over the edge. She came, digging her fingers into his scalp and feeling muscle contractions all the way down to her toes. The wave went on and on, leaving her limp and gasping.

He peered up at her face. "Do you always come when someone nips you like this." He moved his mouth to her other nipple and sucked it into his mouth, biting harder this time, twisting it between his teeth.

"No. I—don't." She had never orgasmed with a man, ever. As he sucked her peak farther into his mouth, the moisture between her legs ran down onto her thighs. "Is it unusual?" Her hands left his hair to stroke across his broad shoulders. His skin felt warm, and she found herself wanting to dig her fingers into the tensed muscles at the base of his neck.

He released her nipple with a pop and pushed himself up on his elbows. "Are you serious?"

She drew a shuddering breath. *Don't give yourself away, Julia. He may not want you if he finds out how inexperienced you are.* "Yes—no, I guess not. I only know it's never happened to me before."

"Me either." His broad smile and the twinkle in his eyes captivated her, and she reached a hand to his cheek, guiding him to her kiss. He rolled to the right, taking her with him so that she was on top straddling his hips and very aware of his erection pressing at the juncture of her thighs.

Chapter Three

*S*he was so wet. He pressed the length of his penis along her slit, moving his hips back and forth, enjoying the heat and the wide-eyed look she gave him. He'd been told he was bigger than average, was he scaring her? "Julia, is everything okay?"

Her grin reassured him. "More than okay, it's wonderful." She bent to give him a quick kiss.

"Slide forward." He put his hands under her ass cheeks, guiding her up his chest until her pussy was right in front of his face. She smelled so good, and he inhaled deeply, drawing the perfume that was Julia into his chest. If ever there was a woman he wanted to taste, it was her; and he brought her to his mouth, reaching out to lap up the juices that ran freely from her soft folds. He could hear her short pants as he teased, and when he sucked right on her clitoris, she squealed. She was so responsive, he wanted to make her come over and over just for the pleasure of listening to her.

"Mark, I want…"

What did she want? His long slow licks were apparently rendering her incoherent.

"Isn't there something I can do for you? His prick twitched in response to her incredibly sexy voice.

"I think so." He waited to see what she had in mind, his breathing growing ragged when she turned, facing away from him and wrapping one silken hand around the base of his rigid staff. He was only human and the things he'd been doing to her had been making him hotter and harder by the minute. Her little hand was almost too much, and he tried to distract himself. Although the view of her neatly shaved, almost hairless pussy was not helping to distract him at all. He shuddered and buried his face in her once again, wallowing in the scents and the sounds she made when his tongue stroked directly on her swollen clit. A squeal from the back of her throat vibrated her mouth over his penis and told him more about her state than almost anything else.

He continued to lap up her juices, but he struggled to concentrate because she had moved her hand to his balls and stroked them, and her lips covered the head of his cock, slipping down over its length, so slowly, getting even for his little nipple game, he supposed. It was torture, as each fraction of an inch of skin was covered by her hot little mouth. Not moving back and forth, almost no motion at all, just a slow engulfing of his prick. He almost stopped breathing when he felt its engorged head touch the back of her throat.

And she stayed like that, for long seconds. The woman was a witch, her cock-sucking technique different than any he'd ever felt before. Just as he thought he might explode right there, she moved, sliding back up so that only the head was in her mouth. She ran her tongue around it in slow circles.

He wrapped his arms around her hips, pulling her right against his face, and began to lick in earnest, fast strokes from front, all the way to her sweet little ass. Fast so that she would speed up, maybe meet his rhythm and ease the torment he felt. So she would pick up on his cue and they could reach their peaks together. He wanted to shoot his load down that beautiful throat, and he bucked his hips. But nothing he did made her change her slow, maddening rhythm.

He turned his head to the side. "Julia, faster, please, I can't stand it. Suck my cock, come on, baby. Ah, hell." He couldn't wait any longer to fuck that beautiful pussy. "Come here." He flopped her beside him on the bed and turned her around so they were lying side by side.

"Come on, Julia." He pushed her legs apart and slipped one finger into her sopping pussy, then two. "You're so ready for me, baby. I'm gonna fuck your brains out. You'll like that, won't you, baby? Tell me you want me to fuck you." He grabbed for a foil packet on the bedside table and tore it open with his teeth, rolling the condom onto his rigid staff.

Her voice broke on a sob, but she said, "I do, I want to feel you inside me, go ahead, fuck my brains out. It's why we're here, after all."

The very tiny part of his brain that wasn't completely controlled by his lust registered that her comment was an odd thing to say, but it was, after all, a miniscule part of his personality. The rest was tied up in the getting his penis inside that welcoming snatch. He propped himself up on his arms, looking down at her intent face, eyes closed again.

"Open your eyes, beautiful. I want to watch your face while I fuck you. Come, on, Julia...Julia are you okay?"

Ψ

She was more than okay. She was completely blown away by the whole experience. But she was a little scared as she felt the large, bulbous head of his penis brush against her entrance. He murmured nonsense syllables against her neck and she opened her eyes as he moved his head back. He wanted to watch her face, and she wasn't sure she was a good enough actress to hide her fear and anticipation of an act that had taken long enough to arrive.

She felt her channel stretching as he pushed in, pushing against that barrier that he didn't know was there. But she did and she felt a sharp pain and gasped as he pushed through the bit of skin that blocked him from fully entering her. He held her gaze with his golden, amber cat's eyes, and Julia was hypnotized. The pain passed, replaced by a sharp wash of pleasure, and she wrapped her legs around his thighs, and her arms around his neck, holding on for the ride of her life. She held her eyes closed for just a couple of seconds, taking it all, taking him in, and when she opened them again, she saw him staring down at her in what looked like horror.

"Julia, dear God, you're not, that is—you were a virgin, weren't you?"

"Yes," her voice was so low even she could barely hear it. But it was pointless to deny what they both knew was the truth. "I was."

He froze, only part of his cock inside her, but her tight passage held it in place. "Then why?"

She lifted her hips and felt him slide deeper. "Just fuck me, Mark. Fuck now, talk later because I'm not interested in a conversation—just now."

And apparently he had no compunction in following her instructions because he surged forward and buried himself to the hilt, drawing a moan from her very core. She had waited so long to feel the ecstasy of a man filling her with his rigid cock and it was more than she'd ever expected.

଼

For a moment he'd faltered. A virgin? On a one-night-stand? But when she'd held him in place, welcomed him, he hadn't been able to think beyond how warm she felt around him, how wet. How incredible it felt to slide his engorged length into her tight, hot pussy. He couldn't help himself, couldn't stop.

Questions could be answered later, at the moment all he wanted was the friction that was rapidly sending him to places he didn't remember ever visiting before. Stars swam before his eyes when he squeezed them closed. He wanted to stop, wanted to find out why she had spent her virginity in a one-night encounter in a strange city, but his body fought him when he tried. His body demanded he continue. She begged him to go on, holding him tightly against her and meeting his every thrust with her own. In fact, he was extremely turned on being her first, just as he'd loved the feel of her natural breasts and the little curve of her belly.

"Come for me, Julia, can you do that, baby?" He was trying to maintain a rhythm, to keep stroking until she found her release before spilling his seed, but she wasn't quite there, and it was a supreme battle to hold it back. "Julia, are you close?"

Her answer was a long wail and a series of rippling contractions in the passage that held his penis. It threw him over the edge into orgasm, balls tightening and hot liquid shooting from the end of his cock, the two of them bucking and writhing until the endless ecstasy faded slowly back, leaving him skin to skin against the sexiest woman he had ever known.

He rolled to the side, not wanting to crush her under his greater weight, and through half-closed lids, surveyed Julia's sweat-glistening form. Her creamy skin caught the lamp's light and he lifted his hand to trace the outline of a full breast, just touching the edge of her rose pink nipple and watching it peak instantly. He cupped its fullness, so soft, so feminine, and let his hand run down her belly, its slight roundness astoundingly sensual. His breath had slowed to nearly normal, and he had to ask....

"Why, Julia?"

Chapter Four

She had known the moment would come. It was a logical question, and her once reasonable plan for eliminating an inconvenient hymen didn't seem to pertain anymore. How was she to have known what an incredible moment it would be, the joining of two bodies, two spirits. *Damn it.*

"I didn't know it would be like this. I just kind of felt like life was leaving me behind. I was afraid to go on dates because with everyone I had to question whether to go this far, whether to make him 'the one' and it was making me crazy."

"Most girls I've met gave it up when they were teenagers." He shook his head. "I am pretty sure you're the oldest virgin I've ever met."

"Gee, thanks." She grinned, too full of after-glow to get mad, despite the feeling that she should be insulted.

"No, you know what I mean. I just don't know what to think."

"Me either. Particularly after the last couple of hours. I've been missing out."

He grinned. "Thank you."

"You're welcome." She giggled. "How polite we are. I specifically asked for a playboy type, a guy who dated a different girl every week, so he would be experienced, but I probably wouldn't like him that much. And look who they sent me!

Madame has a lot to answer for, sending me a sweet guy like you. And incredibly talented. Oh, that feels good."

He was running light fingers up and down her arm, just barely touching her. But it sent chills down her spine. "You know, I feel like I could use a shower."

"Oh, go ahead." She pulled her arm in to her body. "I'll take one too before we leave." It was over, but she was going to be brave. She'd gotten what she came for, and probably a lot more than she paid for, too. She shouldn't be greedy and hope for more....

He slid off the edge of the bed and held out his hand. "Don't you want to take one together? This room has an incredible shower with jets all over the place. I looked when I first came in."

More! "Oh, yes, that sounds great. I've always wanted to try a shower like that." As he quirked an eyebrow at her with a wicked grin on his full, sensuous lips, she smiled back. "But I think you have more than cleanliness in mind."

Chapter Five

*H*e took her hand and pulled her with him toward the bathroom. "Come with me, Miss Innocent, and I'll show you what I can do for you with all those streaming jets."

Her breath caught. His naked body in the lamplight was sculpture. As if carved from warm, living marble, every plane and angle pleasing to her eye. She allowed him to lead her into the bathroom and stood back while he turned on the shower and adjusted the temperature and jets. As he moved, she watched his muscles flexing under his skin. In this brighter light his olive-toned skin was perfection. Apparently there was no light that wasn't perfect for Mark. The rear view was amazing and before she knew it, she had reached out and put one hand on each of his ass cheeks, digging her nails in slightly. God, was he built.

"Like what you see?" His chuckle was low and vibrated up her arms.

"That's what did it." Her blood sang in her veins. She wanted him again, immediately. And what did he have planned for that shower with its inviting bench on either end?

He looked at her over his shoulder then turned to face her. My, he was happy to see her again. His cock jutted straight out from his body, already completely hard and there was a drop of liquid on the tip. She reached out a tentative finger to touch it, smoothing it around the head of his penis, then putting her finger in her mouth.

He stared, and she wondered if she'd done something wrong, but he pulled her against him and put his mouth at her ear, warm breath caressing her skin. "That's what did what?"

"Huh?" She was lost.

"You said, 'That's what did it.' What did you mean?"

Her mind was blank for a moment. What had she said? Oh, yes, a thought came through the murk. "I meant, when you chuckled, that deep sound, with your mouth on my nipple, that's what made me come the first time."

"Really? I'm intrigued. I wonder where else I could put my mouth and do that...."

Her eyes widened, and she forgot to breathe. "I can think of a place," she said, surprising herself with her quick response.

"Mmm," he nuzzled her neck. "And we'll do that, beautiful, but first let's see what the shower is like."

She followed him into the shower. It was as big as her entire bathroom at home and had at least a dozen jets shooting water into the center. There was a dispenser on the wall filled with a liquid soap/shampoo and he reached over and filled his hands with the slippery substance, rubbing them together to create a green-apple scented foam.

"Turn around." The bubbles were spilling between his fingers, and she faced the back wall, resting her hands on its white-tiled surface. He put his palms against her upper back and began to wash her in big circles, the foam slipping down and running between her butt cheeks. When she trembled, he asked, "Do you like that?" He dropped to his knees and continued to rub the foam down her back until his fingers caressed her ass.

His fingertips moved between her cheeks, caressing just the very top of her crack, and though she tensed, waiting for him to reach further, to her aching pussy, he just continued to wash down her legs to her feet. He stayed on his knees and gave her a little push. "Sit."

He was getting pretty demanding. She liked it though—she

liked it a lot. She wasn't sure what that said about her, but having a hot guy tell her what to do naked was working for her big time. She sat on the bench and he picked up one of her feet.

෮

The shower jets hit all over his body as he knelt on the shower floor, but it felt good, incredible really. And he was so involved with touching every inch of Julia's skin, that he only noticed the spray in a secondary kind of way.

He pumped more soap into his palm, and lifting one of her feet, ran his soapy hands over its top and her arch, between her toes. Her nails were painted a rose pink, so close to the color of her nipples, he thought absently, casting his eyes toward those stiff peaks above him. He held the foot and let the shower jets wash away the soapy foam, then ran his hands slowly up her calves and thighs, massaging gently and loving the feel of her soft skin under his hands. He knew his own skin was rough, but she didn't complain. In fact, when he looked up at her face, her eyes were half-closed and looking down at him, their blue barely showing through her lashes. He went for the other foot, slowly washing that one and moving up her leg.

"Open your legs for me." She parted them and he reached up with sudsy fingers and saw the tinge of blood on her inner thigh. He traced it with a slick fingertip. A virgin! He wouldn't have agreed to meet her if he'd known. But he would have missed out on the best night he'd had in a long time. Maybe ever.

Although she lifted her hips, and he knew what she wanted, he continued his leisurely washing of her lovely, soft skin, running his hands over the curve of belly and on to the breasts he couldn't keep away from. Silicone was highly overrated. Soft, natural breasts like Julia's were definitely the way to go.

Suddenly, the quiet, the lack of conversation made him nervous. The only sound was the hissing of the water jets and their breathing. Julia was more than the body he had become obsessed with. He wanted to know what she was thinking, feeling. That was a new idea for Mark the playboy.

"Julia?"

"Hmmm?"

Shit, he had to think of something to ask her, and he didn't know what he wanted. He wanted to hear her voice.

"Is the water warm enough?"

α

Her eyelids fluttered open. "What? Yes, oh, yes it's fine." It was hard to form words, for some reason. Every bit of her attention was focused on following his hands as they soaped and explored her body. He was washing her arms, soaping from her shoulders down to her fingertips, and she felt completely boneless. Boneless but tingling.

"Okay, I just wanted to make sure you were okay. You're so quiet."

"Oh, sorry." *Was that the right thing to say?* Damn her inexperience. Between the water hissing and her heart pounding in her ears, the shower stall seemed pretty loud to her.

He pumped some more soap into his hand and sank down onto the bench beside her. "I want to wash your hair." She turned away and he massaged the shampoo into her hair, then took a moveable showerhead off its hook and rinsed it away.

"I think I'm pretty clean," she said. "Or at least most of me."

His eyes met hers, and he smiled. "I saved the best for last."

"Well, I think you will have to wait."

He frowned and she grinned, feeling more confident in the face of his chagrin. "I think only one of us is clean. Stand up."

He obediently stood in front of her. This put one of his more interesting assets right at her face level and she took a moment to look more closely at his cock. It jutted toward her face, and she decided to tease just a little and took the head into her mouth, licking around twice before releasing it.

"No, don't stop," he said, reaching out for her, but she shrugged under his arms and stood up.

30

"Sorry, I'd love to keep going, but I don't want to be accused of slacking. You just spent a very long time washing me and now it's my turn." The look on his face was priceless. Powerful stuff, this sexuality was, and she began to realize that and enjoy it. She followed the same path he had, back first, then legs and feet and up the front. Skipping the one area she knew he wanted touched the most. Turn about was definitely fair play—and fun, too.

But besides that, she found that running her soapy hands over his body was incredible in itself. The play of muscles under his skin, the coarse hair on his legs, she was learning as she went and paying very close attention to his reactions. When she pinched one of his dark-apricot guy nipples, his dick jerked and bumped against her stomach. *Interesting.*

But by the time she was done with all but the most interesting parts, his patience seemed to be thinning. She soaped her hand and ran it between her legs, then over his rock-hard cock.

"Julia!"

She fought to contain her giggles at the strain in his voice. "Yes?"

"Enough, I can't stand it. Come here." He pulled her against him, pressing that hard cock back into her belly. "I want you now."

"Oh, sure. Now that we're clean and all."

He glared at her and she let her giggles free. "You spent a very long time torturing me with those talented fingers of yours. I just wanted to repay the favor."

"It's not funny," he said, but the corner of his mouth twitched. He shifted her in his arms so they were kissing, streams of water hitting them from all around. He was no longer behaving as though he had all day, but was urgently prying her mouth open and ravishing it. When her tongue tangled with his, he shifted his hands down to her ass and lifted her so that her feet were off the floor. He braced his hands under her thighs and pressed her back against the shower wall.

She gasped and he broke the kiss to look down at her. "What's wrong?"

She pointed and he looked down to see he had placed her so that one of the jets was shooting directly against her clitoris.

"Oh, no." He made as though to move her away, but she punched his shoulder.

"No, don't move, it's so…it's so…."

"Good?" He held her in place as her body shuddered and she clung to his shoulders.

"I really need to remodel my bathroom," she said, holding tight until the world stopped spinning.

Before she could do anything else, he lifted her slightly and drove his cock into her quaking passage. "I can't wait any more." He slammed it in, two or three times, then slowed, gliding in and out, over and over, so that his tip hit a place inside her she had only read about.

"Yes, Julia, there is a G-spot," she murmured into his neck and then screamed his name as she came again. "Mark, oh God, yes, yes."

He shuddered as he spilled inside her, finding his own release yet again. "I can't even believe how tight you are, Julia!" He held her up with her legs wrapped around his waist for another moment, then collapsed with her on his lap onto one of the benches. Water streamed over them, hitting from all angles, and suddenly the heat, the water beating against her skin, the steam became overwhelming.

"Mark, please turn it off. I can't stand it."

He reached over and turned off the shower. "Are you okay? I should have thought—it was your first time. You're sore, aren't you. I'm so sorry."

She shook her head then laid it against his shoulder. "It's not that, I'm not sore. It's just that all of a sudden it was like sensory overload. Good, bad, intense. I didn't know what to do with myself."

He laid his head back against the wall. "Oh, that I understand. Let's get out of here and get dry. I think I might need to lie down for a bit. What a workout."

She dropped a kiss on his neck and stood on shaky legs. "Okay, I think I might be able to make it that far. Stepping out of the shower, she handed him a towel and tucked one around herself, wrapping another around her hair. "So, that's what everyone's been talking about," she said, shaking her head. "I can't believe I waited this long to find out."

Chapter Six

*T*owel around his waist, he followed her out of the bathroom. "Julia, that's not, I mean, tonight is not what everyone is talking about. I've been just the playboy you asked for, a different silicone babe every week, and I can assure you, it's never been like this."

She tilted her head and looked at him. "I'm sure you're right. I couldn't possibly keep up with girls like that."

"That is not what I mean. Those girls, I don't know how to explain the difference, but they aren't like you. You're real, every soft, curvy, cuddly, exciting inch of you. Not one of them could keep up with you." He hoped she understood how extraordinary she was, but was afraid his poor words weren't carrying it well enough.

She smiled at him. "I had a good teacher. But prof, I'm awfully sleepy. Do you think we could lie down for a while?" She undid the towel in her hair and unwrapped the one around her body. "I should find my bag. I brought a sexy nightie to sleep in."

He held out his hand and took the two towels from her, tossing them, and his, into the bathroom. "Don't get the nightie. Just come curl up with me and we'll take a nap. It's been quite a night."

She yawned then looked startled. "I completely forgot you ordered the drinks. And what is on the covered dish?"

"If you like, I'll pour us some champagne."

"I'm awfully sleepy...what's in the dish?"

"Take a look and see if it's anything you like."

She stretched her arms over her head and walked over to the table. "I don't know, I think I'm too tired to...strawberries! Strawberries with brown sugar and sour cream. Oh, I'm hungry. Go ahead and open the champagne—I just got a second wind."

She carried the plate with its booty over to the bed and plopped down cross-legged against the headboard. "How did you know?"

"I didn't. Madame said there would be refreshments in the room. I've never seen strawberries with sour cream before."

"I had it at a party once and fell in love." She took a big, red strawberry dipped it in the cream and then the sugar. Dark gold crystals clung to the sides of the berry. "Taste." She took a glass of champagne from him and held the treat up for him to bite. She was so delighted, he didn't want to say no.

He chewed and swallowed, closing his eyes as the sweetness of the sugar and the tart sour cream collided with the rich berry juice in his mouth. "That is amazing." He sat down on the edge of the bed next to her and smiled. "Who would have thought?"

"I don't know, somebody very smart." She finished the first berry and dipped another, offering it to him. He looked at her, sitting cross-legged and naked on the bed, holding up the red fruit with its sugary coating. A one-night-stand. And Mark, who had one-night-stands several times a month, felt melancholy flutter its wings around his heart. Someone was going to be very lucky when this woman decided who she wanted forever. But it was going to have to be someone better than him. He didn't deserve her, and he wasn't kidding himself that he did.

Enough. He drew a deep breath. He had her for one night.

Julia sighed and pushed the nearly empty plate away. The champagne flute she put on the bedside table, and she slid down and curled onto her side. "I need to close my eyes, just for a minute." Mark lay down behind her, spooning her and wrapping an arm around her waist. He tugged her closer as her limbs softened and her breaths became long and even. Quite some time passed before he joined her in sleep, his mind moving over possibilities, ideas foreign to his playboy mentality. One night with Julia was not going to be enough.

Chapter Seven

She woke with a start, for a moment panicked. Where was she—then she remembered. The arm across her waist was a clue. *Mark*. Her one-night-stand. But through the open drapes she could see a fine line of light along the eastern horizon. Daytime was coming and with it, reality.

She slipped out of the bed and padded to the window. Las Vegas lay below, still flashing its lights for her admiration, but she knew the sun would be up soon, and it was time for her to go. She grabbed her overnight bag and slipped into the bathroom to dress.

When she came out a few minutes later, the sky was noticeably lighter. She set her bag down and pulled the heavy drapes closed. No reason for Mark to have to wake up early so far as she knew. He was draped across the bed, arms spread wide and a slight smile on his face. She hoped he was having a good dream. She paused for a moment by the desk.

Julia leaned over the bed and pressed a very soft kiss on his bristly cheek. "Don't forget me," she said, almost under her breath. "I sure won't forget you."

She slipped out of the room and rang for the elevator. If that couple from the night before was still there, she would get on anyway. Her newly advanced level of sophistication would carry her through.

℘

He slept until ten. That was the time on the small clock on the bedside table when he opened his eyes. Stretching, he sat up and looked around. He couldn't remember the last time he'd slept so well. The hotel bed was luxury itself. Oh, and the little encounter last night didn't hurt either. Speaking of which...where was she?

"Julia?" There was no answer, and he had actually known there wouldn't be. It was a one-night-stand and the night was over. He'd met the one woman who could reach out and touch his heart without even trying, and she was gone.

Sighing, he stood and stepped into his boxers and jeans. He couldn't face the shower again, not after making love to her beneath the jets. He reached into his bag for his socks, found a folded piece of paper and smoothed it out on his lap. "Dear Mark," the note began. "I hope I'm not breaking the rules of 1NightStand by doing this but I wanted you to know how to reach me..." A grin spread across his face as he tucked it into his pocket.

THE VIRGIN AND THE BEST MAN

"Kate Richards took the ending to a place I certainly wasn't expecting."
You Gotta Read Reviews

"You'll find yourself glued to the page."
Night Owl Reviews

Chapter One

"Julia, there can't be two twenty-something virgins in one family." Mark leaned through the open bathroom doorway. "It's statistically impossible. Seems like the kind of thing you'd have mentioned earlier." He grabbed his toothpaste and aftershave and stuffed them into his shaving bag. "You tell me everything else about those crazy relatives of yours."

"First of all, there aren't two twenty-something virgins among my relatives—anymore. *You* saw to that." Her giggle carried in to him, as he pulled open a drawer and saw her diaphragm in its plastic case. They were leaving it behind, ready to take their chances in the baby pool. He steadied himself on the edge of the sink. He'd never expected to be saying his "I dos" so soon after meeting Julia, or to be excited at the thought of starting a family. His pleasure didn't completely eliminate the anxiety at the rapid changes his life had taken.

He wouldn't go back to his freewheeling single days for all the money in the world. He loved every inch of Julia's curvy body, every strand of her light brown hair, every…. God, must be wedding nerves turning him into a sentimental idiot.

He returned to the topic at hand.

"That doesn't explain why Karin's late bloom hasn't come up in conversation before," he said, returning to the bedroom to deposit his sundries in her mammoth suitcase. Since she planned to check luggage—a practice he'd never adopted—he could take his regular shaving cream and deodorant instead of the annoying FAA-approved travel sizes he could carry on the plane. "You don't mind, do you, sweetie?"

"No, not at all." She opened the closet and pulled out another, even larger bag. "It just means I need another case." Plopping it on the bed, she flipped it open and dumped in an armload of folded clothes.

"Julia, you don't need two suitcases, do you? My razor and aftershave don't take up much room." In addition to the airline's ridiculous fee for the bags, he'd have to wrangle them, plus his own, at both airports. And judging by her actions, both bags would be overweight—Vegas Airlines would love that. How much did they charge for extra tonnage? His temples began to throb. "And why do you need so many clothes for just a few days away?"

"I'm a bride, darling." She swept past with an armload of dresses and paused to glare at him. "And what do you mean by 'late bloom'? I wasn't exactly sixteen when we met either! And I thought you were so happy to have been my first." Her full lower lip thrust out in a sexy pout. "I thought...I thought...."

He paused, trying to follow her convoluted responses. Ever since the wedding plans had ramped up into full speed this past month, she'd been on an emotional roller coaster. One moment Julia laughed and smiled, relaxed and fun to be with, the next she fussed and fretted until he didn't know what to do to calm her.

He'd been more than glad she'd never taken another lover, once he'd recovered from the shock of finding out. He'd never imagined the woman Madame Eve at 1Night Stand set him up with would be a first-timer, much less the love of his life.

Just the idea of another man laying hands on Julia clenched his fists. He began to respond, but she had fluttered back to her packing and let him off the hook. For once.

She stood away from the bed, cheerful again, her forefinger pressed to her rosebud lips. "Maybe a third bag would be good."

He paused, wondering if their luggage would even fit in the

cab. What could she be taking when she'd had him ship so many of her things already? The dress and veil. His tux. Overflowing boxes of "wedding necessities." Parting his lips to argue, he thought better of it and snapped his jaw shut. His married buddies—the ones who'd dared him to sign up for 1Night Stand to start with—had warned him. Don't mess with the bride.

She'd spent so many hours on the phone with Leah Castillo, who had volunteered to arrange things in Las Vegas, he was amazed she hadn't asked the hotel owner's wife to be her matron of honor.

But no, the honor had fallen to Karin, her first cousin—petite and dark haired with long lashed, violet eyes. A gorgeous girl, funny and friendly. But a virgin? Was it genetic? A librarian in her small town an hour north of the Bay Area, maybe a little shy with strangers, but not withdrawn or anything. Of course, there'd been nothing wrong with his bride, either. Nothing a night with him hadn't been able to fix. *There's my old arrogance coming out again. Guess she hasn't cured me entirely.*

Julia piled lingerie and a jacket in the third bag. *A coat for Vegas?*

"I don't know why—" He bit his lip. He'd almost said something stupid. Again. "You take whatever you need."

Julia dropped to sit on the bed, covered her face with her hands. "I'm so much trouble, but I just want to make it a special day for us. I don't know why you're even marrying me."

Her shoulders trembled, and his heart thumped. He knelt in front of her and pried her fingers from her damp cheeks. "Shhh, don't cry, Julia."

The wedding meant so much to her—she'd worked herself to a frazzle for months, making every detail perfect. He'd done virtually nothing to help—not even stay out of the way and not upset her as his dad had suggested. Not that she'd let him do a thing...but still.

Planting baby kisses on her forehead and the tip of her nose, he pulled her tight against him. "You know why I want to marry you, but should I tell you again?"

She sniffed, wiping her wet face against his white T-shirt. "Yes, if you don't mind."

"Okay." He moved to sit next to her and lifted her into his lap. "I love you because you are smart and beautiful. I love you because you make me laugh at myself, because you always see the bright side of any situation. You're everything I never knew I wanted in my life and more. I want to marry you because I never want to wake up anywhere but beside you."

She relaxed in his arms at the familiar litany, snuggling closer with a sigh while he stroked her back in long, comforting sweeps.

Her soft warmth gave him other ideas. The side of her breast pressed into his ribs, and her rounded ass was planted directly over his cock, which stood up to take notice. Craning his neck to the side, he did a quick calculation and grinned. A small portion of mattress remained free of luggage and piles of things waiting to be packed. He rolled her onto the white eyelet bed cover she loved so much—the replacement for his worn, red and blue plaid flannel comforter.

"Mark," she shrieked, tears forgotten, as he stood, stripped his T-shirt over his head, and unbuttoned his jeans. "We don't have time for this."

Boxer briefs disposed of, he sat next to her and began to help her out of her clothing. She struggled a little, her wriggling hips sending his cock to complete readiness.

"Honey, when we don't have time for this, I will worry about us." Top and shorts off, she wore only a pale aqua demi-bra and.... "No panties? Mmmm." He stroked a finger through her slippery softness. "Bad girl, Julia. And so wet for me."

"I was just packing," she protested, squirming to sit up. "It's not like I left the house like this." Her cheeks bloomed with red.

"No, I think you were hoping I'd find out." Mark stretched out beside her, trying to decide what to do first. She was right about time—they didn't have a whole lot—so he had to make it count.

He leaned in and kissed her, slow, smooth, as if they had all day. No matter how quick a quickie, her kisses were too special to rush. Bringing a hand to cup her breast, he flicked her nipple, and she stopped squirming. Encouraged, he rolled the hardening point between his fingers and released her mouth.

"When we leave here, I want you to remember this." He bent and drew the stiffened peak into his mouth, circled it with his tongue, and smiled at her gasp. With a quick peck to the other side, just to be fair, he moved lower, pausing to nip at her bellybutton before burying his head between her legs, sucking on her clit and gliding two fingers inside.

He didn't like to rush, but circumstances being what they were, he laved her with his tongue and drew hard until her back arched then he crept back up her body to plunge his cock into the heat of her pussy.

She reached for him, tugging his lips to hers. He obliged her, reveling in the tight heat around his cock.

"Julia, I won't last long." He grasped her hips, thrusting balls deep, again and again.

She shuddered, but laughed. "Where have I heard that before?"

He wanted to protest, to remind her of the long, slow lovemaking that happened all the time, but her clenching muscles and sharp cry drove him over the edge with her, and he buried his face in the curve of her neck, riding it out.

"It gets better all the time," she gasped, her heart thundering against his chest.

He glowed with pride and rolled over so she straddled him. "Let's do it again."

She grinned at him then glanced to the side and leapt away, as if he'd burst into flame and burned her inner thighs. "The taxi will be here in twenty minutes. And I'm not nearly ready." She fled into the bathroom and emerged wearing a wrap dress that enhanced every curve and dip of her figure. "I'm worried about the gifts we have for Karin and your brother."

"Well, Ray is sure to appreciate a 1Night Stand date, but with the new information about Karin, I hope Madame Eve is as intuitive with her as she was with us."

"If she is, Ray will get a showgirl. He's a worse playboy than you ever were." When he didn't respond, she turned her glare on him. "Isn't he?"

He winced. "Julia, what's past is past, but, yeah, he's pretty bad."

"I hope Karin doesn't hate me. It's not like she has to have sex with the guy, right? It's just a date, a chance to meet someone nice...it will have to be okay." She shoved a few more things in the suitcases and sank onto the bed with a sigh. "Well, I guess that's it. I know I'm forgetting something, though."

Mark scrambled into jeans and a polo, and shoved his feet into loafers. "I'll take the bags down to the foyer while you try to remember." He zipped the suitcases closed and lifted them, his breath whooshing out at the weight. "Vegas Airlines is going to make a killing off us."

"I'll take your duffel, and we'll be ready when the cab comes. We still have to pick up Karin on the way to the airport, so we can go over the details of the party tonight." She skipped past him and scooted down the stairs with his single light bag, while he trudged along, trying not to let gravity drag him to the bottom with the tonnage in hers.

A horn honked at the curb, and he reached for the doorknob, but Julia rested a hand on his arm.

"I just realized what I forgot," she said. "It's kind of funny." To his amazement, she opened the door and stepped out.

"Julia? Honey?"

"Hmmm?" She paused on the walkway. "Come on, we don't want to miss our flight."

"But don't you want to get what you forgot?" He hovered in the doorway.

"Not really," she said, bringing her lips to his ear. "I don't need panties anyway." At his sharp inhale, she grinned. "Serves you right for taking advantage of a girl before the wedding. Shame on you."

Crap, now he was going to be thinking about her smooth, shaved mound with no underwear the entire flight. "That's no fair, Julia."

"There's always the mile high club." Her laughter floated back to him as she hopped into the cab. Evil woman. He couldn't wait to marry her.

Chapter Two

*K*arin sat cross-legged on the steps of her college roommate's apartment building, where she'd spent the night to save travel time. Her home in the sticks lay over an hour away, so she'd stayed in town after the bachelorette party, excited about the trip to Las Vegas and anxious not to miss a moment of the fun.

Julia had hinted about a very special maid of honor gift, with a glint of too much glee in her eyes.

Julia had a warped sense of humor on occasion, and she'd always been more like a big sister who knew what was best for Karin, than a cousin. The combination made for interesting gift-giving. Like the book "Your Body and You" when Karin was twelve or the permanent marker, full color hand drawn tattoo of a skull when she was six. Of course, she'd also come up with her first pair of high heels when Karin was fifteen. Just a little older, Julia led the way into the big world for her country cousin—with a few interesting twists.

She bent forward and peered down the street. No cab in sight yet. She pulled her phone out and texted Mark.

Where r u?

Almost there, J took 4ever getting ready.

Mark—always the cut-up. But mad about her cousin. She rolled her eyes. Had they stopped for a quickie on their way out the door? *Like bunnies!* The thought brought back something she'd shared the night before when she'd gone drinking and dancing with Julia and her friends—a local bachelorette outing for the girls who weren't going to Vegas. Casual and lots of fun. The martinis had flowed, and after slugging down a delightful, tart key lime version, Julia had informed the group Mark had been her first and only lover.

In the spirit of friendship and under the benign influence of her fifth bourbon, Karin admitted she had yet to do the nasty with any man, and at twenty-two, she wasn't about to give it up unless the guy had the potential to be everything to her, like Mark was to her "wonderful, wonderful cousin."

When the giggling women silenced, their wide eyes focused on her, Karin had understood her mistake. It was one thing for Julia to have *been* a virgin too long. Everyone knew she and Mark couldn't keep their hands off one another.

"But guys hit on you all the time," protested Sue, one of Julia's work friends. "Just now, on the dance floor...?"

Yes, a half-drunk creep had tried to cop a feel, but she'd fended him off. Still she felt the need to defend her—apparently—oddball state. "I'm picky," she said. "Not disinterested."

Charlotte, the only other member of the wedding party present, patted her hand. "Don't let them worry you. You don't have to sleep around to be a fun person. Julia was always fun."

Sue nodded. "And before Charlotte met Birdie, she had her share of women in her bed."

Elegant, confident Charlotte glared at her. "How do you know who spent time in my bed, Sue? I never shared that information at work."

"Well...I just...that is...." She lifted her club soda with a slice of lemon and took a sip. "Oh, don't mind me, it's the hormones, makes me say stupid things." She batted her eyelashes, and Charlotte burst into laughter.

"Shut up, Sue. Don't you blame your gossiping on that innocent baby in your belly." Charlotte shook her head. "If we didn't love you so much, we'd never put up with you. It's lucky Birdie is meeting us in Vegas. You'd convince her I was a total tramp."

The conversation turned to Charlotte's impending transfer and move to Reno. She'd be living with Birdie on the ranch they'd bought together, telecommuting. Karin listened, relieved they seemed to have forgotten about her unfashionable status.

The women were anxious to hear all about the place, and Charlotte pulled out her cell phone and passed it around, while they all oohed and aahed over the pictures of the gorgeous mountain backdrop and spindle-legged colts frolicking in dark green meadows.

Everyone but Julia, who still hadn't said a word. Was she upset nobody was paying attention to the bride? No...not her, she never tried to be the center of attention. But she stared at Karin as if she'd grown horns.

"Julia? Is everything okay?" She couldn't be judging; she didn't have a leg to stand on.

Julia blinked and licked her lips. "Oh, no, nothing for me. I'm not done with this one yet."

"What?" Karin leaned close and spoke in her ear, her words hidden from the others by the thumping bass of the club rap. "Are you dreaming about your wedding night? I'm no expert, but how different can it be from every other night—and day—with Mark? When I stayed at your place that night, when we had all that wine, I thought your headboard was going to crash through the wall."

"Oh my God, are you kidding me?" Julia covered her eyes.

"Yes, and I'm just an innocent—you could have debauched me."

Julia grinned. "Oh, little cousin, you're so right. Run away while you can, before my evil influence brings you to the dark side."

Another round of drinks arrived, and the women got up to dance, the rest of the evening passing without further embarrassment. But Karin still wondered what had made Julia react so strongly to her announcement. Deja vu?

A taxi turned the corner. The bachelorette party had been a blast, even if the limo had dropped her off so late she'd only been able to grab a few hours' sleep. She would catch an early night after the family dinner at the hotel.

As the cab stopped, Julia leaned out the window and waved. She and Mark were a perfect match—they had moved in together almost right away and never looked back.

A lingering fear surfaced. The longer Karin waited for Prince Charming, the less sure of her plan she became. Maybe there was no special person for her, seemed as if lots of people never met their one and only—at least not someone who made them glow like Julia did.

"Get in cousin-in-law," Mark said, hopping out and waving her into the back seat. "I'll ride with the driver and let the pair of you complete the plans to shackle me."

"Have you two taken up bondage now? Glad I stayed at Angie's, or I wouldn't have slept at all." She laughed at his startled expression and slid in, giving Julia a big hug. "Excited?"

"You have no idea. The rehearsal dinner is at eight tonight, giving us about five hours to get everything ready." Julia yanked her phone out of her purse and typed in a few words. "I just want to make sure the florist has confirmed the order."

"I'm pretty sure Leah has that covered."

"She's amazing. I couldn't do this without her." She bent closer to the screen. *Flowers fine, will be delivered in the a.m. Chef Gina already working on your cake and the food. Relax!*

"She's right, you know," Karin said, leaning over her shoulder. "It will be a beautiful wedding. Did your folks get there yet?"

"I don't know!" Julia lifted the phone again, but Mark reached over the seat and plucked it from her grasp.

"Honey, we'll be in Vegas in a couple of hours. Anything left to do, you can handle then, okay?" He held her gaze while Karin watched. This Prince Charming could calm her slightly hyper cousin with a moment's glance, melt her into a puddle with a touch. Not that she was jealous of Julia—well, maybe a little—but she wondered whether she'd snapped up the last good guy on the market.

Nobody she'd gone out with had made her feel like Julia looked—like she'd gotten all the cake and ice cream at the party. She let the anxiety go. This was her cousin and Mark's weekend, their special time, and Karin would do everything in her power to make it the best wedding ever. Kind, generous Julia, always watching out for everyone else. She deserved every ounce of happiness she got...and the hunk who smiled at her as if she *was* the ice cream and cake, with a cherry on top.

Leaning back in the seat, Karin exchanged a glance with Mark as Julia babbled on about details for the ceremony and the small, elegant reception to follow. Happiness looked good on her.

Chapter Three

*M*cCarran International Airport had changed since Ray last flew in. Most of his trips were in short hops around Washington State, occasionally Oregon, and he'd been fascinated to see the growth of the Las Vegas Strip. Daytime didn't hold much of an impact, but maybe he'd find time to take a quick night flight before he returned home.

As a commercial pilot, he'd been pressed into service to transport his parents, sister, and a few assorted other relatives into town for his brother's wedding, arriving the day before. Their mother and father were crazy about Julia. They'd kept him on edge at the incredible Castillo brunch buffet, speculating on how soon they could expect a visit from the stork and waxing ecstatic that their wild son had settled down. Well, one of them, anyway.

Once they focused on his sis, asking when she'd be finding a nice grandchild-producing husband, Ray had volunteered to meet the bride and groom at the airport. Sophia had glared daggers at him as he made his escape—but when his parents began with "I don't think it's too much to ask to have our children happily married before we die," it was everyone for him or herself. Soph just wished she'd thought of the airport trip first.

Dang Mark for raising their expectations anyway, bringing

home a treasure like Julia. Looks, brains, kind to animals and children.... Hell, if he could get one like her, he'd whisk her off to a Vegas chapel today.

But he'd never met another like her, and likely wouldn't. So he was safe to spread his wings and fly, free as a bird with a girl in every town.

The hotel limo pulled up in front of the terminal, and he hopped out and headed for baggage claim. Despite a bit of jealousy at Mark's good fortune, he valued his freedom and wouldn't trade it for a home and family for a long time.

"Over here." Mark emerged from a long tunnel and waved. "Glad to see you, bro. I just expected the chauffeur." He approached and wrapped Ray in a bear hug.

"He's outside. I decided to come along and meet you myself." Giving Mark a slap on the back, he stepped away. "Where's the ball-and-chain-to-be?"

"I beg your pardon, brother-to-be? Are you referring to me?" Julia appeared, beaming, and Ray hugged her, too, lifting her off her feet.

"No way, he made me say it." He pressed a kiss to her cheek. Her dark blue sundress enhanced her curvy figure and made her eyes almost indigo. "You sure look pretty. Way too pretty for him. You sure I can't convince you to marry me instead? I'd fly you anywhere you want to go, anytime."

She giggled. "Tempting, but I think I'll keep Mark." Taking a step back, she hooked her arm through her fiancé's. "He's just getting broken in."

As the pair got lost in one another's eyes—again—another woman stepped forward. "Well, if nobody wants to introduce me, I'll do it myself." She extended her hand. "I'm Karin Smith, Julia's cousin and maid of honor." She paused. "And you must be Ray?"

He nodded, bemused. "Mark's brother and best man."

Where Julia had curves to spare, this woman was small and delicate as a mountain violet. In fact, her eyes were the color of the tiny wildflowers in the meadows he loved. Far away from the crowded cities. When they bloomed in spring and he flew over them, a whole section of the range might glow deep purple, velvety with their massed petals.

She let her hand drop to her side, and he hated to see her disappointment. He cursed his distraction.

"I didn't mean to be rude," he said, reaching for her and smoothing her fingers between his hands. "It's been a rough day with the family." He could have told her the truth, but she might get the wrong impression—think he was hitting on her or slinging a pathetic line. *Your eyes are like meadow flowers.* How lame could he get?

She smiled at him and extricated her hand. "I understand. Wait until you meet our folks. They should be driving up to the hotel about now. Dinner with them is bound to make your people tolerable by comparison."

He grinned back, enchanted by her lovely face and sweet tone. "We'd better stick together, then. The bride and groom will be useless to us. We can help keep one another sane." As a horn blared, the couple in question turned to the baggage carousel.

"It's a bargain," she said. "How about a signal? If you need rescuing from your folks, just text *help me,* and I'll come and say you're needed to do something weddingy. Give me your phone."

"Kind of bossy, but I'm not going to look a gift horse—er, buddy—in the mouth. Even if she does have the sexiest one I've seen in a long, long time." *Couldn't keep from flirting if my life depended on it. If something I do upsets the bride, Mark will knock my block off.*

She batted her eyelashes at him and took his phone. "Why thank you, kind sir. I'm glad you don't think I'm a horse." Punching a few buttons, she handed the device back. "There, my number is in your phone, and if you call me, I'll save it in mine."

"Then our plan is set. Just don't tell—"

"Sshhh, here comes Julia."

"Ray, would you please go help Mark with the carry-ons and my bags? He's so macho sometimes, treats me like a princess, which is a good thing, as long as he doesn't hurt himself."

He chuckled. "Sure thing. You know, I think I'm going to like having a second sister. One who won't try to tell me what to do."

"Of course I won't," Julia said, waving him away. " And get Karin's things, too, okay? Now, could you hurry up? We don't have much time before the wedding. Scoot!"

He sighed and joined Mark at the carousel. So much for his theory. "Give me one of those, we're in a rush."

Mark pointed to a bulging bag at his feet. "Be careful, it weighs more than my lovely bride. The extra fees were astronomical."

"No worries, bro. Wouldn't want the groom unable to perform on his wedding night due to a back injury. It's not like I have any plans after the reception."

"Right." Mark flashed him a shit-eating grin, and Ray's stomach churned. "Of course, you don't." What was he up to?

He lifted the bag and huffed. "I'm amazed this thing didn't bring the plane down. What's it full of, rocks?"

"I have no idea, but maybe shoes."

"Cement shoes?" They laughed.

"We'd better get going before Julia melts down." Mark adjusted the duffel strap over his shoulder, tucked his laptop satchel under his arm, another carry on in one hand, and lifted a floral imprinted bag in the other. From the expression on his face, it had to be nearly as heavy as the one Ray hefted. "Can you also grab Karin's carry-on?"

The two of them trudged over to the women, who turned and led the way out the door.

"I'm a gentleman, Mark, but do you think they could help with anything?"

"Look at 'em, Ray." Mark shifted his load and followed the ladies. "Do you want to make them carry heavy loads? Mess up that hip action?"

"It is a nice rear view...."

Mark's voice dropped. "That better not be my future wife you're talking about."

"Nope, I'm not that stupid, bro." He dragged the heavy bag,

grateful for the rollers, while taking in the other woman's form. What was she twenty-one, twenty-two? Her long, dark hair swished across her back in time with her steps. As petite as she was, the ebony weight of it seemed almost too much. Still, white short shorts made her legs go on forever. No, not looking at the bride.

The limo driver opened the trunk, and they helped him pile the luggage in while the women disappeared into the back compartment. In twenty minutes, they would arrive at the hotel and be surrounded by family and friends. He wanted to enjoy the quiet time with his brother and Julia—and Karin—before they plunged into the fray.

Following Mark inside, he dropped into the opposite seat, next to Karin. "Help yourselves to drinks from the cooler. I think there's even champagne in there."

"I'm so happy you're both in our wedding," Julia said, plowing through her giant shoulder bag and pulling out a tablet. "Not only do we love you, but Karin is incredibly organized and trained in rescuing me from Mom when she gets pushy." She tapped on the screen a few times, murmuring under her breath, and glanced up, a smile tilting the corners of her lips and a twinkle in her eyes, giving him a glimpse of the sparkle Mark saw in her. She arched a brow.

Karin, twisting the top off a bottle of chilled water, froze. "What are you up to?"

Julia pouted, pushing out her lower lip. "Why would you think I'm up to something? Can't a girl be happy on the eve of her wedding?"

"Jules, I've seen that expression so many times, and it always means trouble for me."

Ray glanced from one woman to the other, wondering what could be wrong. Julia turned to Mark and whispered something, and he ran a hand through his hair then shrugged.

"I thought we'd wait until later, but sure, go ahead and tell them."

"Really?" Julia tilted her head. "Maybe we should wait."

Karin groaned and gulped her water then fixed her with a glare. "Tell us."

Ray held his peace—how bad could it be? Were they going to have extra wedding responsibilities?

"It's not a bad thing! We bought something special for each of you. Gifts for our maid of honor and best man, and—" She rummaged through her bag again and withdrew two thin envelopes. "—here they are."

Karin took hers and tugged on the flap, but Julia grabbed it back. "You can't open it until after the dinner tonight. It's a special surprise."

"Then why did you give it to us now?" They glared at one another until Mark chuckled. "Let them open the presents. Don't tease."

Ray accepted his and pried the envelope open. At his side, Karin fumbled in her hurry to do the same. He found an engraved card with the words 1Night Stand and an email address. He stared at it, not understanding right away, but Karin did.

"Oh, dear heavens, you set us up with dates? From that Madame Eve woman you two used to meet each other?"

Ray stared at his brother. "Are you kidding me? You thought I needed a date? I go out all the time."

"Yeah, you do," Mark said. "All the time, but rarely the same girl twice. I want—we want you two to have a chance to meet someone special, picked out just for you."

"And when are these dates supposed to happen?" Karin's voice squeaked. "Do we just email to set it up when we get back home?"

Julia smiled. "No, we wanted to give you what we had, the first time we met." She leaned on Mark's shoulder, and he dropped a kiss on her hair. "An evening with your perfect match at The Castillo, Las Vegas."

"So." Ray tried to put it all together, to decide if he was happy, upset...insulted? "We'll have these blind dates tomorrow, then? Because the next day, I'm flying everyone back to Seattle."

The bride and groom exchanged a glance, and Karin sank back in her seat.

"No, tonight," Mark said.

Ray laughed, waving the "gift" in front of him. "There's no way it could be tonight. We have the rehearsal dinner and probably a hundred other things to do with the families. You do mean tomorrow, right?" Of course, it could be the perfect excuse to escape from a lot of those things.... No, for once he'd be the perfect brother, the perfect best man. *I wonder what she looks like?* "The only reason I didn't bring anyone to start with is because I wanted to be here for you. I don't need you getting me dates."

"Well, neither do I." Karin grimaced, her eyes narrowing. "If it's tonight, it will have to change. I'm the maid of honor, and I have a lot to do. Maybe we can arrange something for another time. It's very sweet of you, but—"

"No buts, cousin," Julia said. "It's tonight, it's all paid for, and your date will be expecting you."

"Oh God, no. I'm supposed to go to your rehearsal dinner, go out on the town, and then be up early for all the festivities tomorrow?"

"Yes."

"It's not even possible." Karin's shoulders slumped, eyes half closed. Suddenly, they opened wide. "Julia! Aren't these one-night stands? Doesn't that mean both parties expect to have," her voice dropped, "S-E-X, with a complete stranger?"

Her pale skin flushed, the blush creeping down her throat to the round neckline of her black T-shirt.

"Are you okay?" he asked. A strand of hair fell over her eyes, and he pushed it over her shoulder. "Take a sip of your water." He glared at the happy couple snuggled close on the opposite seat. "Tell her she doesn't have to have S-E...sex with anyone." The very idea enraged him. A delicate beauty like her, in the arms of some brute while he—

It wasn't going to happen. Not if he could prevent it.

Julia sighed. "Karin, it's a date. You'll have a nice time with someone special."

Mark grinned. "Yeah, not like my brother here. He'll probably get a woman ready to leap right into bed."

"Come on," he protested. "You don't want my new sis and her cousin to think I'm a total dog."

"Well, aren't you?" Mark asked.

He opened his mouth to deny it, but could only muster a grunt. Maybe not a total canine, but he did go out with a lot of girls in the most casual way. Still.... "Don't listen to him, ladies. I just haven't met the right woman yet."

Julia smiled and rested her head on her groom's shoulder, looking like the cat that got the cream. "Don't worry, Mark was a real playboy, too, once. All his friends' wives couldn't wait to tell me tales when I met them."

"But not now," Mark said. "I have one girl, and she's almost more than I can handle." He bent to take possession of the girl's lips, and the kiss went on and on, leaving the maid of honor and best man in uncomfortable silence.

"So, what do you do, Ray?"

Grateful for the distraction from the lovebirds, he answered. "I'm a pilot."

"How interesting. Do you get to fly at night much?" Her question surprised him.

"Some, when we have clients who need to go places in the evening. Why do you ask?"

She turned to look out the window, but he caught the blush on her cheek. "I was originally an astronomy major. I like the idea of being up closer to the stars."

"Originally? What made you change?"

"Oh, my parents convinced me librarian was a more practical major for a small town girl."

"You wanted to work in a big observatory?"

"Not exactly, but...."

He admired the curve of her cheek, the dark sweep of lashes, another stray lock of hair he longed to smooth back then he started. What on earth? Was Wedding Fever contagious?

Focusing, he cleared his throat. "How did they convince you—your parents, I mean."

"Oh, they reminded me my grandmother was getting older and so were they, and if I wanted to go to grad school in Houston, where I'd been accepted, they would have nobody to help them with her." Her head dipped. "Grandma had Alzheimer's."

They'd held her back, how unforgivable. But he supposed people with a serious illness to cope with sometimes put their offspring's best interests second to the person who took so much time and energy. And it hadn't been her grandmother's fault.

"So you stayed home, became a librarian, and helped take care of your grandmother."

She shook her head, a slow, sad wag. "No, Grandma died about the time I got my degree. But by then the dream seemed too far away. I'd turned down the scholarship, and I couldn't have made it without that. My mom and dad don't have a lot of money."

"So your dream got stolen for nothing?"

Karin turned to face him. "No, not for nothing. I like my job. I just miss the stars. I think Grandma is up there, you know, sometimes when I am out in the desert or on my friend's sailboat in San Francisco Bay. I think one of those winking lights might be her. And she's proud of me anyway."

His breath caught at the watery smile she showed him. She'd unselfishly chosen a career to let her help her family and given up her own desires. He didn't think he could have made such a hard choice. Of course, his pilot's license let him be anywhere he needed to be with little notice. But still....

"How do you like being a librarian?"

She brightened, a twinkle in her eye surprising him. "I like it. Especially when the children come for story time, or after school asking me to help them pick out a new book to read. For a second choice, it's not bad at all."

Before he could continue the conversation, the limo pulled up in front of the magnificent façade of the Castillo Hotel.

Then there was no time to discuss careers or anything else, as relatives and friends anxious to begin the festivities swarmed the car.

Chapter Four

A date. Her heart hammered at the thought, the romantic in her ready to meet the mysterious stranger.

Jostled by her relatives and friends, Karin wanted to get checked in. She needed a little privacy to send the email and find out when and where to meet Mr. 1Night Stand. Her baggage unloaded, she kissed her mother and promised to come back down as soon as she was unpacked.

"Fine, darling," her mother said, beaming at her, "go get settled. But you won't mind taking Jeannie and Ann with you, would you? They came at the last minute, and so of course, they don't have a reservation, and I thought—"

"Oh, I'd love to...." Karin's mind flew. Two giggly eighteen-year-olds as roommates? Taking up the bathroom and gabbing all night? *Oh, hells no.* She cast about for an out then found one. "But I only have a single." And a need for privacy.

Her mother's beaming smile dashed her hopes. "I changed it, dear. Now you have two queen-size beds. And the girls don't mind sharing one."

Crap on a cracker.

❧

A few hours later, already late, she tucked the 1Night Stand gift card in her evening bag with her wallet and a few other necessities and scooted for the elevator, the chatty pair bracketing her, oohing and aahing over everything from the décor to the romantic way the bride and groom had met.

Rather...the *story* Mark and Julia had told their parents and everyone but a few of their nearest and dearest. Knowing the real version, Karin had a hard time remembering their blind date that ended with a kiss, so she just nodded and smiled and hoped her blue-violet silk dress matched her eyes, as the sales girl had claimed.

She'd had the pencil skirt hemmed to a few inches above the knee, because at her height, she wanted the world to see her long legs. A floor length gown, no matter how formal the occasion, made her look squatty. A *C* cup added to the problem, and the wrong dress could give her the top-heavy appearance she probably deserved but didn't want, but the strapless bodice should draw eyes to her shoulders instead.

In any event, a glance toward the mirrored back of the car reassured her the strappy aubergine stilettos she'd destroyed her budget to buy had been worth every penny. They made her sigh each time she saw her freshly pedicured toes peeking out. And they matched the gorgeous, purple beaded clutch bag.

When they emerged in the lobby she let the giggle-boxes dash ahead and took a moment to prepare herself for the evening. If she had a date after the dinner, she needed to stay pretty and not eat anything with garlic. Even if she didn't plan to sleep with the guy—and of course she didn't—she planned to exchange witty remarks and didn't want to worry about her breath.

Julia waited outside the private dining room, her face anxious. "Karin, thank God. I'm so nervous. What if our families hate each other? What if the food isn't good? What if I'm making the biggest mistake of my life?" She stopped on a gasp.

Karin took in her soft rose dress, the long skirt tight at her tiny waist then falling to swirl around her ankles. The off-the-shoulder bodice top emphasized her long, swan-gorgeous neck. She tried to think of something to say to reassure the nervous bride, but her own inexperience and awe at Julia's beauty silenced her.

Ray arrived and saved her. "Mark is the luckiest man in the world. What did he ever do to deserve such a gem?"

Julia's frown dropped away, a flush of pink coloring her cheeks. She smiled, her wide blue eyes twinkling. "Thanks, Ray."

As Julia was borne off by an arriving gaggle of dinner guests, Karin sighed. "She's worried about so many things...."

"Not really," he said, taking hers arm and proceeding across the room toward the bridal party's table. "She just wanted to know she looked pretty."

"But she's so much more. She's stunning, always has been. She got the looks in the family."

Ray turned her toward him and tipped her chin up. He reminded her of Mark, with his classic features and wide-set eyes, but stood an inch or two taller. And, she noticed now, he had one dimple cutting into his cheek, and his crooked incisor made his bright smile a little winsome. The boy inside the man. She swallowed, her mouth dry.

"Is that what you think, Karin?"

Her mind muddled, lost in his eyes. "What?"

He cupped her cheek, seeming to see inside her, his gaze compelling. Like he could know things about her, her deepest secrets. Her insecurities, wish to be taller, fear of the unknown, the bad relationship two years before that made her doubt her own judgment.... Did he know?

"Don't sell yourself short, Karin."

He leaned toward her, and her focus shifted to his mouth, drawn in, wanting to find out if he kissed as good as he looked. She lifted even higher than the stilettos took her, closing the distance, the noise around them a dull buzz—

"Come on, Ray, don't monopolize the maid of honor." Reality came back in the form of an Amazon princess, nearly as tall as Ray and Mark, red waves spilling around her shoulders and green eyes snapping with impatience. "They won't serve until the whole bridal party is seated. So sit."

He sighed. "Coming, Soph. You really do have great timing."

The magic spell broken, Karin shivered. *What did I almost do?* She allowed him to lead her the rest of the way and pull out her chair. Julia, showing no signs of her earlier nerves, was entertaining the table with an anecdote about Mark's proposal while a phalanx of waiters in white dinner jackets delivered salads of delicate greens and baby vegetables.

All so normal. By the time the entrée arrived, she'd forgotten her concern with her breath and happily dipped the grilled garlic shrimp in melted butter, sharing family stories and trying not to make her interest in Ray obvious. The bride and groom's contagious happiness brought the two families together in a blissful mélange.

She basked in the warmth of their love, sneaking glances at Mark's brother across the table from time to time. Had she been about to kiss him? What would her blind date think?

With a sinking sensation in her stomach, she realized she would be spending the rest of the evening with a total stranger and—worse—so would Ray. Unlike her, he'd be getting naked with his stranger. That shouldn't bother her at all, but it did. A lot.

Ray kept an eye on the maid of honor. The brief contact with her on their way to the table had shaken him. When she'd looked up at him, her violet eyes had held secrets. Her guarded look made him wonder who had hurt her. Somewhere along the line, someone had shattered her trust. Yet they'd almost kissed—and she didn't strike him as a girl who got up close and personal with every man who crossed her path. A wash of feelings confused him. He wanted to protect her, to litter her path with rose petals to keep those small, cute feet from harm. And he wanted to peel her dress from her and cover her smooth, white skin with kisses—starting with the swells under her pretty purple dress.

She laughed at the barely funny jokes, the teasing about the honeymoon night. Although nobody in their right mind thought it would be a first, he supposed tradition must be upheld. No amount of persuasion had gotten Julia and Mark to agree to spend the night before their wedding apart. The groom insisted there could be no bad luck associated with seeing his bride before the nuptials. Anytime he laid eyes on her was good fortune of the highest order.

Ray supported the theory. If he ever found someone he loved like Mark loved his Julia, he'd never let her out of his sight. He'd need to marry a pilot, so they could fly the skies together, he supposed. Assuming *his* "Julia" was out there at all.

And nobody he'd dated so far had made him want to take it past casual. Depressing thought.

A bearded man strolled past, and Julia whispered, "Is that the guy you were telling me about, Mark? The professor?"

"Yeah, Lukas!"

The man came to his side. "Hey, Mark."

"How was the drive down from Reno?"

"It was fine, I had to pick up some supplies anyway."

"Glad you could make it. Julia, this is Lukas Gerard, professor of geology at University of Nevada, Reno, and predictor of the imminent end of the world. He's a prepper. Also my oldest friend."

Lukas shook his head. "My research has uncovered some disturbing things I am not bringing up at your rehearsal dinner. I'm on my way to the bar to have another drink on your nickel." He took Julia's hand and slapped Mark on the back. "Great party."

The table was quiet for a moment after he left.

"Mark, you don't think he knows something we should be worried about?" Julia's voice trembled.

"Of course not. You know how scientists can be."

Ray cursed under his breath. "Lukas gets all caught up in his research, don't let him bother you. Besides, he's a geologist. They think of time in terms of millions of years."

"And it's not stopping him from drinking his weight in free

Scotch." Mark chuckled. "He's a good guy, just a little quirky. One day we'll have to visit him and take the tour of his bunker."

"He has a...?" Julia waved her hand. "Enough. I want to hear more funny stories. If the world is ending, it will have to be after tomorrow."

Sophie grinned. "I have one."

Ray focused on the lovely maid of honor and lost track of the conversation until Mark's roar of laughter drew him back.

"And then Mark told Mom he only wanted to see what Ray looked like as a girl, so...."

Horror filled him. "Soph, shut *up*. Don't be telling everyone that silly story. Besides, I'm not even sure it's true."

Mark agreed. "Oh, it's true. But you were three, so you might not remember."

"Just shut up, okay?" He jumped up from the table, flush with anger. How dare they embarrass him in front of everyone, in front of...Karin. If he'd had the slightest interest in her—not that he had—he could forget it now. She'd be picturing him in the damned pink dress, with bows in his hair. So much for his manhood.

But as everyone at the table roared with laughter and begged him to stay, he saw one person wasn't chuckling. She set her spoon on the saucer under her chocolate mousse and stood, her purple purse clutched in her hand.

"Excuse me, please. I'll be right back." She took off across the room.

Waiters began to circulate with champagne flutes, and she ducked around one, nearly bumping him in her rush. Where was she going in such a hurry? Oh...crap. The gift. Was she going to meet her date? He hated the idea like poison. Surely she wouldn't leave during the dinner...would she? A flicker of unease reminded him of his own commitment, but he couldn't stand Karin going off to spend the night in the arms of some other guy. The whole thing made his stomach churn.

And why did he care so much? He'd never been a knight in shining armor...or worried so much about a relative stranger's welfare. But she was so attractive, sweet and funny.

Aw, hell. He took off like a shot, weaving through the room, ignoring several relatives who called his name as she headed down a short hall. He followed her through a doorway, and he froze when he realized his mistake.

He stood in a small lounge, with a couch and a curved table topped with a large, gilt framed mirror. Through an archway, an array of porcelain and marble. An older woman shrugged past him with a snort, but it was too late to turn back. These bathrooms were only accessible through the banquet room, so nobody outside their party was likely to be there, and a quick, hot-faced glance showed him no legs under any of the stalls. He turned and spun the lock then faced his quarry.

Holding her phone, Karin stared at him, her brow furrowing. "Is everything okay, Ray?"

"Umm, yes." Now he didn't know how to explain his mission. *I just slammed into the ladies' room to stop you from going on your date, or texting to find out where to meet the bastard. It's okay, I'm not going to call mine either. Want to go out for coffee?* Lame. Again.

"This is the ladies' room." She dropped her phone into her purse and snapped it closed. "I think you made a wrong turn." She tilted her head to look past him at the door. "But you might have guessed when Aunt Estella walked past you."

He nodded, still at a loss of what to say. *That's new.* Shifting from foot to foot like a teenager, he watched her come closer until she had to tilt her head back to speak to him.

"Is something wrong? Do you feel okay?"

He cleared his throat. "Yes, I feel fine. I just wanted to talk to you."

She shrugged, but her eyes flicked to the side. "All right. Let's have a seat." She moved toward the pink brocade couch, and stopped. "If we stay in here, they're gonna be beating the door down."

"This won't take long. Do you mind if we sit?" He feared if they emerged into the press of family and friends, he'd lose his opportunity and nerve.

She bit her lip and glanced at her purse. *The phone.* "No, I guess it's okay, as long as it doesn't take long. I need to email Madame Eve and find out about my date." Sinking into the plush cushions, she patted the sofa. "So, sit, talk to me. What's wrong? Are you nervous about giving the toast tomorrow? Has your mom been driving you crazy?" As if she'd known him forever....if not for the way his pulse raced when he got within three feet of her, they could be old friends.

He sat next to her, close but not touching. Afraid of a repeat of their near miss in the banquet room. After all, he'd seem a hypocrite if he tried to get her to cancel a date just so he could drag her to his own room and ravish her. "That's what I wanted to talk to you about. You see—"

Her eyes widened. "Oh, my God! Did you text me? Was I supposed to rescue you?" She clicked her purse open and fished inside. "I didn't see a message from you."

Covering her hand with his, he drew a deep breath. *This is for her benefit, her safety. Has nothing to do with the sweet curves of her cleavage and my desire to scoop her breasts out and bury my face between them.* He cleared his throat, forcing the image into obscurity. "No. My sanity is more or less intact, so far."

"Then what?" Her brow wrinkled. "The toast?"

"No, the date."

She cocked her head. "What about it? Did you find out about yours?"

"No, not yet." He tightened his fingers around hers, so small and soft. He would not imagine them wrapped around his cock. "I wanted to try to talk you out of going on yours. It's not right for a girl like you."

Chapter Five

What the hell? Prying her hand free, Karin scooted into the corner of the couch. "Why don't you want me to go on my date? And what do you mean 'a girl like me'?"

What had he heard? Julia told Mark everything—had he shared her secret with his brother? Heat flooded her cheeks.

"Nice women don't do one-night stands." He patted her leg, and she jerked away, but he didn't seem to notice. "Just about anything could happen. You'd be in over your head with some strange guy. So, you shouldn't go."

"Just like that?"

"Hmm?" He frowned, his eyes locked on her thigh, bared most of the way by her new posture. "Oh, yes. Men can't be trusted."

She tugged her skirt down, as far as it would go—which still left a fair amount of unprotected leg. "I see what you mean. But I thought Madame Eve would match me with my perfect date. Certainly not be a wolf who would gobble up an innocent lamb like me."

He swallowed hard, his Adam's apple moving in his throat. "Maybe not, but why take the chance? I don't like the idea of you spending the night with someone you just met."

He didn't seem to know her secret, but she couldn't be sure.

Mostly he was just arrogant, and missing the warning signs anyone in her family would have seen. She didn't like being told what to do. By a virtual stranger. Patronizing. Thinking he knew what was best for poor little Karin from the back of beyond. Assuming she didn't know what she wanted—what she needed.

"Oh, okay." Sarcasm—warning sign number one—coated her tones. "So, I should go back to my room with my teenage cousins and do our hair and talk about cute boys."

"Yeah." His tense shoulders sagged. *Relief? Idiot.* Irritation began to turn to rage.

"And you'll go on your date, of course." The set of her jaw would be warning number two, and any of her boy cousins would have shut up by now.

"Well, sure, why not?"

She balled her hands into fists, nails digging into her palm...number three. As a teenager she would have gone from there to slugging the offender. Lucky for Ray, she didn't slug anymore. Of course not.

"And," she kept her tone sweet, clinging to the last of her self control, "you'll sleep with her, if the opportunity arises."

"Umm, I might...you're changing the subject." His gaze flicked to the side, and she pressed her advantage, desperate to end the conversation before she did something she might regret. He had such a handsome face, and Julia would kill her if he had a black eye in the wedding pictures.

"Am I really? I don't see how. Just because I'm a virgin doesn't mean I can't go out with whomever I want and have sex with him if I like. I'm over eighteen, and I have my rights." Heat rushed from her toes to the top of her head.

An expression of gape-jawed astonishment marred the handsome face.

Dear God, what did I say? He hadn't known.

But he knew now.

She rose to flee.

Loud pounding on the door added to her horror. "Hey, what's wrong with this thing? Marty, go get security with a key.

Somebody locked the door!" Cousin Irene. The biggest gossip in three counties.

Spinning to face him, she hissed. "Hide. If she finds us in here, that's all anyone will talk about for the rest of this event. She'll tell everyone I know." She grabbed his hand and tried to drag him off the couch while he looked wildly around.

"Where?"

Towing him behind her, she marched into the main restroom area and opened a stall door. "In here, quick." She shoved in behind him and, grabbing his arm for balance, stepped onto the toilet seat. With her heels hanging in space, she transferred her hold to the top of the dividing wall and whispered, "Up, come on!"

He climbed up with her and she kicked the door shut. "Now, be quiet. They can't know we're here."

"Did you unlock the door?" he asked.

"No, but someone will bring a key, and we just have to stay in here until the coast is clear." She wobbled, and he steadied her. She shrugged him away. "Just be quiet, okay? God, I won't need to blow off my date if this gets out. Who will want to go out with me after I spent the evening slumming in the bathroom with you?"

What an interesting predicament. Despite her concern for both their reputations—hers, anyway—the humor still made it hard to maintain his stance on the wobbly seat. And his head rose higher than the wall, meaning if he didn't want to be seen, he had to crouch. Fighting to keep his balance, he grasped her around the waist, and in the ensuing weaving dance, his face wound up pressed between her warm, sweetly scented breasts. Before she could remedy the situation—because he made no move to do so—the bathroom door crashed open, and the room filled with bustling women.

Chatter and giggles, clicking of heels, stall doors slamming. If he'd straightened, they'd have seen him for sure. As the door next to them opened, Karin pulled her fingers from the connecting wall and held onto his head. If she hadn't been so angry, it might have been an intriguing situation. As it was, her heaving breaths against his cheek sent a message to his cock. Once his face got up close and personal with a pair of tits like these, the below the waist parts of him went on red alert. And her lack of experience had no impact on his reaction.

Unfortunately, the hard-on was pinned against his leg in a most uncomfortable way, and he shifted to try to avoid the pinch. Karin's breasts heaved, and her fingers tightened in his hair. Was she crying?

A virgin all pressed up against a strange man in a bathroom stall, his nose in her cleavage. How embarrassing for her—although he still couldn't quite process the fact that a woman in her early twenties had not taken even one lover. Especially one as feminine and appealing as her. Or one who smelled like vanilla and the violets that matched her irises. Closing his eyes, he drew in a deep breath. Lovely. Their awkward location aside, position was everything. And his remained just this side of Heaven.

His distraction fled as someone yanked on the door of their hideaway.

"No," a piping voice said, "I can't get it open."

"Use another stall." An older voice, perhaps the child's mother? Karin trembled harder, how upset was she?

"They're all full, and I can't wait!"

Another woman spoke. "I don't see any feet...is anyone in there?"

He pulled back to meet Karin's face, tears running down her cheeks. Alarm raced through his veins before the rest of her expression registered. Mirth. The girl was laughing! He tightened his grip on her waist and stared at her in shock.

She let go of his head, steadied by his hold, and pointed down, her mouth agape.

"Mommy, why is there a man and a lady standing on the toilet in here?" A little face stared up at them. "Are you guys done? I have to go number one now!"

"We'll be right out." Karin spoke before he could even begin to think what to do. How had he ever believed they could carry this off without getting caught? He helped her down from their perch and stepped to the floor, moving to the back while she slid the lock and pulled the door open.

"Follow my lead." She moved out of the stall and into the bathroom like a queen, shoulders back and head held high. He trailed behind, looking neither right nor left, cheeks flaming, gaze fixed on the diminutive figure gliding through the staring women. The little girl scooted past them, apparently having lost interest in favor of her ultimate goal.

It felt like years but took seconds before they were in the main banquet room again.

Karin picked up the pace, her high heels clicking on the hardwood floor as she made a beeline for the French doors leading to the patio and gardens. Ray did as she'd ordered and followed, allowing a few feet between them as they wound through the crowded room.

Dinner over, the other guests had left their seats and mingled, chatting and laughing, involved in their conversations. The two families seemed to have hit it off, the party in full swing. Passing the last table, he pretended not to notice his sister waving at him and dodged out into the warm desert night.

Karin let the door swing closed behind them and breathed a deep sigh. "Fun."

He nodded, falling into step beside her as she descended a flight of stone stairs at the side of the patio. "I wouldn't describe it that way, exactly. It isn't good for my reputation to be caught cowering on a ladies' room toilet, but I guess no major harm was done."

She made a choking sound, but he feared to look her way and find she was laughing at him this time. A man had his pride.

At the bottom of the flight, a gravel path wound out of sight through some cottonwood trees and desert plantings. As they moved along it, they entered an area where blank walls on two sides blocked the bright lights of the strip and the hotel. They strolled for a few moments in silence.

"The little girl was my second cousin, Marika." Karin's low tones blended with the balmy breeze bending the tree branches. "Irene the Gossip Queen's daughter."

He blanched. "Ouch."

"Yeah," she said, no hint of emotion coloring her words. "I can never go home now."

He tried to discern whether she was serious, but her calm voice gave nothing away, so he reached for her arm and stopped her, turning her to face him. The moon rose above the trees, its full light shining on her face. Her look of despair wrung his heart.

"This is a big problem for you, isn't it?" he said, folding her hand in his two much larger ones.

She nodded. "Yeah, it is. I can't begin to imagine how she will embroider the story. I will be the only fallen woman/virgin in three counties." A wry grin turned up the corner of her lips. "But, I suppose that has its own status."

"You can have T-shirts made. A scarlet V." He traced the letter in the air with a flourish, watching for a reaction.

She giggled. "I'm probably overreacting, but Irene has a big mouth. I am a librarian."

"And what do you mean?"

She shrugged. "I live in a small town. People judge."

"Screw them!" Bastards who dared to judge Karin!

Her eyes widened. "I don't screw anyone, that's the point. I work and go to the gym, visit my parents two towns over where they moved a while ago, and live a virtuous life."

"Nothing wrong with being virtuous," he said. "You're an example for us all."

"I'm dull, boring, and too blah to live." She jerked away and began to walk toward the party. "I might as well go back and face the music."

And her date. Unless he could use the new situation to talk her out of it.

From halfway across the garden, the festive site of the rehearsal party glowed. People flitted past the wide windows, their happy faces making Karin feel even worse. She tried to snap out of it, shrug her embarrassment and despair away. This night was about Mark and Julia and their joy, the two families meeting and getting to know one another. Not about little Karin's problems.

Her role had been simple. Attend, eat, drink, and leave to enjoy the very generous gift the happy couple had bestowed upon her. Instead, she'd gotten into an argument with the best man, Mark's brother, and created a scandal in the bathroom.

She could imagine what Irene would make up to embellish the story. Maybe they'd been kissing...or worse! By now, everyone in the room would know. There had been at least eight women and one very chatty child present to witness her humiliation. *Can you believe...? Yes, Karin, such a nice young lady. Standing on a toilet with the best man.*

And they had the bathroom door locked.

The worst part. *Who goes into a bathroom with a man and locks the door unless she intends to...?* God.

She stopped and turned to face Ray. "I can't go back in there."

He nodded. "Okay, where do you want to go?"

Her options limited, or maybe, for the very first time, they were not. A fallen woman had greater latitude. With a ruined reputation, or one about to be—as soon as Irene got home to spread the word, she'd either be laughed at or shunned, or both. The library director, Miss Sarah, was the last of the great spinsters. She'd hired Karin for her spotless reputation. If she heard her paragon was fooling around with strange men in public restrooms, she'd fire her on the spot. Call her a bad influence on all the children and upstanding citizens of the fine town of Delta. One of the downsides of living in a small burgh. In a big city, a librarian didn't have to be Miss Marian from *The Music Man.*

She'd have to move to an urban center somewhere. Shrugging away the worries of tomorrow—or next week when she'd be out of work—she made a decision. "I want to go to Hell in a handcart."

"What?" He laughed. "How about we have a drink in the hotel bar?"

"Okay," she said, lifting her chin. "It's a start."

Chapter Six

*T*he girl could hold her liquor. Why he'd thought her claims of virtue extended to teetotalism, he'd never know. When he'd suggested a drink, he'd thought she'd have one, get a little loopy, and be more amenable to his suggestion she forget her 1Night Stand date and go to bed.

Instead, she'd proceeded to drink him under the table. No girlie cocktails with fruit and umbrellas. She laughed at the idea of the pomegranate martinis on special that night. Straight bourbon, top shelf, two fingers at a time. Ray considered ordering his usual lager, but had joined her in the hard stuff and had begun to realize his mistake.

While he spoke with care to avoid a slur, the little girl with the violet eyes tossed back another and launched into a story about Julia and Mark and their sex-like-bunnies episodes. At least the booze seemed to be loosening her inhibitions. While she didn't swear, her tales grew more graphic with each drink.

"...and they don't know this, but I wandered into the bathroom to get my makeup bag, and then I heard these sounds, kind of a squishy splashing noise. I backed out of there so fast!"

He scratched his jaw in disbelief. "They never found out?"

"No, lucky I never thought of it before after a few drinks." She beamed at him and waved to the attractive blonde bartender. "Another round, please. Charge it to my room." Tipping her glass back, she swallowed the last drops. "In case you haven't noticed, bourbon makes me chatty. And less than discreet." She giggled.

"Maybe we've had enough." He had, even if she hadn't. And he'd made no progress toward getting her to give up the date so he could go on his. He wasn't in the greatest shape to meet a new woman at this point anyway. The situation grew progressively worse.

"Oh, no. I can go on all night."

The bartender approached with the bottle, but Ray held his hand over his glass.

"None for me, thanks. I'm done." He waited as Karin tossed back the fresh one, and then he nodded in her direction. "And so is my companion. If we have any more, she'll have to carry me to my room."

The server laughed, tossed her ponytail, and gave Karin a wink. "If you're looking for someone to finish the evening with, I get off in an hour. After he goes night-night." She smiled and moved down the bar, where a pair of men in business suits were trying to get her attention.

Karin's eyes were as wide as saucers. "Did she just hit on me?"

Ray covered his mouth to hide his grin. "Yes, I believe she did. Are you interested?"

She leaned forward to watch the woman flirt with the customers. "I think she treats everyone the same way."

"She probably does, a little, for tips or to keep from being bored. But I think with you she meant it." For a moment the idea flew through, maybe his lovely companion had waited so long because...was she not attracted to men?

"Gosh, I hope I didn't do anything to lead her on." The hint of worry in Karin's tone reassured him, although in his state of intoxication, his instincts were less than trustworthy. "I better go tell her I like boys."

He breathed a sigh of relief. Now...did she also find sparks with him? And how to ask?

"No, it's okay," he said in a low voice. "She was only fishing. As long as it doesn't go any further, no harm no foul." And if the bartender did push the issue, he'd shut it down for her. Why did everyone in town, bartenders and blind dates, want to bed this innocent tonight? If it kept up, he'd never convince her to go back to her room and behave herself.

"All right, if you're sure." She dug in her purse. "I'd better find out where I'm supposed to meet this date of mine—and you should do the same." She paused. "Unless you already texted Madame Eve?"

Ray panicked. He needed to distract her for—he glanced at his watch—another hour or so. It was nearly midnight. Soon, she'd have to agree it was too late. They had to get up early to help with the final wedding preparations, and once it hit one o'clock or so, there'd be no way she'd be able to have a date without being exhausted and useless in the morning.

He covered her hand with his, tangling their fingers together. "Sure, but first I want to show you something." He reached into his pocket and tossed a few bills on the bar for a tip. Catching the bartender's eye, he pointed at the money. "Thanks for everything." *Everything, yeah. Hitting on my date.*

She's not my date. But she's not someone else's either, not if I play my cards right.

"What?" Karin asked.

He stood, keeping her delicate fingers in his big paw. "Huh?"

"What do you want to show me?"

He had no answer for her, as he led her toward the lobby, his slowed brain trying to think of something interesting enough to distract her from her mission. He could drag her to another casino, maybe take her to see the lights on the strip. His best tool, the one he used for his most successful seductions, was his pilot's license. A short flight usually brought women to his bed, but the amount of alcohol he'd consumed made flying a no-go. He'd need another tactic this time. Plus...he sought to distract her, not seduce her. No matter how much he wanted to slide her purple skirt up her thighs and cup her ass and....

Stop it! The idea was to keep her out of a stranger's bed. But what if the stranger was him?

Focus.

What would occupy them for an hour? What did this woman find interesting?

The plan appeared out of the alcohol fog in his brain. *The stars.* And since he couldn't fly her to them under the influence, he had another idea.

Chapter Seven

*T*hey strolled through the lobby, Ray leaving Karin standing by the elevators while he strode to the information desk. He had to make sure the venue in question remained open before sharing his brilliant plan. If he couldn't distract a thwarted astronomer with the Castillo's brand new observatory, he didn't know what else he could use.

"Hi," he said to the young woman in the neat blazer and button down worn by many of the employees. "Is the observatory open at this time of night?"

She pointed to a small sign listing the facility's hours. "I'm afraid it's just closing. But it opens in the morning at nine, if you'd like to check back then." Disappointment flooded him.

"There's no way I can get in for just a few minutes? It would mean a lot." Ray glanced over his shoulder at Karin, who wandered the lobby, looking at the artwork and pausing to check her watch.

"I don't think...wait." She waved to a woman crossing the marble floor at a fast clip. "Leah, do you have a second?"

The petite woman paused and moved toward them, clutching a sheaf of printouts in both arms. "Sure, but I have to keep moving. Big wedding tomorrow and I'm the planner...somehow." She laughed. "It's not my usual job, so I'm afraid of missing a detail."

The information clerk pointed to Ray. "This gentleman asked if we can keep the observatory open just long enough for him to show his girlfriend. I explained it's about to shut down for the night."

Leah turned toward him, about to say something, and stopped. "Andrea, this is the best man from the wedding tomorrow. Mark's brother...Ray, is it?"

He'd encountered Leah Castillo, the owner's wife and Julia's friend, for only a moment when they first arrived, so he was pleased to be remembered. Maybe it would help his case. "I would very much appreciate anything you can do to help me."

Leah's eyes narrowed. "You have a girlfriend, but I thought—"

He winced. Was she aware of their unusual arrangements for the evening? Would Julia have confided in her—maybe. He remembered something about Leah and her husband meeting through the same dating service he was probably blowing off. Not that he hadn't intended to go on his date, but keeping Karin from hers was making keeping his impossible. He hoped Mark and Madame Eve would forgive him.

Karin arrived at his side. "Ray, if we aren't going to see whatever it is you want to show me, I need to go follow up on you-know-what."

"Karin!" Leah smiled. "Is this who your date is, Ray?" She glanced from one to the other. "You never know. In that case, let me just place a call upstairs, and I'm sure we can accommodate your...desires."

She pulled a cell phone from her pocket, juggling the files in her arms, and spoke into it in a soft voice. Pressing a button, she beamed at them both. "There you go! Never let it be said the Castillo stood in the way of romance." She scooted away, calling over her shoulder. "Wait until I tell Jackson. He'll be so amused."

Karin stared after her. "What did she mean, I'm your date?"

He shrugged. "She didn't give me a chance to correct her. But she did make it possible for me to show you something special. We can let her know tomorrow, if you find it necessary, but I think she'll be busy with the wedding."

"The wedding. How late is it? I have to check in with my real date, or I won't have any time to go on it."

"Oh," he said, taking her arm and leading her to the bank of elevators, "this won't take long. And Leah went to so much trouble to arrange it for us. I know you'll think it worth your time." The bourbon buzz was wearing off, replaced by the high brought on by the pleasure of her company.

She glanced behind her, as if she expected to see someone— her date?—but allowed him to lead her into the glass elevator marked, Observatory and Rooftop Gardens. The doors closed behind them, and the car shot upward.

Karin pressed her face close to the wall. "Look at the strip all lit up. Beautiful, isn't it?"

"Almost as beautiful as the company." He moved nearer to her, turning her toward him. Her face tilted up toward his, like a flower, with her rose red lips parted.

"Where are you taking me?" she asked. "I didn't see this elevator before."

"You didn't see the sign, then?" He released her arm and slipped his around her waist. "I'm taking you to the stars."

"This is the elevator to the heavens?" She rested against the glass, smiling at him. "You do have connections."

Ray's face was shadowed, the occasional light from outside flashing across it as they rose higher. "Apparently so, are you impressed?

Impressed, yes. Giddy with his touch. Short of breath at being alone in the small space with him. All of the above and more. With his broad shoulders, his hands big enough to engulf hers when he took them. With his humor and his handsome face. "Well how could I not be? Are we meeting God himself in Heaven?"

"You'll see, we're almost there."

"Can't wait."

The elevator slowed and stopped, the doors opening onto a broad terrace with more desert landscaping. But this garden featured a shimmering reflecting pool in the middle of its patio of multi-hued stone. She slipped away from Ray and moved toward it, hypnotized. The height dimmed the Strip's lights, as did the waist-high walls surrounding the paradise they'd entered. The plantings were different from the other garden. Desert, but not like anything she'd seen in Nevada. Exotic trees with long draping branches touching the ground, low-growing bushes whose exotic fragrance tickled her nose. And the pool itself, reflecting every star in the never-ending night sky. Her breath hitched.

"Like it?" Ray came up behind her and rested his hands on her shoulders. "The heavens captured for you, in a bowl."

"Can I take them with me when I go?" She relished the breeze stirring her hair.

"I will put them in my pocket and carry them wherever you want them."

She turned to him, her soul alight. "I will have to follow you, because you'll have my heart in your pocket."

"Excuse me, sir? Miss?" They spun to face the voice, a man in a blue jumpsuit, similar to an astronaut's, stood in an open doorway. "I understand you are the couple who requested a private showing in the observatory?"

She laughed in perfect happiness. "I didn't even know they had an observatory at this hotel. I thought the lights of the strip would make it impossible, even if they wanted one."

"We're very high up, and our telescope is powerful." He beckoned them inside. "I will turn on the equipment and then go and leave you alone. If you need me, just hit the buzzer on the side of the seat and I'll come in." He waited as they found their way to seats in the middle of the room, and clicked some keys on a control pad by the door. "I'm turning on the evening show, the 'date night' version instead of the educational one we use for families during the day. Have fun."

Ornate sconces along the walls dimmed. Karin settled into

the cushioned seat and blinked as it tilted back until she lay nearly flat. Beside her, Ray's chair did the same.

"Nice," he commented, chuckling. "I'd heard it was special up here, but the Castillos never do anything half ass."

"I guess not," she replied. The room went dark and suddenly the ceiling above them glowed with constellations gliding by in an ancient, implacable dance. A low voice announced, these were the skies seen by Scheherazade and her king, when she told her tales over a thousand and one nights. Those heavens inspired the romance and magic that turned her king from a threat to her life to her most ardent admirer.

There were no more words, only a swelling music she thought might be Middle Eastern in origin, classical but with a haunting lilt.

"*Caravansary,*" Ray whispered. "Kitaro."

"Oh, I don't know it," she said. "But so lovely."

"Do you mind?" He lifted the arm of the seat between them so it rested behind their chairs and took her hand. "Look at the way they move." He pointed to a thick grouping above them.

"I was going to be an astronaut," she said, linking her fingers into his. "I was going to go there."

"To the stars."

She sighed. "Yes." Her mourning for the loss of her dreams had ended forever ago. Except for times like this.

"Why didn't you go back to school and finish your degree?"

"Oh," she spoke in a voice as hushed as his, not wanting to break the spell. "It's too late. The scholarship is gone now, offered to the next applicant in line. I'll just have to keep my feet on the ground." She'd never lose the sadness that swelled whenever she made the flip comment, but perhaps she could keep it from showing.

From his nearly prone position, Ray turned to the side and reached toward her with his free hand. He touched the skin under her eye and held his finger in front of her, the tear he'd captured glimmering in the starlight. "You can't give up your heart. You aren't a girl whose feet belong on the ground."

She laughed, her throat closing, nearly choking her. "But I don't have any choice, not anymore. I can't be an astronaut. I'm a librarian."

Dropping her hand, Ray slid his arm around her shoulders and tugged her against his side. "Let's watch the show for a while and enjoy. I think you were born to reach for the sky."

Her date would have to accept her apologies tomorrow. The man next to her was worth her time, and she'd begun to think he might be interested in more than just protecting her from the stranger she'd been set up with.

Chapter Eight

*T*he little librarian was a stargazer. A sweet-smelling, soft, warm, wanna-be space jockey. "I thought you had to be in the military to get the training to be an astronaut."

She tilted her face toward his, and he watched the starlight play over her smooth cheeks. "Oh, not anymore. And I wasn't planning on NASA. My scholarship came from a private company looking to staff their future flights. They are planning on tourist ventures as well as exploratory flights to nearby asteroids and maybe even planets to search for resources like minerals and oh, I don't know what all. My undergrad degree in astronomy was just a basis for the advanced one I wanted in astrophysics."

"So, you were going to be an onboard scientist but not fly the ships?"

"No, I would have been both, at least as per the plan the recruiter discussed with me. They were going to send two-person teams on the scientific missions, so they needed both members to be scientist/pilots."

"Interesting." So, she would have plied the universe in the name of science and commerce all alone with some guy. The idea raised the hackles on his neck until he took in the wide eyes fixed on his face, and he smiled. They were alone in the observatory, too late now for either of them to follow up on their dates, and he had begun to enjoy her company too much to want to do it anyway. Her breast pressed against his chest sent ideas to his cock, which hardened in anticipation of more contact.

But no, not with this virgin. The responsibility of being her first—she deserved someone who would be with her forever. With the stars swirling in the sky/ceiling and classical music in the background, if he'd had a romantic bone in his body, he'd have kissed her.

God, no he wouldn't. The girl was an angel, but one grounded in her town in California, not someone who could fly with him.

"Ray, you okay?"

He'd tensed, and she'd followed suit. He stroked her back, up and down in slow, comforting sweeps, and she relaxed.

"Sure, I'm fine. Are you enjoying the show?" Not that he was focused on it.

"It's great. Thank you for bringing me up here." She shifted to lie on her back in the chair, but stayed against his side. "All these planets and stars and asteroids. The universe is out there to be discovered."

The longing in her voice struck his soul. Beyond sensible thought, he did the only thing possible, rolled to the side, and kissed her. She made a squeak of surprise or protest and he began to move back, but she lifted her arms to circle his neck and held him there, her soft, full lips parting to his demands.

Under the influence of the atmosphere, his head swam. When the tip of her tongue teased his lower lip, he groaned and deepened the pressure. Nibbling and laving, he explored the warm cavern of her mouth as if it were the deep space she sought to penetrate.

Penetrate. His dick became even harder, if that were possible, and he shuddered when her thigh rubbed against it. For a girl with no experience, she seemed to know just how to arouse a man. His conscience told him to hold back, but he stroked her bare shoulder and moving down to cup her breast through the fabric of her gown. Palming it, he felt a sense of satisfaction at the sharp nipple poking through her dress.

As long as he didn't go too far, where was the harm? He wouldn't take her to bed. They were only making out a little.

Like high school kids.

He kissed her some more, loving the taste of her, the way her arms tightened when he rubbed circles on the tips of her breasts. Leaving her lips, he dropped pecks on her cheeks on the way to her ear and the sweet warmth of her throat. Every inch of her fascinated him. She dropped her head to the side as he sucked at her neck. He nibbled there. A low sound of pleasure encouraged him to continue.

Forcing his doubts down, he pushed her dress off her shoulders and confronted the scoop-shaped bra offering her creamy mounds to him, half-moons of delight. He'd keep it above the waist, play a little more then return her to her room no worse for wear.

Satisfied with his plan, he snapped the clasp on the front of her bra and gazed with pleasure as her dark tipped nipples came into view. Cherries on snow. He hesitated, where was that poetic crap coming from?

"Ray?" Her voice seemed to come from far away, and to give him some sort of permission.

He took one breast into his mouth, flicking the nipple and growling in satisfaction when she gasped. Her heart pounded, and he sucked on his prize.

Releasing it, he rubbed his cheek over her chest. "Say no anytime, baby."

"No."

He jerked away. "I'm sorry, I...." *I what? Ravaged you in the name of protecting you?*

She laughed. "I mean, I won't say no." Tangling her fingers in his hair, she tugged him back toward her bared breasts. "Please don't stop."

The words galvanized him, sending lust surging into his groin. "No," he said, fighting his base instincts with every ounce of his self-control. "You were right to start with."

"I want you."

Dang the woman was persistent. But she didn't know what she was saying. "Honey," he said, reaching up to remove her hands, "if we go much further, I won't be able to stop."

"I don't want you to." She tightened her grip. "Keep going."

"This isn't high school, and I'm a full grown man. I can't just kiss you and suck on your tits, and then call it a night."

She jerked her hands free and jumped to her feet. "Nobody asked you to."

Karin set about straightening her clothes. From his prone position, the stars swirled over her head, and he felt a pang as her dress settled back on her shoulders, hiding her lovely skin from his eyes.

It was all for the best. He gave himself a mental pat on the back for his valor and strength.

"Let me walk you to your room."

She laughed. "You really do think I'm a little girl, don't you?" Bending, she hit the buzzer and called out, "Hey, we're done here. Leaving. Thanks."

The heavens dimmed, the music faded. The sconces glowed again.

"I'm a virgin, Ray, not a child. I can see myself home, thank you." She stalked toward the wide door as it swung open. "I am going to text and find out how to contact my date. If he can forgive me for being so late, I am sure he won't think I'm a little girl." She moved outside, calling over her shoulder, "I'll see you tomorrow, Ray. After my one-night stand."

She disappeared.

Images of her in the arms of another man filled his imagination. The faceless stranger touched her body, and rage propelled Ray out of his seat, which was rising to upright again. He stumbled and regained his footing, but by the time he raced out into the garden and toward the elevator, the doors were closing behind her. Crap.

He had to find her. Glancing around, he saw a sign for

"Emergency Use Only" steps and started for them, then realized opening the door would likely set off alarms. Besides, so many stories up, it would take him much longer to get down than for the elevator to return. So he waited, in a fury of impatience, pacing and hitting the button to call the glass car every time he passed it. As if it would bring it faster. After an eternity, a chime sounded, and the doors opened. He leapt in and began the interminable descent to the lobby.

He didn't know her room number, but he would find out from the concierge.

When he reached the bottom floor, he tore out of the elevator and headed for the information booth. Another young woman in a blazer, her blonde hair in the longest braid he'd ever seen, stood behind the podium, sorting through the contents of a voluminous folder. She looked up and smiled when he arrived.

"Sorry, I'm helping with some final details of a wedding tomorrow. I swear you'd think the couple was European royalty, the way Leah has pressed us all into service." She giggled, rolling her eyes. "But you don't care. How can I help you, sir?"

"I need to get someone's room number."

She frowned. "Giving out room numbers of other guests would be a security breach. Can I do anything else for you?"

His mind raced. He couldn't be sure she'd be there, but she'd go back to freshen up before meeting her "date." Wouldn't she? "Are you positive? I need to find her before she calls some other guy."

"Oh, I'm positive. I would lose my job." She didn't seem inclined to budge despite his off-the-wall comment, and if it meant her job, of course she wouldn't. He nodded and turned away, trying to think of another solution and coming up empty.

"Yes, sir," the girl spoke again, from behind him. "That's the man over there, he seems quite distraught."

Shit, she'd called for backup. Someone to throw the stalker out of the building. Turning to face the person behind him, he encountered not a uniformed security guard, but a tall Latin man in jeans and a fitted black T-shirt. Ray opened his mouth to explain...what? He had to stop the woman he'd become obsessed with from having sex for the first time in her life with a stranger? He wanted to rip the head off any other man who touched her? That should convince the hotel they had a crazed stalker to deal with. This was not normal behavior, especially for him. He hadn't thought jealousy part of his makeup until he'd laid eyes on Karin.

"Hi, maybe I can help."

Promising. He hadn't said, *I need to escort you outside.*

"I'm looking for a friend of mine."

The man laughed. "A friend, huh? Your expression doesn't say 'friend.' It says you're looking for your woman. I'm searching for mine—my wife—she's still down here somewhere, dealing with the details of a wedding instead of upstairs in our bed where she belongs." He extended a hand. "Jackson Castillo. Walk with me while I look, and you can tell me your story. Maybe we will find your lost one, too."

He shrugged. "Sure." Maybe he would find her. Although, he was fairly sure she would be upstairs in her room. But if the hotel staff wouldn't tell him where she was, what could he do? Call one of their relatives and demand the information? Such a call at this hour of the morning would raise a flag. And draw questions. *Sorry for waking you up, I just want to find Karin so I can screw her brains out before some other guy does.* That should go over well with her friends and family. Even Julia—who he shouldn't wake on the night before her wedding—would not think highly of him under those circumstances.

Jackson strode off across the lobby, and Ray took a quick extra step to catch up. "So, what's the story? You and your girlfriend have a fight?"

She's not my girlfriend. Nothing to be gained by admitting it. Wait. "Did you say Jackson Castillo? And your wife is planning the wedding? You're the owner here, aren't you?"

"More or less, yes." They entered the casino, late night gamblers still plying the machines, lights flashing, and bells chiming. A shriek rang out from across the room. "There's a happy winner."

Ray glanced, but quickly lost interest, his focus back on Karin. With every passing moment, the brute of a one-night stand could be closer to her. "If you own the place, you can tell me Karin's room number."

Jackson paused at an archway leading to the long hall lined with elevators. "Why would I do that?"

Why would he? The question struck deep. What did Ray have to offer Karin? A quick night in bed? The loss of her virginity to a different stranger? Despair filled him. He had no answer.

Jackson slapped him on the back. "Let me make it easier on you. You're Mark's brother, Ray, aren't you? From the wedding that's made my life a living hell for weeks?"

He grimaced. "Yep."

"And you are looking for Karin, your date."

How did he know? But she wasn't his.... The sliver of his brain not too tied up in jealousy and desire surfaced. "Right."

The man grinned, his white teeth gleaming. He could do toothpaste commercials with his smile. "Let me make a call." Pulling a cell phone from his pocket, he pressed a button then spoke a few words into it. After a moment, he said, "Thanks," and slipped the phone back. "Okay, still looking for Leah." He took a step away.

Puzzled, Ray grabbed his arm. "Wait. Weren't you getting me Karin's room number?"

Jackson moved forward, and Ray's hand dropped away. "Of course not. Besides, she's not in her room."

Ray followed. "Where is she?"

"The woman at the security desk told me she's with Leah. They were last seen heading toward the banquet room."

"Together."

"Yes, and I've had just about enough. I am going to get my wife and take her upstairs to our bed. I can't sleep without her there." The man pounded a fist in his other palm. "I'm putting my foot down."

Reassuring.

"I suggest you do the same."

Ray gulped. "Put my foot down?"

Jackson laughed and reached for a door handle. "If she'll let you. It's never worked for me yet. She just lets me boss her a little because she's crazy about me."

They entered a large room already decorated for the wedding reception with ribbons and streamers and a large bunch of pale pink and white balloons hanging from the ceiling. The tables were covered with white cloths and set with gleaming plates and glasses.

"You want to boss me around?" A petite platinum blonde approached and lifted her face toward Jackson. He bent and gave her a kiss then wrapped an arm around her shoulders. "If I'd known you were in this mood, I'd have come up sooner."

The picture of wedded bliss, the two stood facing him. But his gaze drifted to the smaller shape across the room. Karin stood by a gaily-decorated table, twisting a bit of ribbon in her hands, and she wouldn't meet his eyes. He tried to take comfort in the fact she had been doing wedding things with Leah instead of out on her date, but the set of her jaw didn't give him hope for much more.

After a long moment, Jackson gave Leah a squeeze and a peck on the nose. "We are going up to bed, and you two should do the same."

"Jackson!" His wife elbowed him in the ribs. "Let them work this out for themselves. Don't be rushing them." She ruined her glare with an impish grin. "But we do have to get upstairs. Tomorrow will be an exciting day."

Jackson bent and whispered something in her ear, and she colored.

Unable to stand their happiness when the woman who'd managed to worm her way into his heart in a few hours looked so miserable, Ray nodded. "Good night. We will see you both tomorrow."

Karin approached and gave the couple a hug. "You're making

everything so perfect for Julia and Mark. I'll never be able to thank you enough."

"My wife is nothing if not perfect." Jackson flinched as the elbow hit home again. "You are, my dear." He spoke to Leah, but his eyes focused on Ray. "Opportunities to find perfection are once in a lifetime. Goodnight, my friends. I hope you enjoy the rest of your evening and your stay. Be sure to let the staff know if you need anything at all." The pair left, their laughter drifting down the hall behind them. Domestic bliss Castillo style. They made it look good.

"I suppose he's right," Karin said. "It's going to be an exciting day tomorrow, and I'm going to bed." She brushed past him, but he wrapped his hand around her wrist and tugged her to face him.

"I thought you were going to go on your date."

Her jaw tightened, but she kept her gaze on the open doorway, as if ready to make her escape. "At this hour? It's three in the morning. That ship has sailed."

"Sorry you missed out."

She jerked her arm away. "Really, and your date? Where is she?"

His date? He hadn't thought of it—her, whoever—in hours. Keeping Karin occupied had taken up all his attention. "Oh, I guess it's too late to get in touch with her now."

"You can try tomorrow and see if the offer is still open."

Would she? Had he spent the whole night stopping her from doing something she'd just do the next evening anyway? He'd used every trick in his arsenal and several he'd made up on the spot. For nothing?

Chapter Nine

What an idiot he was. Karin had trailed around after Ray all evening while he tried to distract her from going on her date, while he tried to get her drunk enough to...what? Send her off to bed...seduce her himself, maybe? She'd followed like a puppy from location to location, and why?

Because I am a bigger idiot.

In her stupidity, she had thought he might like her. That he protested too much. Why should he care, after all, if a woman he barely knew went to bed with someone else? But then, why should it matter to her whether he did?

All the while she'd gone along with his plans, they had served her own purpose of keeping him occupied. For some silly reason, she hadn't wanted him to go on a date with someone else either.

In the observatory, she'd thought....

Screw it. Life had to start sometime.

She brought her head up to meet his blue eyes and lifted off her silly high heels onto her tiptoes. While he stared, she twined her arms around his neck and smiled up at him.

"Enough. Come to my room with me." She followed up with a kiss she hoped told him her intentions. She'd decided hours ago, before the observatory, to let the other date go by. She hadn't ever been this attracted to a man. Her heart raced every time he'd taken her arm to lead her from place to place through the hotel. Couldn't he tell how attracted to him she was?

Sometimes inexperience sucked.

But it didn't keep her from knowing what she wanted. She wanted Ray.

He held back for a moment, while she moved her mouth over his, hanging from his neck then, in a move that stole her breath, he took control. Wrapping his arms around her waist, he lifted her off her feet and ground his lips on hers, forcing them to part. His tongue met hers, stroking in a sinuous pattern. He cupped her breasts through her thin dress and bra.

He spoke against her mouth, his breath teasing and warm. "If I come to your room, there is no turning back. I'm staying all night."

Her blood thumped in her ears. But she'd heard him. "I hope so." Karin clung to him, dizzy and limp.

He broke the kiss and set her away from him, taking her hand. "Let's go."

In a daze, she allowed him to lead her out of the banquet room and toward the elevators. She'd made the decision of a lifetime. There were no guarantees, no promises of an eternity together, but Ray had touched her in so many ways already, she'd worry about that in the morning. Tonight, she would take him to her room and...*shit!* She stopped, dragging him to a halt, too.

"I can't take you to my room."

He faced her, such a look of horror and disappointment on his handsome face she fought back laughter. "I understand. You've changed your mind. I'll just take you to your door. It's too late for you to wander the halls alone." Releasing her hand, he turned away.

She did laugh, and he spun back, frowning.

Before he could react any further, she moved into him and hugged his waist. He tensed, and she stroked the broad back under her fingertips. "No, Ray. We can't go to my room because it's full of teenagers. I can hardly send them in search of other accommodations."

He relaxed. "My room?"

"Unless your mother has also imposed half the kids in the family on you, yes." She snuggled closer, her cheek against the heavy cotton of his shirt. "Let's go to your room."

"Sounds perfect." He laid his arm across her shoulders. "I might have something to show you there, too."

"Do tell." She felt more comfortable with his banter, now her decision was made. "I think I might like to have a look. Etchings?"

"Hmm, no, although I think there's some kind of art on the walls if you want to check it out. It is a nice room."

"Oh." She stood at his side while he pressed the button for the elevator. "I can't guess." Heat rose in her cheeks. Not used to such repartee, she feared she wouldn't be able to keep up. A man like him must be used to women a lot more worldly than a virginal small town librarian. But his hand slid up her side to her ribcage, his fingertips resting on the edge of her breast, and fire spread throughout her body, centering between her legs.

The enormity of her decision overwhelmed her, but so did the rightness. Ray was sexy, fun, and had taken her to see the stars. Nobody else had ever seemed to understand what the heavens meant to her. Certainly not her college boyfriend who used her for meals and cheated with her roommate because she didn't put out. Somehow it seemed too important a gift to give someone in a hurry. Yet, look at her now.

"I wish I could take you up in my plane," he said, almost reading her thoughts. "But if you make a habit of getting me drunk, that won't be possible."

"Some other time?" She'd never been in a private plane, only large commercial jetliners. "I'd like it a lot."

"Sure," he said. "I'll be down to visit Mark and Julia sometime, I'm sure."

A pang hit her belly at the reminder this was a one-night thing—unless they happened to connect when he came to visit his brother, and the odds weren't in their favor there. She didn't live close.

"Is there an airport in your town?" He knew she didn't live in the same area as her cousin? Mark must have told him.

"Yes, outside town. Some of the ranchers fly in to check on

things, but it's pretty small."

The elevator arrived, and he guided her inside. "Good to know."

Whatever that meant, it still made her glow with pleasure. Although, she warned herself not to read too much into it. In the tight space, he seemed to loom over her. With such a large man standing at her side, she felt small, maybe a little fragile. She giggled, and he stared down at her.

"What?"

"Nothing. I was just hoping I'm not too small for you." *God, what is he going to make of my comment.*

He arched a dark brow. "You're just the right size. Although I wonder why all that hair doesn't tip you over. Isn't it heavy?"

She wagged her head, sending the heavy mass shifting from side to side, brushing the base of her spine. "Not so far." The elevator continued to rise. "Wow, what floor are you on?"

"Penthouse. I got a suite because I expected to get stuck with a lot of the family looking for a place to party after the event tomorrow. My aunts and uncles and cousins never know when to quit. I had thought they'd end up there tonight, but I got a bit distracted at the dinner."

"Did you, indeed? I thought you just got misdirected—ending up in the ladies' room and all."

"Misdirected, huh?"

The doors slid open to a wide hallway, and she stepped out onto carpet so deep her spike heels disappeared.

"I think I'm back on track. And it worked out for the best because if they had gotten the key from me, they would still be here." He punched a series of numbers into a keypad, and his door clicked open.

She stood in the corridor, her heart in her throat. There would be no turning back from this point. A surge of bravery loosened her limbs, and she followed him into the luxury suite. "I am glad they aren't."

As the door closed, he flipped a switch, and the room flooded with soft light.

"Can I get you anything to drink?" He moved toward a dark wood bar with a row of sparkling glasses suspended upside down from a rack over it. "Bourbon?"

She paused in her wanderings through the palatial rooms. "Hmmm? Oh, no. I'd fall right asleep if I had a drink so late...or is it so early?"

Two bedrooms, a bath with a tub the size of a small swimming pool set in an alcove surrounded on three sides with windows.... One of her favorite fantasies come true. Lying back against a strong man, watching the city lights from the warmth of the bubbling water. The man had been faceless until now.

"I hate to think I'd put you to sleep," he said. "Coffee, then? Or a soft drink?"

She flinched, scooting back to the living room. "I didn't mean...well, it's three in the morning after all. At least, I think it is."

He glanced at his wrist. "Later even."

"Can I get some kind of sparkling water?" She drifted into the bathing area again. There was also a regular bathroom, through a doorway to the left, with an ordinary, although elegant, shower. "This is an amazing tub."

He joined her in her admiration of the Jacuzzi. "Nice. Looks like it could fit two quite easily."

She turned to him, startled. Had he read her mind? "Yes, it does. Would you like to take a swim with me?"

"A swim?" He handed her a glass of sparking water. "I'm afraid I don't remember where I packed my suit."

His grin gave her confidence, and she entered the game. "Why, mine is back in my room. Whatever shall we do?"

Ray's eyes gleamed. He reached past her to turn on the faucet and water began to gush into the tub. "We will think of something, I'm sure." He waited while she took a sip from her glass then took it back and set it on a wide ledge above the bath.

Karin faced away from him. "Well, I can't wear my new dress in there, anyway. Can you help me with the zipper?" She held her breath, proud of her boldness but a little scared when the fabric parted under his touch. As the violet silk fell to the floor, she stepped out of it and gave it a gentle push to the side so it wouldn't be trampled.

Ray's breath caressed her bare shoulders. "Look at me."

Karin sucked in a breath and turned around.

He fell into her thickly lashed violet eyes. Resting his hands on her shoulders, he promised himself to take it easy, not rush her. For a girl with little to no experience, her offer of a Jacuzzi together was a daring move. Her rosebud lips parted, and he bent to take slow possession of them.

"Last chance to back out, baby." He spoke against her mouth, loath to move away from her sweetness.

"Mmm, you keep saying that."

He chuckled, stealing another kiss. "I do, don't I?"

"I'm going to start thinking you don't want me."

He folded her closer, wishing her bra and his shirt into oblivion. "Never." He put her away from him and unbuttoned his shirt, holding her gaze. "I want to savor every inch of you." He bent and removed his shoes and socks.

She unclasped her bra, the lacy garment falling to the floor. Dressed in a tiny pair of black lace panties and her high heels, she dropped her hands to her sides and stood while he slipped his shirt off his shoulders and reached for his belt.

"Can I do that?" A slight tremble betrayed her agitation when she opened the buckle and pulled the leather free from the loops. She unbuttoned his waistband and tugged the zipper down while he held his breath. His slacks fell to his feet, and he kicked them away.

Her hands rested on his hips, and he waited for her to proceed, determined not to rush her. But his erection held the front of his boxer briefs away from his body, and Karin's focus seemed to be slowing the process.

"I can," he said, at the end of his patience.

"No, no I want to." She took hold of the elastic and moved it downward. Finally it, too, lay on the floor by the tub. A long silence held them both until she swallowed hard. "Are all men so...big?"

"Well...." How to answer such a question? He wasn't the largest man on the planet, but probably a little better endowed than most. Glancing past her, he noticed the bathtub nearly full and reached to turn the faucet off. "Ready to take a swim?"

She nodded and sat on the side of the tub. "I need to take my heels off, though." She held one out. "Help me?"

He dropped to one knee, his cock bobbing against his belly. Resting her foot on his thigh, he opened the strap binding her ankle and slid the shoe off. He lifted her foot and held it. As delicate and refined as the rest of her, with pale lavender polish on her toenails. Ray massaged her arch. "Those high things must have been hard on you with all the wandering we did tonight."

She moaned. "Not too bad. I wear heels often, although not usually stilettoes." She smiled at him. "Amazing, but maybe you could do it in the tub? I'm going to melt into a puddle if you keep this up, and end up hitting my head."

He pressed a kiss on her instep and reached for the other shoe. In a moment, he'd freed her and helped her stand. She bit her lip then grasped the tiny sides of her panties and shoved them down her thighs. Standing, she faced him, her eyes fixed on the floor between them, her arms crossed over her belly. A brave attempt not to hide anything, he suspected.

"Look at me."

She tilted her face up, her lovely white skin even paler.

He took her hands and held them away from her. "I want to admire you, okay?"

Karin nodded. "I guess so."

"You're beautiful." Framed by her wealth of long, dark hair, her skin glowed. Her heart-shaped face with its dark violet eyes, smooth cheeks, and short, up-tilted nose struck him as the most perfect he'd ever seen.

"No," she protested, but he gave her a serious look.

"Don't argue. I'm the expert here."

She tugged at her hands, but he held firm.

"No, you said I could look."

Her clothes disguised how long and elegant her limbs were,

and her breasts, with their deep rose nipples, peaked in the air conditioning—or dare he hope from arousal?—had him making plans for spending a lot of time getting familiar with their taste and texture.

"How long can it take?" she asked, a wobble in her voice. "I'm not that big."

"No, but you're perfectly proportioned." He grinned at her. "Longest legs I've ever seen on a woman under five foot two."

She laughed. "Thanks. Now, if you're done making me incredibly uncomfortable, can we take our bath?"

"Sure thing, baby." He released one hand but held onto the other and helped her into the warm water. Once they were settled, facing each other across the expanse of the huge tub, he reached under the water and came up with one of her feet.

"Hey, what are you, a foot guy?" She sank until only her head and shoulders and the rounded tops of her breasts showed above the water, but she didn't pull away. Encouraged, Ray massaged from heel to toe, digging his thumbs into the arch.

"No, I think I might be a Karin guy. I am only starting with your feet. Doesn't it feel good?"

"So good," she admitted, sighing. "So, proceed."

"Happy to." He reached for the other and repeated the massage then moved to her ankle and calf, taking his time, wanting to know every inch of her. His cock twitched, and he struggled to keep his calm demeanor.

"I am surprised," she said, sinking deeper and resting her head on the ledge.

"Surprised? Why?"

"I kind of thought things would move faster, you know...."

"Hmm, well if you want them to." He let her leg slide back into the water and lunged for her. Karin squealed when he caught her wrist and tugged her toward him. Her skin was warm and slippery, and she laughed as she fell onto his lap. "Fast enough for you?"

Her back pressed against his chest, her rounded ass cheeks directly on his rigid cock. He counted backward from one hundred by sevens.

Suddenly, all play was gone and lust roared through his body.

Chapter Ten

*K*arin fought to assess the situation without panic. She was sitting on a naked man's lap. Her naked butt on his naked penis. There were very few directions in which she could go with this other than directly to sex. Yet, when she searched her mind for fear, for reservations, she found a warm pool of desire. Ray's chest against her back provided solid reassurance she'd found a strong man, one she could rely on to take her through her first time.

He kissed her neck, and she tilted her head to the side to grant him better access. Her belly fluttered. "Nice." Small word for such an incredible moment.

"Yes," he replied, bringing his hands forward to take a breast in each. "At least nice—more like heavenly. Do you mind if I feel you up a little?"

His careless words made her grin. "Please."

Her days shut up in a stuffy library, in conservative clothes, high-necked blouses, and neat slacks faded as warm palms rubbed her nipples to tingling awareness, and her blood sang in her ears.

If she'd imagined this moment—and of course she had—she'd pictured herself as a maiden under the hands of a masterful teacher, showing her the way. But a Siren she hadn't known dwelled inside her took over the show. Instinct led her to turn in his arms and face the man who would be her lover. In her new position, her breasts pressed against his chest and his penis along her pussy.

Ray groaned. "Baby, if you keep this up, we're going to have a short night."

The water gave her buoyancy and grace she never had on dry land, and she rocked her hips, resting her hands on his shoulders for balance.

"You don't like this?" Karin shifted down his thighs and slid up again, her belly tightening at the sensation of his cock brushing past her virgin orifice. "Is this better?"

"Oh, I like it." He grasped her around the waist, holding her in place. "Too much. Are you sure you haven't done this before? Because you're awfully good at it."

She smiled and wriggled against him. "I'm feeling like a mermaid, slippery and sleek. Out of the water, I'm kind of klutzy." Doubts faded into the background. On top, she had a control that made her confidence soar. Along with his compliments. He could keep those going all night if he wanted.

He buried his face in her neck, licking at droplets of water and taking a nip of skin. She yelped.

"If you're going to be a mermaid, I might be a vampire." He bit again, sharper, and she lurched in his lap. His cock slid inside a fraction of an inch, and he pushed her away. "Not yet. I want this to be good for you." Tightening his grip, he lifted her onto the side of the tub. "Open your legs, baby, I want to taste you."

Oh, God. The ledge was pretty wide, but she still feared she'd tumble off if she got any more boneless with desire. Ray nudged her thighs wide apart and knelt between them. He stroked one finger over her pussy, and finding her clit, he pressed hard.

Karin gasped at the sensation, which went straight to her core

Grinning up at her, he brought his face closer. "I know you're a virgin, but has anyone ever eaten your pussy?"

"No." She swallowed, more thrilled by the .

"Interesting." He rubbed his thumb up and down, finding one sensitive place after another. "So when I do this," he dropped a kiss on her shaved mound, "it's a first?"

"Yes." Her legs shook.

"And this?" Another, lower, and a pinch to her clit.

The shaking climbed to her hips. "Yes...."

"Mmm, let's try this." He buried his face in her, working her with tongue and lips and teeth until she had to tangle her fingers in his hair and hang on to remain upright. Incredible pleasure she'd never thought possible. Her only experience some mild make-outs and—she'd rather die than admit this to him—a small device purchased in the city, used alone in her bedroom. They were no comparison at all.

Her blood ran thick and slow in her veins, pounding in her ears as heat built between her legs. She rode the feelings, waves lifting higher then receding until she didn't know where to go with it, where it was taking her. When he tightened his lips around the sensitive nerves of her clit and sucked, she reached the top and tumbled over, clinging to his hair and shaking from head to foot. "Don't stop, don't ever stop."

He didn't, not right away. As she rolled down the back side of the mountain into the valley, he continued to eat her pussy, slower, until she shuddered to a stop. He worked her hands free and used them to tug her back onto his lap with a splash.

He cupped her chin and brought her lips to his kiss. Still half lost in the place he'd taken her, she dreamily responded, sitting facing him with a bent leg on either side of his torso. As her mind and body returned to her, she became aware his cock jerked against her opening with some urgency.

She gasped and sat up straight. "Don't you need to get a condom or something?"

Ray pulled her back against him. "Shh." He held up a torn foil square. "I put it on before you got back on my lap. Feel." Guiding her hand down, he rubbed it along the rigid length. "Safety first."

"Is it okay I'm on top?"

Was it? Did one deflower a virgin while she was in the pilot's seat? He rather liked the idea; it gave her more control—and since he didn't have much experience with first-timers, he was making it up as he went along anyway.

"Well, if you were on the bottom, you might drown."

She giggled and caught her breath. Clasping her hips, he lifted her and inserted the tip of his cock into her tight heat. "Oh, you're right." But her eyes were wide and her cheeks pale.

"Put your hands on my shoulders." As she did, he bucked his hips, going a bit deeper. "You have full control. I don't want to hurt you, but rumor has it the first time can be uncomfortable."

"Just do it." Her fingers dug into his skin, but her set jaw held determination. "I want you inside me. Now."

Feisty virgin. Holding her waist, he rocked his hips up in a sudden, strong thrust and surged deep inside her. She tensed, then fell forward against his chest, panting.

"You okay?" he asked, worried.

She tilted her face toward his. "Oh, yeah, I'm fine."

He bent to her lips, giving her time to acclimate to his penetration, but after a moment, she broke away and moved her lower body, and he needed no more hints. She weighed nothing, a feather in the water on his lap, and he lifted and lowered her, until she took up the motion herself. Her hot channel held him like a velvet glove. He tried to stay still, let her find her rhythm, but the little minx twitched her hips and tightened her muscles. With a shout, he thrust one more time and shot his cum into her, shuddering until finally, he drew her into a long, slow kiss.

They rested together. He never wanted to be anywhere else. Their long evening together had wound up where he'd never dreamed it would. Was she as pleased about it as he was? Or as surprised?

The water cooled around them, and with great reluctance, he set her away from him. "We'd better get dry before we catch pneumonia in the air conditioning."

"Oh," she said, drowsy and sexy. "We never even washed."

He chuckled, lifting the drain and rising to his feet. "I don't think we're too dirty after all this time in here."

She sighed but smiled. "I suppose not." She accepted his proffered hand and stood, too, stepping onto the floor. "I wonder what time it is?"

Did she want to leave? Go back to her room? He generally didn't mind if a woman left after loveplay—he had a history of "early flights so I can't stay over." Yet, the idea of Karin leaving struck a melancholy chord. Still, he grabbed a towel and padded across the room to find his cell phone. "It's a quarter to five."

She wrapped a towel around her and patted herself dry, shaking her head. "Even my teenage cousins should be asleep by now. I hate to wake them."

He grasped the opportunity. "I don't know why you would. Can't you just stay here for what's left of the night?" *Say yes.*

"I suppose, if you don't mind?" She'd been hinting. Her impish grin gave her away.

Ray struggled to stay serious. "Oh no, you don't hog the blankets, do you?" He moved closer to her, dropping his towel to the floor.

"All the time." She stepped back. "You'll probably kick me out of bed."

He followed her as she put the bed between them. "Yeah, I might."

Backing up, she held a finger in the air. "But I don't know if you want someone who drools."

"Oh, you drool?"

"Maybe, I haven't had a sleepover since I was a teen. Are you willing to take the chance? Maybe I kick or talk." She kept the bed between them as he prowled after her.

He lunged across the mattress and grabbed her, tugging her down next to him. "I'll take my chances." He pressed kisses all over her face until she laughed and struggled to get away. "I snore."

"Oh no!"

"Yep," he said, untucking her towel and flinging it onto the floor. "Right in your ear, all night."

She lay still, and he propped up on an elbow, looking his fill at her body. Her long dark hair, damp from their frolic in the tub, spread about her like a cape and set off her pale skin. He traced her straight brows and down her cheekbones.

She began to speak, but he placed his thumb on her lips "Shhh, I'm taking inventory."

Her brows knitted, but she held her peace. Tension tightened her shoulders, and he replaced his thumb with his lips, moving over hers. He could explore with his mouth, too.

Leaving her face behind, he pressed a kiss into in the hollow of her throat, feeling the beat of her pulse. Her life force. After a moment, he was drawn to lower places and trailed his fingertips over her nipple. As it rose to meet him, he bent and took it in his mouth, savoring the fast breath she took. True, little remained of the night, but since it was all he was sure of with her, he intended to enjoy every moment.

While he lapped at the treat in his mouth, he pinched the other nipple to attention, making it ready. So responsive, for one so new to the arts of love. When he moved his lips and tongue to the new spot, he applied a light pressure to her lower belly with the heel of his hand.

She moaned.

"If you like," he took her nipple between his teeth and tugged, pleased when she jerked under him, "we can just go to sleep. We have a busy day tomorrow."

A long pause and his confidence ebbed. If she could say no, what would she say when he proposed getting together again?

"Stop and I'll kill you."

The kitten had claws. Excellent. "I'm at your service, baby. All night long."

She pushed him away and sat. "No, you've already served me. I want a turn. Scooch up against the headboard."

He wondered what she had in mind—he had an idea—but he'd let her take the lead. "Scooching, ma'am." Sitting propped against the pillows, he watched with fascination as she crawled between his legs, pushing them apart as she went.

"I've never done this before, so I might not be very good." So far, her inexperience hadn't slowed her down.

"Just go for it. I can't imagine having your head in my lap could be anything but a pleasure."

She paused, palms flat on his thighs. "I'm afraid I'll hurt you." She reached for his cock and stroked one finger over the head, catching a drop of pre-cum. While he stared in amazement, she brought it to her mouth and wrapped her lips around the digit, her cheeks indenting as she sucked it clean.

Lust surged through him, threatening to blow the top of his head off.

"Hurt me like that, and I'll never let you go."

Her eyes flicked to him, wide and startled. "Let's take it one night at a time."

His heart sank. She didn't want to see him again?

"You don't know if I'm any good at this. Wouldn't want to take on a pig in a poke, would you?"

Despite his rigid cock and desire to fling her to the mattress and ride her to fulfillment, he chuckled. The lovely Karin...a pig. A swan, maybe...or some other graceful creature, but never a member of the swine family. "Let me be the judge here. What did you have in mind?"

She propped her head on her folded arms, which were on his upper thighs. "I don't know. I'm a fly-by-the-seat-of-my-pants kind of girl. Shall I just get started and we'll see where it goes?"

"Okay, fine." He choked out.

"And you'll let me know if you don't like it?"

He nodded, beyond words.

Her even tone and matter of fact jabber drove him insane. His dick jerked, and she reached for it, stilling it by closing her hand around its middle. Rising a little, she brought the shaft down to her mouth and took a lick.

"A little salty, but not bad." She licked again and again, laving the head and stroking her tongue down the front and up the side then over the prominent vein. Too much and not nearly enough. He fought the urge to grab her hair and push her mouth over his prick, to make her deep throat him.

Way to freak out the virgin—well, former virgin.

Chapter Eleven

*K*arin had often wondered what women found so enticing about sucking a guy's dick. In the romances she picked up in the library—the more erotic ones—the heroines went on and on about how much they loved the taste, the textures...to her dismay. She'd never envisioned herself enjoying such an activity.

But that was before she got her hands, and her lips, on Ray's penis.

Long and smooth, arcing up toward his stomach, the pole held charms she'd never imagined. He lay still while she explored, but his tense abs and the hands fisted at his sides gave away his agitation. She glanced up the long, lean line of his torso, over his muscular chest. "Am I doing this right?"

He nodded, lips pressed tight together. She shrugged.

"I'll get better with practice." With him, she hoped, but even after his flip comment about never letting her go, she knew they only had this one night to count on. He didn't want to get tied down to some girl he hardly knew, when he probably had girls in every town he flew into. But maybe, if she played her cards right, she could wangle an invitation back here after the wedding reception.

For a little more practice. Having taken the big step, there'd be no stopping her. She could sleep with any guy she went out with. Licking her way down his penis, she paused.

She couldn't imagine doing this with anyone else, even if there were any single guys in town she wanted to date. He'd ruined her for all other men. *Dramatic, Karin.* And unlike her. Still....

Ray made a noise deep in his throat and brought a hand to stroke her cheek. "Don't stop."

She forced her attention back to the moment. Tomorrow—and the day after, when everyone went home—would have to take care of itself. She was wasting precious time worrying about the future.

At the base of his cock, she took a moment to lift his balls in her hand and rolled them. With romance novels as her research, she tried to remember if guys wanted a girl to get her mouth on them as well. Should she ask? Or just.... She took a delicate lick, surprised by the slight scrape of stubble across her tongue. He shaved—she waxed her own pussy, enjoying the smooth feel of her skin, but his roughness felt masculine and sent a throb of heat between her legs. Had he liked it?

She lapped again and jerked back as the sack seemed to move. Good or bad? Tired of being careful, she decided to move forward and be assured he'd let her know if anything hurt. Sucking one of his balls into her mouth, she held it gently and toyed with it a little then moved to the other and did the same. Not a word from Ray, but if trembling thighs were any indication, it was a good thing.

Encouraged by his reaction, she left his testicles cradled in the palm of her caressing hand, and moved back up to his cock. She brought her mouth over its bobbing head and closed her lips around the tip. Tentative at first, then with more confidence, she dropped lower, taking it in by centimeters. Smooth, warm, and solid. She explored it with her tongue. A bulge, the vein she'd seen on the way down, protruded, the blood vibrating under her touch.

She couldn't imagine how she'd get it all in, but she

continued to work her way down until it touched the back of her throat before starting up again. Slowly. Wanting to know him this way and loving the clean, salty musk of him. When she got to the top, she began to lower her mouth again, and got a bit farther this time.

His girth filled her to her cheeks, and she relished the stuffed feeling; although she chose her actions, having his cock overflowing her lips implied a certain vulnerability. Focused on this specific body part, learning its topography, she jumped when Ray's grasped her hair and held her in place.

"I can't stand it, baby, faster." His hips rocked, and she tried to allow him to fuck her mouth as he pleased, but when he pushed deep, she choked and struggled in panic, trying to get away. He released her immediately. "I'm sorry, did I scare you?

He drew her toward him and cradled her in his lap, stroking her cheek and smiling down at her.

"No, I'm sorry. I was doing it wrong." Karin's passion cooled in her embarrassment. How could she have thought she could please him when she didn't have a clue what she was doing? Books could take her only so far.

"Wrong? God, you did it so right, you were driving me over the edge. And while I loved it, I got too excited." He hugged her closer. "I wouldn't want to make you afraid to do it again."

"No danger." She returned his grin, relieved by her success. "I need more practice." She moved to pull away, but he held her firm.

"Not right now, you don't. I'd come in two seconds." He guided her face closer and drew her into a long slow kiss. His tongue urged her lips apart and moved into her mouth to engage hers in a dizzying dance. After a long moment, he broke away. "Are you sore?"

"What?" Fuzzy, she tried to process his question.

"From before. I'd like to fuck you again, in bed this time, if you aren't too sore from before."

She focused on the warm throb between her legs. "I don't think so."

"Excellent." He laid her beside him on the sheets and dropped a quick kiss on her forehead. "Let me get another condom." He disappeared and returned in a moment with a foil package like the one she'd seen by the tub. Tearing it with his teeth, he withdrew the rubber and rolled it on his cock.

She quivered with anticipation. Ray knelt and parted her legs. This was how she'd expected her first time to be, on a bed with the man on top. She'd had a most unusual deflowering—she smiled at the thought and sobered when he arched a brow at her.

"Something funny?"

"No, not funny in the slightest. So far, I'd describe tonight as amazing."

A smile turned up the corners of his mouth, and his eyes held a soft glow. "Me, too." Rubbing his thumb in her juices, he bent and dropped a kiss there. "Mmm, I'd love to eat you again, you're so sweet. But I'm afraid my lusty friend here won't wait, so it'll have to be another time." He straightened and took hold of his penis, bringing it to her pussy. "Be sure to say if I hurt you. You're new at this, and I'm new at having my way with virgins."

As he pushed inside, a fresh flood of desire surged through her, and she wrapped her arms around his shoulders and hung on. His first thrust sent her flying, and by the time he found his rhythm, she was ready to come again, with a hard clench of her internal muscles that made her scream his name.

He pumped harder, dropping his head to devour her mouth, and took her up again, higher and higher, her thighs wrapped around his hips, nails digging into his back. She'd never imagined it could be like this, would never have held out so long if she had.

"I can't wait any more, going to come," he said, tearing away from the kiss and arching his back as he shot into her, and she came again, her hips slamming into him over and over again. They held together for a moment at the peak and fell to the bed, rolling to the side.

Panting, they lay there, wrapped tight in one another's embrace.

Through the sheer curtains over the window, the sun began to rise, light flooding the bed. The night was over. They'd spent it together, but what now?

She didn't want to make him think she demanded anything of him. He lived states away, a glamorous life filled with airplanes and excitement while she sat in her small library full of dusty books. *Take what you've got, Karin. Treasure it and don't try to make it more than it was—an amazing first experience. Be grateful.*

Ray pecked her on the cheek and rolled away. He stopped on the way back from the bathroom to tug the heavy drapes over the window then crawled onto the bed next to her. "I think, if we're lucky, we might be able to get an hour or two of sleep before the wedding craziness starts."

She groaned. "It's going to be a long day, if we don't."

Ray pulled her into a spoon position, his arm draped over her breasts. "We'd better go for it. Night, baby."

"Night, Ray." She lay next to him, listening to his breathing even out. She doubted she'd be able to sleep, but after a while, her eyes drifted closed, and she followed him into deep rest, secure against the broad chest of the first man she'd ever made love with—and, the uneasy thought followed her into slumber— maybe even loved.

Chapter Twelve

Ray snuggled his cheek deeper into the soft pillows, aloft on a dream of a violet-eyed, dark-haired goddess sitting co-pilot in his cockpit, soaring through the clouds. Heaven. She was telling him something about a lake high in the Cascades she wanted to fly to, and he was changing the coordinates, entering those for the destination she sought. Anything to keep his woman, his partner in business and life happy. Contentment was rapidly replaced by desire when a silken thigh brushed against his cock and it surged to life. The dream images faded, and he lost the threads, remembering only flying...and Karin.

His eyes blinked open. Dimness held the room in its grip, with a thin line of light penetrating between the closed, blackout drapes. The warm figure in his arms stirred, and he refocused on the delight at hand. Long strands of dark hair spread over the pillow, surrounding a face he found even more beautiful than the day before. Ray struggled to keep from touching her. He should leave her asleep. They couldn't have been out for more than a couple of hours. He would be content to wake with her every morning, but their lives were so far apart. Sure, he could fly in and visit with her from time to time, but long distance relationships, even for a guy with his own plane, were difficult.

She had her job and her family.

She shifted, snuggling closer, and he sighed. It would be difficult to change his base of operations to the Bay Area, but maybe things could be worked out. No...all his contracts, ones it had taken years to set in place, were in Washington. He'd be starting from scratch, and the payments on his plane wouldn't allow it. Besides, he didn't know how she felt. Whether she'd want to pursue more with him...?

Content for the moment to hold her, he tried to retrieve the dream. Elusive, it stayed just out of his reach until suddenly the fog cleared, he remembered all of it, and he knew what to do...if Karin also wanted to see where their relationship might go.

Karin's brain swam back to awareness. Still not fully functional, she tried to figure out where she was. Not home... Not her sunny bedroom with the cheerful bird chirping and an early morning breeze stirring her curtains.

The hotel. Julia's wedding. And the big arm slung across her belly belonged to Ray, who had led her a merry chase to make sure she didn't go to bed with a stranger then seen to it the stranger she went to bed with was him.

"Morning, sleepyhead." The deep growl of his voice hit her right in the pit of her stomach.

"Good morning." She swallowed her nerves. If this was the only time she woke with him—and she had no reason to think otherwise—she wanted him one more time. One for the memory books. Now, how to seduce a man?

He cupped her cheek and dropped a soft kiss on her lips, one on each cheek, her nose, her forehead. "Mmm, you look sexy in the morning. Want to play?"

Ohhhkay. Maybe she could just let him do the seducing. Six of one, half dozen of another. She held up her arms, "Love to," then gasped as he pulled her on top of him.

Karin sat astride his waist, hands braced on his chest. Just like in the tub, only this time she didn't have the buoyancy of the water to lend her grace. Hesitant, she remained where she was until he lifted her by the waist, as if she weighed nothing, and set her back down on top of his cock. It rubbed against the sensitive tissues of her pussy, and she gave a tentative slide.

He hissed.

Encouraged, she moved back and forth a few more times, closing her eyes to concentrate on the exquisite sensations. She circled her hips, oh, even better. So good, her moisture lubricated them both, and she became lost in the pleasure, in finding the places his shaft felt best, gliding against her again and again.

"Ummm, babe?"

Her eyes flicked open.

"I need to get a condom on or we're gonna be doing this commando." He held up the circle, and she took it from him.

"Can I do it?"

"Sure," he said. "Just hurry."

She rolled the rubber slowly over his cock, smoothing it down the length and sitting back. "Is this right?"

With a muffled roar, he flipped her onto her back and followed to lie between her legs. "You tell me." He plunged inside her in a single smooth move, driving all the air from her lungs. "Tell me if I hurt you, if this is too much, but I want to fuck your brains out."

She wrapped her legs around his waist and gripped his shoulders, excitement surging at his words. "Brains are overrated."

He choked back a laugh—at least she thought it might be a laugh—and drove into her again. She held on tighter, overwhelmed, a little sore, but wanting everything he could give. If this was their last time together, she wanted it all.

She met him thrust for thrust, over and over, faster and faster until the sensations riding up her spine peaked in her brain and she came, tightening around him, muscles spasming, heart pounding so hard she feared it would burst.

"Dear God, Karin." He shoved hard into her and held still, shuddering and shaking under her hands, then fell to the side, panting.

She smiled. It might be all they had, but it was quite a lot.

He gathered her close and dropped a kiss on the top of her head. "So where do we go from here?"

Starting from her languor, Karin bit her lip and tried to think of what to say. She didn't want to ruin the moment. *But what other moment do I have? He might want to spend tonight with me, but won't it just make parting harder?*

"I don't know. What do you have in mind?" *Smooth, what a woman of the world.*

"I'd like to see you again." He tucked her head against his shoulder and stroked her hair. She didn't purr...quite. "Would you be willing?"

Sadness weighted her limbs. Willing? Yes. But how could they have more than an occasional booty call at the airport motel? "I don't know. You live too far away."

"I know it's a long shot, but I have a proposal for you."

She jerked away, and he tugged her back.

"Don't panic, I'm not insane...it's not a marriage proposal. Not yet, anyway. I would like to know a girl for at least a full twenty-four hours before tying the knot."

Confused, she shrugged. "Okay, what kind of proposal?"

"Business." He hugged her closer. "I think you're in the wrong line of work."

Epilogue

*R*ain poured on the tarmac, making it slippery. There couldn't be a worse day for a pilot to take a check ride for her commercial license. Ray paced inside the small terminal. How much longer could it take?

Mark and Julia's wedding had been everything they both dreamed of. The bride gorgeous, the groom beaming, and the families applauding when they kissed.

He'd basked in their happiness and danced with Karin at the reception. By the time the party was over and he'd convinced her to return to his suite—to which he'd invited no relatives—he'd known he could never let her go. In twenty-four hours, he'd gone from freewheeling bachelor to a one-woman man.

Karin had taken a huge leap of faith, leaving her dusty library behind to learn to fly planes. But from the first time she'd taken the stick, her innate talent delighted her instructors. He'd flown in whenever he could to help her get the hours she needed, and to spend time together. Long cozy evenings of quizzing her on the rules and regulations for the written and oral exam. Getting her Class 2 Medical Certificate had been the easiest part—a straightforward doctor's exam had found her healthy as a horse. He'd never seen anyone so determined to complete the requirements in record time. Her delight in the sky matched—in a way he wasn't sure was entirely flattering—her enthusiasm in bed.

"Would you sit down, son?" His dad sat surrounded by the sections of the Sunday paper, looking nearly as jumpy as Ray felt. As a retired pilot of giant jetliners, he'd given Karin a few lessons himself and had insisted on coming to offer moral support. Ray's mother was waiting by the phone at home. Mark and Julia texted every five minutes. "You're going to wear out the floor."

"I think I hear them coming in. Do you hear them?"

"No, but why don't you go outside and look. You're only making yourself and me crazy in here."

Ray grabbed his slicker from the rack by the door and headed out into the weather. The windsock stood straight out; she'd be landing in a crosswind. Tough even for more experienced pilots. He should never have let her go up in this. But the instructor had said it would be at least two weeks before he could return, and Karin had refused to put her test off. And it had only been a drizzle when they took off.

Pacing outside was worse than in. Cold and wet, he scanned the skies to the south. Was it? Yes! A small plane broke through the cloud cover and approached the runway. Smooth, pretty smooth. His girl could fly.

But only the examiner could give her the certificate to be his co-pilot. He had no way of knowing how things had gone during the rest of the test. She'd come through her private pilot's exam with flying colors and flown all the required hours with only a few difficulties and no life-flashing moments. But even the best beginner could crack under the scrutiny of the final flight.

As she landed, the wheels kissing the airstrip, the sun broke through, its rays glinting on the silver sides of the small craft. The runway still held rivulets draining off to the sides, but she didn't slip or skid at all. The plane taxied to a stop, and he headed toward it, forcing himself to walk and not run. *Be cool, Ray. If she didn't pass, if anything went wrong, she'll just take the test again.* He arrived as the door popped open and the examiner stepped out. His expression gave nothing away. But the next face he saw was Karin's, and it glowed.

Ray held up his arms, and she fell into them. "I passed. Can you believe it?"

"Of course I do. I never doubted you for a minute."

She laughed. "Don't lie, I saw you down here walking in circles. And I saw your face...but I did it! I did it! Is your offer still open? Do you still need a co-pilot?"

"Of course I do! But first, we need to take a trip and celebrate. There's a lake in the Cascades I'd like to show you, in a valley surrounded by fields of violets. If you'd like to see it."

She smiled and caressed his cheek. "I'd love to see it. And the weather is promising clear skies tonight."

"Of course."

She never tired of flying at night, of being near to the stars. He didn't get all that close to them, but he had some calls in to a business associate who was investing in commercial space flight. Seemed they were looking for pilots with a commercial license to train for some upcoming ventures. And with a little luck....

Virgin Under Ground

"Friendship, love, heat, and authentic connections. Seriously, what more could you ask for in a romance?"
Delphina's Reviews

"There is an interesting combination of unique characters and a perfect romance."
Night Owl Reviews

Chapter One

*J*ane Ann Summers heaved the bound copy of her dissertation into the backseat of her dusty sedan and slammed the door. "Where to, Sue?"

"Somewhere we can get a drink and celebrate, *Doctor* Summers." Professor Susan Wright grinned at her protégé and slipped into the car. "Aren't you going to call your mother and father?"

"Dad probably knew my dissertation had been accepted before I did...or at least Akari did. My sweet step mama has spies in every department." Gunning the motor, she pulled out of the parking lot and headed for Highway 395, the main route anywhere in the Reno area. "And I'll text Mary when we stop. So anywhere in particular?"

"How about the usual, the Bar S? They make those great fizzy drinks." Sue leaned back in the seat and laughed, sounding half her age. Sometimes Jane couldn't believe she hung out with her mother's old college roommate—other times she couldn't believe her mother had.

"Those 'fizzy drinks' pack a wallop, and it's three in the afternoon."

"Here it is." Sue grabbed her arm. "Come on, you've been working hard and if we don't want to drive home, I'll call Don to come pick us up."

Jane shook her head, but took the turn into the parking lot beside the old, white frame building recently converted from a real estate office to the hottest off-campus watering hole for University of Nevada, Reno students and faculty. "One drink, then I need to get home and start packing."

"Your mother hoped you'd spend at least a few years more here...or somewhere with a social life."

Jane turned off the ignition and released her seat belt. Sitting sideways, she faced her mentor. "Not another word. There's plenty of social life in the Marshall Islands."

"That social life is why your mother packed you up and shipped you out so fast." Sue opened the car door and they headed toward the two-story building. "I never heard her so upset."

"I guess. But I did nothing every other girl didn't. It's a coming of age thing, a rite of passage in a lot of the local tribes."

The cool shadows of the lobby wrapped around them, a welcome change from the sun's bright glare. "But you're not a member of—"

"Let it go, Sue." Jane pushed through the saloon doors into the barroom and the rest of what she intended to say died on her lips.

"Surprise!" A drift of blue and silver balloons—UNR colors—fell from the ceiling as family and friends pelted her with confetti and good wishes. Her father swept her into a hug, his wife, Akari, standing behind him. "My daughter, the doctor. We are so proud."

"Thanks, Dad." She buried her face in his tweed jacket, tears pricking her eyes. "Your support means so much."

Strange and uncomfortable with him at first, she'd learned to love and respect both her father and Akari while living in their home as an undergrad. And found the Japanese half of herself. Her reserved father's display of emotion touched her. "But how did you know I would succeed?"

"My brilliant daughter never fails at anything she puts her mind to." He set her away from him and smiled, his dark brown eyes—the exact color and almond shape of her own—gleaming. "And now it's time to celebrate that success."

A crowd gathered around and she took in the people her father had invited to her party. People from the university, from her department—Meteorology, his—Sociology, and Akira's Language Studies. A few were regulars at the Bar S, where she'd spent many evenings sitting at a table in the back, studying and enjoying the friendly banter without ever being completely a part of it.

Thank the gods of her friends back home and the one God preferred here, she was done with all the effort, the seven years it took to complete her undergraduate and a combined masters/doctoral program, and could return to the remote science center where she'd grown up.

Champagne corks popped at the bar and the rows of gleaming glasses soon overflowed with bubbles. The guests passed them from hand to hand and when everyone had one, Sanji Tanaka, her proud father, raised his.

"First, a toast to my talented and intelligent daughter who has brought honor to our family by receiving her doctorate in meteorology."

A chorus of "To Doctor Summers" rang in her ears, more corks popped, and the waitresses circled, pouring the sparkling wine. To her surprise, her stepmother made the next toast.

"And to Mary Summers, her mother, who so generously placed her Jane Ann, in our care and brightened our world."

More toasts followed, but Akari's rang in her ears. The woman had opened her home and tried to make a petulant and homesick teenager part of her family. As Jane searched for the right words to say—to try to somehow express her gratitude—a crowd of colleagues wanting to congratulate her swept her away, keeping her glass filled.

Trays of snacks were laid out on a long table to the side, but every time she headed toward them, hoping for a meatball or a few chips, even a piece of celery, someone else caught her and wanted to discuss her plans for the future, or some detail of her dissertation. Apparently the Marshall Islands/Nevada desert weather similarities fascinated all the scientists and many of the other academics in the room.

The bar regulars enjoying free drinks wanted to tell her the long-winded, pointless stories for which they were famous.

And every time she took a sip, someone filled her glass to the brim again.

After a couple of hours, she fell into a corner booth because her wobbly legs would no longer hold her. One by one, the partiers drifted off until only her father, Akari, and Sue and her husband Don remained.

Sue smiled down at her. "Tired?"

"But happy. What a wonderful surprise. Thank you all."

"We'll take her home, Sanji," Sue said. "And her car."

"Thank you." Her father looked exhausted but happy as well. "I believe we will go then." He bent and kissed her cheek. "We're so very proud."

Watching him leave the room, Jane couldn't believe a man she'd never met until she was seventeen had become so dear to her. She'd miss him, but wouldn't allow another two decades to pass before seeing him again.

"Ready, Jane?"

She nodded and pushed up from the padded bench seat, losing her balance and falling back with a giggle. "Yes, but I might need a little help. All that champagne."

"We gotcha," Sue said. Don helped her up, and holding her elbows, they walked her outside and poured her into her passenger seat.

She closed her eyes and when she opened them, the car had come to a halt in front of her building. A little more stable, she hugged Sue, thanked her again, and took the elevator to her loft, hoping to fall into bed and sleep off the unaccustomed alcohol.

Yawning, she dropped her purse on the couch. It chirped. Digging into it, she pulled out her phone. An email from her mother.

Darling,

Sue told me the wonderful news. I'm prouder of you than I can ever hope to express. You have achieved your goal, empowered yourself, and opened the door to a level of research that will bring the installation buckets of lovely government money when you return.

However, I am concerned about one thing. Your father and Sue tell me you don't seem to have much of a social life beyond department mixers and family functions and never date. Before you bury yourself in the back of beyond, you still need to experience life. I'd hoped to be booking your return ticket now, but with this news, I think you need to stay on the mainland a while longer.

Perhaps consider applying for a teaching position at the university? And, honey, have some fun! Go on a date!

I don't want to hear another word about it until you can honestly report you know what you are shutting the door on when you return.

I know what you're thinking, but it's for the best. Go on, enjoy yourself, and if you have so much fun you don't ever want to come back...I'll be sad, but I will know you're where you should be.

Hugs and Kisses,
Mary

Jane's pleasant inebriation fled, leaving her cold and shaking. She plopped onto the sofa, desolation filling every cell of her body. Mary, not Mom. Sometimes she almost forgot she'd never addressed her mother any other way. Practical to a fault, Mary'd had a brief affair with Jane's dad in grad school, the only "life" in her history...*hypocrite.* Or maybe she regretted her own choices? The director of the Marshall Islands Interscience Institute never showed a crack in her professional veneer.

Jane had spent seven years away, going home a few times,

mostly for research, taking classes all year round to hurry her return to the one place on the planet she felt comfortable. Now her mother grabbed it away, stole it from her just as she grasped happiness with her fingertips. And on the most important day of her life.

Way to go, Mary.

In a fit of anger she flipped on her laptop and began to search for other facilities where she might apply. Stay in the city and teach at the university, right! Not a chance. If she couldn't get on her mother's island, there were many others. Millions. As she scanned an exclusive blog where such positions were listed, her fingers slowed.

Sure, she could go almost anywhere on the planet and study the weather trends so dear to her heart. But only on her island home could she find the outlandish changes that matched the one she'd spent four years studying in the Nevada desert. To go anywhere else would be a fresh start. And would mean giving up on discovering why she found such similarities in a remote South Pacific island.

But what options did she have? Would another year or two change things?

Her mother wanted her to date. And while she had been out a few times with colleagues, a fact Jane hadn't mentioned to Mary's spies, none of her experiences had moved her to take it to the next level.

She needed a shortcut home. A dating service.

Switching searches, she stared down the long list of possibilities. Most of them cited their proficiency at finding mates for their clients. Since the likelihood of finding a man who would be willing to make his home on a remote island seemed slight, a regular dating service was not an option. *And then I'd have to love him!* Because even her logical heart wanted someone...someday. Impossible odds.

Just as she considered giving up and calling her mother to beg her to change her mind, she found the answer. *Let a 1Night Stand Change Your Life.* A one-night stand would solve everything. She'd even have a receipt as proof that she'd "lived."

She brought up the website and clicked on the application form.

She'd be home by the end of the month.

☙

The numbers added up. Every time he rechecked his figures, Dr. Lukas Gerard found the same answers. The earth's crust showed some alarming changes. And not over centuries, eons, as geological time implied, but over the past fifty years.

His own research did not extend back so far, of course. But taking into account measurements by his predecessor, Dr. Lang, he found great cause for concern. Enough cause to become a cliché. Not only a member of NAP—Nevada Area Preppers—he was the sitting president.

Stuffing a sheaf of papers and his laptop in his backpack, he grabbed a printout of an email and read it once again.

> *Dear Dr. Gerard,*
>
> *After a year, we have found a match who meets the criteria you stipulated. Jane Ann Summers (photo attached) has just received her doctorate in meteorology. She will, I believe, enjoy the rather unusual date you propose and might be able to work with you to further your research.*
>
> *While I have no reason to think the world is ending anytime soon, I find a certain validity to your conclusions and hope, together, you and Jane can make a difference.*
>
> *Be gentle with her. As you will learn from the attached files, she's had a sheltered life and less experience than most.*
>
> *Sincerely,*
> *Madame Evangeline*

He studied the photograph again. Straight dark hair fell to the shoulders of the most serious young lady he'd ever seen. Her almond eyes suggested a multicultural background, echoed in the golden tones of her skin. Her nose, short and straight, high cheekbones, and natural pout enchanted him.

Lovely. But how could a meteorologist have anything to do with geology? Earth and sky? He tried to recall whether he'd told Madame Eve about his research, but he didn't believe he had.

A puzzle. He loved a puzzle.

She asserted Jane would like the date he had planned for her. He'd begun to think there wasn't a woman on the planet willing to spend a night inside an abandoned gold mine, much less survive with her personality intact the lengthy time involved if what he feared did come to pass.

Why had the government done aboveground testing of nuclear weapons in the desert? A fragile environment to start with, and not only had nearly everyone present died of diseases commonly associated with radiation exposure, some many years later, but they had caused a chain reaction underground he believed could lead to the end of the world as humankind knew it.

The intercom buzzed, interrupting his thoughts. "Yes, Virginia?"

"Four o'clock, sir."

"Thank you." He added the printout to the mass of papers in his briefcase and headed for the door. He would be presiding over an online NAP meeting in an hour. The mostly paranoid members preferred not to meet in person, and many of them lived out in the desert anyway. He'd do it from the mine because he needed to get there early and make sure it was ready. An untidy underground bunker was sure to be on any woman's lists of turn offs.

Chapter Two

*L*ukas shook his head. The weirdness factor in their little group rose every month. He had accepted the presidency of NAP when Professor Lang left the university and the organization and moved to parts unknown to continue his private research. But some days dealing with the membership took more patience than Lukas could spare.

New members often didn't want to accept the varied reasons others did what they did. They waited for a killer tsunami, the poles to flip, or chose to use the resources the group provided to be ready for a more mundane natural disaster, another economic downturn or other political event.

NAP's mission statement, *There's no time like the present to prepare for the future*, was purposely vague. Yet they often attracted the odd prophet who insisted they listen and follow his or her own personal agenda. NAP held pride of place among prepper organizations for sheer longevity. One of their members, Edwin Carpenter, had been born in a bunker during the Cuban Missile Crisis, although the organization was known as Nevada's American Patriots at the time.

Today's thorn in the president's paw, Joshua Bender, insisted he'd received a message from the horseshoe galaxy warning of a devastating meteor shower due to arrive in three months. Their resident astronomer, Dr. James Garland, did his best to dissuade the man—pointing out anything that close in galactic space would be visible on every telescope at every observatory on the planet.

Bender claimed the government was hiding knowledge, and nothing Jim could say would dissuade him. Lukas would have to counsel him. If he impeded a second meeting, he would be thrown out of the group. A firm policy, no questions asked. Yet another reason why they nearly never met in person and had no address list. One unstable individual could decimate years of work.

The only bright spot today was the absence of Arnold—a man skilled in steering newbies to the prepper life in the wrong direction, while insisting he tried only to help. His most recent debacle involved a new member named Oakes who was very upset about Arnold's advice concerning a sheep purchase. Yet another issue to be dealt with, but not today.

They all agreed something bad could happen at any time and preferred to be prepared for the worst case scenario. Lukas cast a glance around the bunker he called home on weekends and vacations. When he'd found the abandoned gold mine for sale on craigslist, just forty miles outside of town, he'd bought it immediately.

"Ladies and gentlemen, we've already run long and I have another appointment. Unless there is urgent business—I know, Sam, everything we do is urgent—I declare the meeting adjourned. Minutes will be available on the website, along with links to the excellent resources presented by the Olsens and Carpenter. Good night."

He clicked the chat site closed before anyone could protest, shutting out all the rest at the same time. He, as president, could access the software to open a full group session and when he closed it, it shut down. Enough.

Given the chance, they would go on all night, and he had to pick up his date in less than two hours. He stood and stretched, then patrolled the great room area. Everything in its place, despite his earlier concern about untidiness, and not a prepper magazine or MRE in sight.

He set the window vid-screens to show a scene of the hills outside on one side and the snowy Sierras on the other. Nothing to indicate they were anywhere but a luxurious high desert getaway.

Clicking a button on the wall next to the door, the screen changed from a view of outside to a mirror. What would she think of him? A desert rat. The lines next to his eyes from years in the sun aged him, he feared, as did the bronze of his skin. He wore his white button down with jeans and hiking boots, appropriate for the "casual evening at my country place" he'd suggested.

Stuffing a blue bandana in his pocket, he returned the mirror to its security scan and checked outside. Nobody in sight, as usual. Clicking it off, he headed for his Jeep.

His reasons for arranging the date fled from his mind until he drove through the long tunnel into the early evening and bounced down the five miles of rough dirt road to the highway. How long would the days be if what he feared came to pass? Weeks, months alone. He wanted companionship, but he'd not met a woman on who he wanted to spend time with. Madame Eve's service could provide women with no expectations beyond a single night. The way he'd set it up, if she didn't seem right, she'd never even know where she had been. But it had taken a full year to meet one woman through 1Night Stand. He might have to resign himself to a long, solitary time in the bunker.

&#x03;

Jane considered again the rash move she'd made. A night with a stranger, just to satisfy her mother. And the odd request she wear a blindfold while traveling to her date's getaway. Madame had assured her he meant no harm, only valued his privacy. Still....

Still, she had no choice. No other man in 1Night Stand's current files had been available for her hurried request, and she'd already booked a return flight—without her mother's knowledge—for the end of the week. She'd show up, receipt in hand, and battle it out if necessary.

If one night with some strange, maybe kinky guy was the price of her homecoming, she'd pay it.

The buzzer rang and she jumped. *Ten, nine...*she pressed the intercom. "Be right down." *Eight, seven...*grabbing her purse, she smoothed her hair and took a deep breath. *Six, five, four...*last chance to change her mind. And then what? Stay in Reno for another year, or two or five? *Three, two one...*blastoff.

Her impetus faded as she trotted down flight after flight of stairs...why hadn't she taken the elevator? At the glass doors, she paused before pulling her shoulders back and strolling out into the cool evening air.

Leaning against a dusty Jeep stood a long, tall, desert god. The security lights spotlighted him in the dusk. He straightened and strode to her side, hand extended. "Jane?"

The words stuck in her dry mouth. "Y-yes. Lukas?"

"Right." He loomed over her, bright blue eyes burning into her soul. "Ready to go?"

"Yes." His big paw engulfed hers, warm and dry and she fought a momentary panic. Her gaze flicked down toward his feet, at least size thirteen in work boots. *God.* If urban legend served, her first time—if indeed things progressed that far—might be overwhelming.

She glanced up again to find a brow arched.

"Everything okay?"

Heat filled her cheeks and she mutely bobbed her head.

"Great, then let's go."

He stood by while she stepped into the car then he cruised around to the other side. The open vehicle, without even doors to hold back the road dust, surprised her. She was grateful to whatever sense had her wearing jeans and a casual top—although she might regret forgetting her sweater on the way back in the cool evening.

Pulling into traffic, he waved toward the gearshift where a dozen colorful elastic bands hung. "If you don't have a hair tie, help yourself. I should have put the top on, but it's a nice clear night."

She pulled a fat orange band loose and used it to fasten her locks at the nape of her neck. "No, I don't mind. The stars are just starting to come out."

"That reminds me." He handed her a bandana. "As soon as we get to the edge of town, I need you to put it on."

The blindfold. So much for stars.

He drove south toward Carson City, then took a smaller highway heading east. The wind made it hard to hear one another, so after a few aborted attempts at conversation, they sat side by side in silence. As the desert drowsed around them, a turnoff for Virginia City flashed past.

"Now?" She waved the bandana in the breeze.

"Yep, now is good." He glanced over as she rolled it up. "You okay with this?"

"Yeah, I guess so...part of the deal, right?" Although now the moment had arrived, she was less okay than she had been. As she lifted the bandana to her face, the car raced along a curve in the road and a gust of wind whipped it out of her hands. "Crap."

"Hang on." Lukas pulled the car over and leapt out. He ran back along the road and off into the scrub a ways until he reached the fluttering blue banner stuck in a thorny bush. Should she be happy he'd found it or sorry? If he hadn't...would the date have been over?

She wanted to ask, but at the same time felt a little afraid to. Despite her initial misgivings, he intrigued her and she wanted to get to know him better. Her mother insisted she enjoy life, socialize...at least she could chalk the evening up to an adventure.

Madame Eve had checked her out six ways to Sunday. If she'd done the same with Lukas, Jane should be safe. As he strolled back to the Jeep, long strides devouring the yards between them, she had one question to ask before she gave up her sense of sight and put herself in his hands.

He arrived at the passenger side and held up the cloth. "It tried to get away, sneaky sucker."

She laughed, but when he lifted it toward her face, she stopped him. "I need to ask you something first."

His brow furrowed, but he shrugged. "Okay."

"Does Madame Eve know the location of your secret place?" Out there in the dark, with the sprinkle of stars to light the black velvet night, the reality of proceeding blindfolded into the desert with a stranger, no matter how attractive, seemed dangerous. If the answer was no, she would ask him to turn the car around and hope she wasn't already too late.

"Yes," he said, in a low voice. "She insisted." When she still clutched his arm, he smiled. "I understand caution, let me show you something." Lukas reached over her to the center console. So close, his warmth and the clean scent of soap went to her head. *Hang on, Jane. Even if he is the cutest guy you've ever met, and smells so good.*

He retrieved his cell phone and clicked to a text message. "Look at this."

I have confirmed the location of your date and we can schedule your evening. I hope you understand the safety of my clients is paramount, yours as well as Ms. Summers'. Thank you for your cooperation. M.E.

Reassured, Jane faced away from him. "Do it, then." She tried not to flinch as the soft cloth covered her face. It tightened and then his hands dropped to her shoulders.

"Okay?" His fingers rested on her collarbones, inches from her breasts. Her eyes strained, but the several folds prevented the least bit of starlight from entering.

"I can't see a thing." But she could still feel his touch moving down her arms, past her short sleeves, and onto bare skin. The desert wind soughed; her heart thumped in her ears. Hyperaware of the man behind her, she waited to see what he would do next.

"Let's go then." His hands dropped away and the warmth at

her back disappeared. His boots crunched the gravel and the Jeep squeaked as he hopped in, and then they were flying down the highway again. "We still have a ways to go."

"Fine." She leaned back and sniffed the air. Sage, mesquite, all the desert plants she knew well intensified as the earth gave off the heat it absorbed during the day. She had half expected to be frightened by the blindfold, but when she searched her mind, she found nothing but curiosity and a disturbing heat.

"I understand you just completed your doctoral studies. I'm surprised we've never seen one another around campus."

"Me, too." She leaned closer, so he could hear her over the wind whipping past them. "You're in Geology, right?"

"I teach Geo 101 and a few other classes every semester, but research is my passion."

"Oh, me too. I did some teaching assisting, you almost have to, but I can't wait to get back to my work. There are fascinating connections between weather in this area and back where I was raised."

"Shit!" The car swerved and Jane flailed for a handhold, grabbing the roll bar over her head "What happened?" She fought the urge to free the blindfold.

"Coyote ran in front of us, chasing something."

"Oh." She blew out a breath. "I thought I was going to fall out."

"Seatbelt should protect you."

"I'm used to doors."

He laughed. "I leave the top and doors off once it starts to warm up. Sometimes I forget people aren't used to it."

"It's fine." Her covered eyes created a lightshow of electric dots and sparkles. "Just try not to scare me, if you can."

The vehicle slowed. "Turning off here. It's a dirt road, so hang on."

Hang on was right. They jounced along a track so rough her teeth rattled and she kept her grip on the roll bar just to stay in her seat. "H-how much longer?"

"We're just about...there." The road smoothed under the

wheels and sloped downhill. She reached for her face, but he grabbed her wrist. "Not until we're inside."

"I'll fall."

"I'll guide you." He slowed and stopped. "Stay where you are." In a moment he took her hand and helped her stand. "Walk with me, it's not far."

"Not up a hiking trail into the mountains or anything, huh?"

He chuckled. "No, nothing like that." In fact, just a couple of dozen steps—she counted. "Wait, I'll open the door." He led her in and she heard a metallic click behind her. Then the cloth loosened and fell away, and gentle fingers pulled the elastic from her hair, smoothing it around her shoulders.

"Wow, I never expected anything like this."

Chapter Three

"*W*hat did you expect?" Lukas stood next to her, taking in her every move. He seemed tense, like a jungle cat about to leap. Toward her or away?

"Oh, a rustic A-frame, maybe. I was hoping for indoor plumbing." She walked around the room, examining the cozy, cabin type furnishings, the warm, wide floor planks.

"There is some indoor plumbing. But I like a big open area."

"Me, too." She took note of the theater seating in the back, a half dozen cushioned chairs facing a screen. "In fact I live in a loft because it reminds me of my mom's place back home. Not too many walls."

"Glad you like it."

"Oh I do! What's this?" She moved toward a mosaic pattern in the floor, small pieces of different woods making up a complex image. "How pretty!"

At a cabinet slam, she jumped. He held up two beakers. "I thought I'd make us some drinks, would you like one?"

"Those look right out of—"

"A laboratory? I ordered them from a science lab supplier. What do you think?"

"Different." But she grinned. "And intriguing." Jane took one and held it up. Her head dropped back. "How high is this ceiling, anyway?"

"Just under thirty feet. Like it?" The deep vibration of his voice ran over her skin.

"A lot. It's amazing." She turned in a circle, admiring the intricate design of heavy wooden beams. Massive. "You could hold up a mountain with those."

"Mmm, maybe so." He opened a cabinet in the wall and pulled out a bottle. "Wine bottled by a friend of mine in Napa. Sound good?"

"Sure." She moved toward him and held her glass up while he filled it then his own. "Ruby red." Jane took a sip and held it, the flavors of blackberry and an undertone of chocolate filling every corner of her mouth. "And delicious. I don't drink much, but I love good wine."

"My friend will be glad you like it. He takes a lot of pride in his vineyard." He grinned. "If you like this, you should try the 2004 merlot."

"Can I?" She took another sip and sighed. "I'll be spoiled for the Two Buck Chuck I usually have at home."

"I'll show you my wine cellar after dinner, if you like."

"I'd love it." She cast a glance around...no bed so there must be other rooms. Quite a retreat for a scholar. Most of the professors she knew had a hard time affording a rustic cabin as a getaway. He hadn't built his vacation spot on his salary alone. "Is the rest of your place this big?"

He shook his head. "Well, not with these high ceilings, anyway. But I'll give you a tour a little later. Are you hungry?"

"Starving." Which surprised her. She'd expected to feel a lot of things, but intrigued, turned on, and hungry surprised her. "I don't see any food though."

"It's keeping warm." When he pressed the corner of a cabinet, the door slid up and recessed into the wall. The room filled with a spicy scent. "I hope you like curry? I took a chance, it's the only thing I cook that most people will eat."

She giggled and accepted a plate from him, sniffing appreciatively. "Love it." She followed him to the far side of the room and sat on a long, deep sofa. Lukas joined her and leaned forward to tap the low wooden table in front of them. The tabletop rose and glided toward them. "You're full of surprises, aren't you?"

He admired his companion as she took her first mouthful of food and chewed. Her eyes closed.

"If this is all you cook well, I'd be surprised. Delicious."

"Well, thank you. I lived in India as a small child, and when we moved to Seattle, I missed the food more than anything." And the MREs and freeze-dried entrees he generally ate in the bunker were hardly special occasion dining.

"India. How interesting."

"My father held a diplomatic post there. I was seven when we came back, but I remember a lot about it."

She swallowed and took a sip of wine. "We have childhoods in faraway places in common."

"I believe your profile said you were raised in the Marshall Islands?" He found the fact fascinating.

"Yes, my mother is the director of a research installation there."

"And your father?"

She smiled. "My father is Sanji Tanaka, and he and my mother had a torrid affair in grad school, of which I was the only lasting result. She sent me here to get to know him while I worked on my degree."

He eyed her. "Sociology, right? I think I've met him once or twice at meetings."

"That's Dad." He'd given her the straightness of her light brown hair and the almond-shaped eyes he found so alluring.

"Well I'm glad she did, or we might never have met." A silence fell while they ate more of their curry. Comfortable quiet, he noted, yet he watched every move she made. Living alone, he cooked rarely—in his townhouse—for colleagues or the occasional friend. He'd never shared his bunker with anyone once the special construction crew left.

A companion took the place to a whole other level...a real home.

"Is there any more of this?" Her comment brought him out of his musings.

"Yes, I can heat it for you, and I thought we'd have dessert later, on the patio." He reached for her plate.

She shook her head with a rueful grin as she passed it to him. "No...I'll save room for dessert, but I wouldn't mind another half-glass of the liquid ambrosia your friend makes."

"Sure." Stacking their dishes, he carried them over to a counter and bumped a bar with his knee, opening a slot in the wall.

"What's that?" She peered around him, her hand on his arm. She'd moved so quietly he hadn't realized she'd even stood.

"Just a dishwasher." With another knee-knock, the opening closed, hiding the dirty plates.

"High tech."

He grabbed the bottle and waved it. "Let's finish our wine and I'll show you some more of the sights."

Back on the wide, deep sofa, he filled their glasses. He tugged her against him.

"I am amazed," she said. "Your place looks so cabin-ish, with all the wood and upholstery, but it's pretty advanced, isn't it?"

She had no idea. The "high tech" technology employed by Be Prepared Systems—a company he owned half of—would stagger even a high-rise designer. Although the bunker they occupied was in a location he believed would be minimally affected, it had been constructed with an earth-altering quake in mind.

He would love to show her, explain it to her...but the big reveal would have to wait, and maybe wouldn't occur at all.

Jane tipped her glass back and glanced at the bottom, her dismay amusing to behold. "More?"

She sighed. "I guess not. I don't drink much, but this is so good"

Lukas took a drink of his wine and licked his lips, wetting them. "Perhaps I should share mine with you, then."

Her eyes gleamed. "What do you have in mind?"

The little minx. His cock hardened, demanding attention. "So many possibilities, but for now, this." Holding her chin between his thumb and forefinger, he bent to her mouth. "Taste."

She kissed him, the first time she'd taken the initiative, even though he'd hinted, maybe even steered her where he wanted her to go. But he welcomed her touch and stayed still, allowing her to direct the action, remembering Madame Eve's instructions to be gentle with her.

Although he preferred to be in charge, he enjoyed the sweetness behind her attentions. Watching her lips part and the tip of her tongue emerge to swipe at the droplets on his lips, his libido surged—when the saucy appendage entered his mouth, he groaned and took control back. With a quick flip, he laid her on her back on the sofa and then began unbuttoned her blouse. He'd not make love to her without revealing—or deciding for sure not to reveal—his secret, but her sweet scent and her heady kisses led him to push things just a bit further.

She wore no bra. Her small breasts stood up, firm and tempting, dark brown nipples erect. Just a mouthful. He licked his lips and bent to them. Sweet. Rolling his tongue over one stiff peak, he longed for the other one and drew it into his mouth. Jane made a strangled sound in her throat and he paused.

Pulling back, he blew on her nipple, watching the fascinating play of emotion across her face. "Shall I stop?"

Her head thrashed back and forth on the sofa cushion. "No. Don't stop."

He savored her trembling sweetness, the beat of her pulse.

Jane's head spun and she closed her eyes to find equilibrium. Things were moving so fast, but she didn't know how to slow them down. And she didn't know if she wanted to. She'd arranged a one-night stand in order to "live" enough to convince her mother she was ready to return to the island. But the idea flashing through her mind, under the influence of Lukas's hands and mouth, gave her pause.

What kind of adult slept with a man in order to please her mother?

She'd had a single goal. To achieve the qualifications to slip back into the comfortable routine with the scientists and tribespeople she'd known all her life. But somehow, her perfect plan was collapsing into a rush of emotions and sensations she hadn't expected.

When he looked at her, crazy ideas replaced her solid plan. She hadn't been lonely—at least she'd never noticed if she was. But from the moment he picked her up at home, she'd been ogling the man. Cataloguing his attributes. Hoping he found her appealing. Was this the "living" her mother spoke of, and if so, how had she walked away? It couldn't have been like this.

And why did he arouse such a bewildering rush of heat...and longing?

She blinked, the soft light of the cabin making a halo around Lukas's head, buried between her breasts. He tilted his face up, his light beard soft against her skin and the blue of his eyes intensified to a deep indigo, gleaming when he met her gaze. His tanned skin showed every one of his thirty-seven years, but it suited him and made her confident she'd landed in the hands of a man, not a boy like the tribal youths she'd grown up with....

She'd never forgotten her first love, Lowakalle, but he'd married a nice girl from a neighboring island and her grief had been far less than she'd expected. Not worth getting sent away for.

And nothing like the heat she experienced with Lukas. She reached for his hair tie, wanting to free his long, golden brown strands, as he had hers, but he held her fingers and shook his head.

"I want to show you around, before we get too comfortable."

She stared at him. He wanted to give her a tour? "Now?"

"Yep."

She shrugged. "Okay, if that's what you want to do." Even with her limited experience, she knew enough from her tribal friends and the other students to know a man stopping in the middle of a sexual encounter indicated a lack of interest. She wouldn't be losing her virginity tonight.

But, she'd lived this long without sex or romance. "Lead on, Lukas." She'd tour his bathroom and bedrooms...game room...whatever. Then home and finish packing to return to the islands. She shouldn't be so disappointed, though. She'd just met him.

He pulled her to her feet, then let go to stride over to the mosaic she'd admired earlier. She started to follow, but he held up his hand. "Stay there for just a minute." Puzzled, she took in the room around her. No stairs or doors presented themselves. Maybe they'd have to go outside to get to the rest of the place...the bathroom? But when he laid his palm on the wall, a low hum sounded and the intricate wooden circle lifted from the floor, bringing with it a glass tube. "Okay, let's go downstairs."

"I don't see any stairs." She tried to absorb what she saw. "Is that an elevator?"

Nodding, he stepped inside. "Yes, although there are stairs, as well."

She held her ground, nervous. "What story...I mean...are we going underground?" Biting her lip, she observed the high tech transport. Like a science fiction device. Her gaze flicked around the room, noting the windows reflecting desert and mountain scenery. Relief flooded her. "Oh you must have built this into the side of a mountain or something?" *He's so clever.*

"More or less, yes." He waited, smiling. "Do you want to see more?"

She did. Very much. And not just the facilities. "Sure...do you take every girl down in your high tech tubie-thing?" *Say no, please. Let me be special.*

"No," he said, his tone low, his expression serious. "You're the first."

Standing next to Lukas in the elevator, which began a slow, smooth descent, she gave a final look around the comfortable high-ceilinged room, the framed windows revealing the starlit desert hills. *I hope I don't regret this.*

"What would you like to see first?" His warm breath caressed her cheek in the narrow space, and she shifted closer, craving more contact . "The wine cellar? The patio? The bedrooms?"

The bedrooms, yes. But shyness made her ask, "You have an underground patio?" She stared straight ahead, the low gleam of a single LED light in the ceiling breaking the darkness. Nothing outside the elevator gave a clue to what they might be passing through for a minute or more. Her fascination with her companion almost overwhelmed her uneasiness at their descent, but not quite. "How deep are we going?"

"We're almost to the next level, but if you'd like to see the patio, it's a couple more down."

"Okay." Curiosity warred with doubts. "This is your getaway? For vacations?"

"Among other things. I get a lot of work done here."

"I can see why, no interruptions." Before she could formulate any of the hundred questions bubbling into her brain, the elevator slowed and stopped. Low lights bloomed around them. "Where are we?"

"Patio." He ushered her out into a cool, moist space. A steaming pool of water held pride of place in a paved rectangle, surrounded by green plants under grow lights. "What do you think?"

"You have a hot tub."

"Natural springs, part of a geothermal energy system." Lukas winked at her. "But we can try it out if you like bubbles."

She glanced at him, yearning to agree, but unsure of herself, then left his side to patrol the edges, looking at the plants. "These are vegetables and fruits. You have tomatoes and peppers...lettuces. How gorgeous, but why?"

Joining her, he plucked a strawberry and held it to her lips. "Taste." He held her gaze while she bit into the fruit and flavor burst in her mouth. "Like it?"

"Love it. So sweet. But you haven't answered my question."

He bent to kiss her, distracting her and when he stepped back, her face tilted toward the ceiling...seven feet above them at most, and carved from solid rock.

"We *are* underground, aren't we?"

"Yes, we are," he replied. "What do you think of that?"

Chapter Four

*W*hat did she think of it? Her answer mattered more than he'd expected. The sparkle in her eye, her eager response to his touch....

"I don't even know what to think. You didn't do this on a professor's salary."

"No. I had a hand in developing some of the technology you're seeing. Lots of people want to build in unusual locations these days and my geology degree is worth more in those areas than at the university."

She narrowed her eyes. "Lots of people do?" He watched the play of emotions on her face before her jaw dropped. "The only people I hear of who want to dig into the earth are the ones predicting the end of the world. You don't...you aren't?"

Question two. "And if I was?"

She swallowed but didn't look away. "Wow, you're a...prepper, right?"

"I suppose I am...which takes us back to what do you think of that?"

"Is there anywhere we can sit down?"

"Over here." They sat side by side on a low concrete bench. Croaking frog and chirping cricket sounds made it feel almost as if it were outside...and in a long term situation such as the one he predicted, such a space would be invaluable both for the food it could provide and for his—and any companions'—mental health.

"So, what do you believe is going to happen? The apocalypse? Polar flip? Financial meltdown? Killer storms?"

He tried to read her tone, but with their short acquaintance, he couldn't. However, her eyes gleamed in the low light, and her parted lips drew him, closer, until her soft breath touched his face and he lost his train of thought entirely.

She drew back. "So...which one? How is the world going to end according to Dr. Lukas?"

His face heated. What kind of woman could distract him from his favorite topic, his passion? A beautiful and intelligent one whose presence in his bunker filled a hole in his life, made it feel like home. *Focus.* "I...I have discovered a new fault in the Nevada desert."

"A new fault? I thought those things were ancient, developed when the earth was young, or when other large events occurred. It's not my area—I know it's yours—but how new?"

Not laughing, or poking fun. And should she deem him too crazy to be part of her life, he'd regret it, but at least she didn't know their location. The worst thing she could do was make him a laughingstock at the university...and with the theories he'd presented at a recent conference, it would make little difference anyway. Not everyone agreed with his ideas. But a tenured professor was hard to get rid of...and he didn't need the money, only taught from love of the work.

He plunged on. "This fault is, I believe, less than a century old and shows virtually no activity. I happened upon it by accident when researching another some distance away."

She tucked a leg under her. "No activity. That's good, right?"

"Bad."

"What?"

"Most faults give off small amounts of energy on a pretty consistent basis. This one hasn't been. And it seems too well-developed for one so young." He looked over, but she didn't seem bored. Encouraged, he continued. "Which is why I'm so concerned."

"How can a fault just happen?" A frown formed between her brows, and he considered smoothing it away, then tracing the line of her cheek, down to the nipples pressing against her shirt. "Wouldn't some extraordinary event have to precede it?"

He let it fly. "Nuclear testing in the 1950s. The tremendous force behind these explosions—if my theories are correct—led to the creation of the new fault. And the unusual buildup."

She nodded, showing no sign of the skepticism his coworkers did. "I'm curious, how would a geologist know to invent all these things? Aren't they more an engineer's type of work?"

Everything she said demonstrated an open-minded interest that turned him on as much as her soft beauty.

"I have a master's in engineering; it seemed expedient in light of the ideas I played with. Even as a kid I loved inventing things, applying new ideas to solve problems."

She smiled, revealing a dimple in her right cheek he longed to kiss. "You are by far the most interesting person I've ever met."

Interesting. "I'm used to other words like...out there. But it's so important to me to help people be ready for the earthquake I expect, or anything else that might happen. It makes me feel good to use my abilities to assist others."

"Maybe I have a slightly different perspective." She frowned again. "So if you're preparing for a big event like an earthquake...in the Nevada desert, why would you feel safe here? Why not just move away?"

He shrugged. "Because I'm studying it. But I selected my gold mine—you have figured out we're pretty far underground, right?"

"I gathered. You don't dig for gold or anything, do you?"

"No...at least not so far. My real gold mine is the patents on my inventions. But to answer your question, my calculations show the likelihood of a catastrophic release of energy in this direction is minimal, and I want to stay nearby and study the fault and the implications."

He waited. Finally she flashed him a grin. "If you're a prepper, everything I've seen so far is pretty and nice...but where are the supplies?"

He winced. "Are you sure?"

Say yes, please say yes. Because if she didn't break and run he was going to carry her to his bed and make love to her all night.

"Oh, it's sure to be the highlight of the tour."

Lukas stood and tugged her to her feet. "This way, then." On the other side of the patio, he opened a door. "No elevator to where we're going. At least, not yet."

"A work in progress?"

"Exactly. But safe or I wouldn't take you there. Just stay close to me and I'll make sure you don't get lost. It's pretty vast under here. There are tunnels I haven't explored yet way back in the mine."

"I'd like to come back for a soak," she said, glancing back at the pool. "Sometime."

"Let's see what you think of the rest of my hidey-hole. Because I'd like that, too."

Down two flights, Lukas tapped a series of numbers into a keypad and a door opened with a whoosh. She peered past him at a long tunnel and bit her lip. Until now, everything had been appealing, well-decorated, and could have been the getaway of one of the rich and famous...and eccentric. Before them lay a dark, rough-hewn passageway, dimly lit with small, floor level LEDs at intervals.

"Ready?"

Doubts began to assail her. Madame Eve had the address, but what could she do if Jane disappeared into the darkness of the mountain's heart? The moment they entered, the door slammed closed behind them with a hollow thud that echoed in her stomach. *Like a tomb.* Their steps echoed and the sound of her breathing rasped in her ears. Along with an intermittent plunk—probably water dripping somewhere—and her heart's thump.

The sounds of Poe's "The Tell-Tale Heart." She shivered. A person could be buried there forever and never found.

She plodded along behind him, trying to fight the claustrophobia she'd never known to be part of her makeup. Every so often, a smaller passageway branched off, and she wanted to ask where they went, but somehow her hyper-awareness of him made it hard to speak. He didn't offer any information, just strode on for how far she couldn't judge. Her teeth chattered, the air at least twenty degrees colder than in the elegant living areas.

"You doing okay back there?" His words carried back to her from a few yards ahead. Her steps had flagged, as her thoughts overwhelmed her. "Give me a minute and I'll come get you."

"Y-yes." She didn't want to admit how afraid she'd become. How a little girl raised in an island paradise in the South Pacific with nothing over her but endless blue sky or billowing clouds had no experience to draw on, no idea what to think about a billion tons—or so—of mountain bearing down on her head. The small lights cast even the low ceiling in shadow, but directly above it was…. "How deep in the ground are we anyway?"

He strode back to her side and bumped shoulders with her. "Oh, below the actual desert, just a few stories." *Not bad.* "Of course we're under the mountain here, so several thousand feet."

A loud rushing in her ears preceded spinning darkness and a shout from Lukas.

"Jane!" At the sharp sound of his voice she forced back the dizziness, shoving away the galaxies of spinning stars at the edge of her vision.

I will not faint like a ninny. No! After all, if solid stone had held up the mountain for eons, it would continue to do so. The strength in his hands when he blindfolded her…the whole evening had been an exercise in trust.

The first person to inspire such confidence in her besides her parents. And, his research held some parallels to her own. The aboveground nuclear testing in the archipelago she called home had been the reason for her changing from herpetology to meteorology. She'd been fascinated by the lizards and other reptiles of her island home since she was a little girl, but the weather changes her mother reported in the past several years had given her cause for worry. Particularly when she worked on her thesis on atmospheric anomalies during the past half century, both there and in Nevada.

Arriving back at her side, he took her arms. "Are you all right?"

She swallowed and fought to steady her voice. Not because of the fear, anymore. The tall man loomed even larger in the small space. "I am, thanks."

"I thought you might be having a claustrophobic reaction to the tunnel and wanted to reassure you we are almost to our destination."

She smiled and tried to hide a shiver. "Well you have to admit it's pretty dark and cold in here, but I'm fine."

He cursed under his breath. "I should have realized you'd be cold. I'll have something for you in a minute." He led her to where the passage ended in a T, paused, and took a right turn. "Close your eyes."

"Again with the blindfold tricks? I assure you I won't be able to find my way in here."

"No." He laughed. "That's not why, although I did like tying it on you."

She glanced at him, the shadows making his smile more secretive, alluring.

"I just want you to experience the full effect."

"Of your supplies?" Bags and boxes and cans...how thrilling could they be?

He pulled her forward a few feet, then rested her palm on a cool, rough stone wall. "Stay here just a minute and don't peek."

She squeezed her eyelids tighter. "Hurry."

His lips brushed hers. Her lids fluttered but she kept her

eyes tight, savoring the sweetness of his touch.

"I'll never hurry with you, Doctor Summers." He moved away, the absence of his heat in the cold cave leaving her gasping.

Never hurry. Her heart slammed against her rib cage. She wanted it, wanted him. "Hurry," she whispered again. "Just this once."

After a moment or forever he returned to lift her hand. "Open your eyes."

She blinked in the sudden glare.

"It's quite a use of power, all the spotlights...but, every so often...."

"It's...it's unreal." She stood at the edge of a great cavern. "This isn't any kind of storeroom."

"No," he murmured. "We found this when we were tunneling back into the mountain to build the supply depot." He spoke with a reverent tone, as if they stood at the edge of sacred ground, and she understood why. "Broke through a wall, and poof."

Stalactites hung from the ceiling, great icicle-like structures almost meeting the stalagmites reaching up toward them. The walls glittered with minerals...gold, silver...she had no idea. All that was missing was pipe organ music. "So beautiful. Is that sparkle at the bottom water?"

He nodded. "Yes, a natural underground river provides us...me...with all the drinking water I could need. Crystal clear and delicious."

"Amazing, like something from a fairy tale."

Lukas rested his hands on her shoulders. "Which one? Beauty and the beast?"

"No, one with a handsome prince. Maybe Snow White...can't you see the dwarfs in here, mining precious gems?"

He nuzzled her neck and a shiver ran down her spine, this one for desire, not temperature. "Yes, but they'd be dressed for the chill. Heavy tunics and boots." Big hands rubbed her bare arms. "We can go down there later if you want, but for now I have just what you need. Come with me."

Jane filled her gaze with the magic cavern in front of her. A prepper's water source, but the most magical one possible. The bright lights flicked out and the display disappeared. With a sigh, she turned.

She felt no fear, but.... "I can't see a thing."

"Hang on." Once again her cold fingers were swallowed up in his warm grasp and she followed him, blinking in the gloom. "Your eyes will adjust in a moment. I travel in here often, mine just seem to do it faster."

He led her down what she thought was the left side of the T, the floor level lighting a relief to her straining vision. While the walls still lay in shadows, the ability to see the ground under her feet lent her some confidence. They soon arrived at another heavy steel door, another keypad. "This is the heart of the place. This and the control center."

"Control center? Can I see?""

"Another time."

She leaned against the doorway while he flipped on a light and waved her forward. A steel-walled room about half as large as the cavern held shelves and cabinets. Every shelf filled with white buckets or heavy cardboard boxes, cans or bags. A huge freezer unit next to a propane tank. "How many years do you plan to be stuck down here? Looks like one person could live ten years on this."

"Not just for one."

A pang. Who would he bring?

"Worst case scenario, the quake could sever the continent just west of here. Food will be a problem. I hope to help others."

Of course. "How many?"

"As many of my colleagues as I can. Just because they doubt my theory doesn't mean I want them to starve. And other survivors will need their knowledge."

She strolled the perimeter of the room. "Oats, wheat, beans...popcorn?"

"Sure, it's nutritious and cheering at the same time. If you go through that door at the back, there's even more." He reached past her for a parcel wrapped in brown paper. "But this is what I wanted to pick up." Handing her the package, he pulled a multi-tool from his pocket and cut the raffia tying it closed. Jane unfolded the layers of paper and gasped.

She held it the tightly-woven blanket to the dim light. "I love it. Look at the lovely shades of browns and grays, and," she stroked the folds, "it's the softest thing I've ever touched."

"Myra is quite the weaver."

"Yes, she is...is she a prepper, too?" *And is she someone special to you?*

He took the blanket from her hands and laid it over her shoulders. Under its welcome weight, her shivers ceased. "She is part of the community, but I don't know her well."

Pleased, she caressed the soft weave. "She's talented."

"If you like this she has a little shop downtown or you can buy on her website as most of our group do. Internet with a blind credit card, sent to a post office box or general delivery."

"And you?"

"I just have everything sent to my apartment in town, or my company warehouse in Carson City." His face lit as he explained his world to her.

"Lukas, how many people have you brought here?"

"Since construction completed? Besides my employees?"

"Right."

"None."

Jane dragged the blanket closer, tugging the ends together and lifting the bottom so it wouldn't drag on the floor. "And what did you intend to do with this cover?"

His glance settled on the wall behind her. "It's for my bed."

Her muscles, tight from shivering, relaxed as she snuggled into the woolen coverlet. And when his eyes focused on her, the last of the cold slipped away and heat bloomed in her cheeks. But she had no doubt where she wanted to be.

"Then let's go put it there."

He searched her face, and she wanted to reassure him.

Although she worried about what he might think when he found out he spent the night with a woman so inexperienced—and what if she couldn't please him?—she had to try.

"You sure?"

She smiled. "Never so sure of anything in my life."

He pulled her against him and kissed her. She struggled to embrace him in return, but her hands were tangled in the blanket, so she leaned back and went with the flow. His beard tickled her chin, but his lips were soft against hers, reverent. She'd never met a man who made her want him more.

If her feelings continued to build, how would she leave him behind to return home?

When he lifted his head, she asked, "Ever wanted to live on an island?"

"And leave here? No, why?"

"Never mind." She'd take the night and all it could give and be grateful.

Chapter Five

*T*he tunnel would take too long, so Lukas led Jane, instead, to the back staircase up to the living areas, holding tight to her hand. He seemed to be doing that a lot. Her beauty drew him, but her mind—the curiosity and interest in his studies—provided an even stronger lure. Other spaces remained to show her, but the insistent ache in his groin—and dammit, his heart—refused to be denied. It had been all he could do to stop from bending her over a sack of grain and taking her right then and there. Only his respect for her and desire to make their first time together good for her stopped him.

"Aren't we going to take the elevator?"

"We can, but it would take longer to go all the way back down the tunnel. This is more work, but quicker." He lifted her fingers and kissed them, rubbing them against his cheek. "I don't want to wait any longer to make you mine."

She followed him, but as they climbed flight after flight, stairs he took on a regular basis to save the large amount of energy consumed by the elevator, she began to flag.

"Just a minute." She halted and pulled free, leaning against the railing, puffing. "I'm not used to climbing skyscrapers."

He glanced back at her and laughed. "Sorry, I forget not everyone climbs hundreds of steps on the weekends."

She shook her head, and sucked in air. "You're wearing me out."

He grinned. "I have plans for you." He bundled the blanket around her and scooped her up in his arms, ignoring her squeak of protest. "You're going to need all your energy."

He made short work of the remaining few flights—because even he wouldn't have tried to carry someone up if they hadn't been almost there—hoping his plans and hers meshed.

She clung to his neck and buried her face in his shoulder. He liked her there, his protective side rising to the forefront. His muscular frame had no trouble supporting her slight weight. The soft, sweet-smelling bundle in his arms would be in his bed as soon as he could get her there.

Reaching the top step, he punched the code into the keypad and when he heard the click, leaned into the door leading to the control room, the bathroom...and his goal.

No codes were necessary, but he had to shift her to free a hand to open the conventional door. "Low lights." The darkness retreated to reveal a space he hoped would please her. Letting her slide to her feet, he turned her around.

Small sconces lit the walls and Jane took in the room where her life would change. She'd finally "live," which was fine, if a bit frightening. But she feared she'd lose more than her virginity there. With each moment with Lukas, she lost a bit more of her heart.

His bedroom reflected its owner as she was coming to know him. A low, wide platform bed covered with a blanket in a similar style to the one she clutched to her, shelves along one wall, where hardback tomes from his dual fields of geology and engineering shared space with Shakespeare and Dickens, Poe and Faulkner. Classics—like him.

"'The Tell-Tale Heart,'" she murmured, lifting the book to page through it.

"What?" He came to her side and took the volume from her. "Oh, Poe."

"Yes." She swallowed. "That's what it sounded like in the tunnel. My heart pounding in my ears, no other noise...."

He put the book away and turned her to face him. "When you

fell behind?"

She shivered. "I'd never felt so alone in my life."

"When I came back to you, I thought you were about to faint. I feared you couldn't be under the earth with me, maybe you were claustrophobic."

Shrugging, she tipped her head back to meet his blue gaze. "I thought so, too. For a moment. I've never been in a situation like this, you know."

"And now?" He laced his fingers at the small of her back, searching her expression. "How do you feel about my place?"

"It's amazing." Safe. Secure. The result of her growing faith in the man whose hands supported her while she watched the changing emotions on his face. What did he want from her? A promise of forever?

"And you think you can manage to stay here with me all night?"

All night. We signed up for a one-night stand. Her heart sank, but how could she protest when her plane left at the end of the week. Back to the Marshall Islands and out of his life.

She forced a smile. "Sure I can. Turns out I kind of like being here, with you."

"It's mutual." He tightened his grip and brought her against him. She rose on her tiptoes, eyes drifting closed. "I'm glad you're staying."

I wish I could. But for how long? A week? A month? She could postpone her flight...if he wanted to see her again.

I do want to live. Even for one night. Screw practicality; nobody ever dies from a broken heart...do they?

"I'm glad I am, too." She waited for his kiss, amazed how she'd grown so used to it already. But to her shock, he released her and lifted her again, striding with her across the room. Her eyes opened wide. "Do you carry all your dates around like this?"

"I don't date. Much. Haven't for a long time."

She parted her lips to ask why, but his flat tone didn't invite questions. "Me, either."

"Good."

She stared as he bent to lay her on the beautiful blanket.

"You're glad I'm a wallflower?"

"I'm glad not to picture you with other men." Fierce. Possessive. Thrilling.

"No worries there." Hinting, but she didn't want to tell him. He sat beside her and removed her blouse. Not new territory there, but her nipples remembered his attention and peaked in anticipation of more. He didn't disappoint her, cupping her breasts in his warm palms and dipping his head to blow hot breath on each, then draw one into his mouth, sucking stroking it with the flat of his tongue. She jumped when he nipped, flicking his gaze up to her.

"You're so sweet." Moving to the other side, he worked his delicious magic on her other nipple, pinching the first between his finger and thumb to her delight. After not nearly long enough he pulled away and left her wet peaks exposed to the cool cave air.

He unbuttoned her slacks and slid them down her legs. She lay there in her tiny, white lace panties, feeling so vulnerable. Her belly fluttered. What would he think of a PhD in her mid-twenties who hadn't even had sex with a single cute boy in her class. The closest she'd come was back home, but it hadn't gone far, just kissing and a little petting. And the coming of age ritual sent her away.

She swallowed panic. She'd never believed she'd get this far, had she? Not even when she went to the salon, in anticipation of the evening, and the waxing girl oohed and aahed over her art. She considered asking him to turn off the lights. The tattoos were sacred, a gift to the woman's intended, to make her beautiful for him. If she'd never see Lukas again, she shouldn't let him see them.

They weren't for the casual eyes of a one-time lover.

But, Lukas wasn't casual to her. She fisted her hands and waited. He reached for her panties and then stopped. Along with her heart.

"Something wrong?"

"No," he said, standing again. "I just need to grab something." Reaching into one of the cabinets over the bed, he retrieved a strip of foil packages. She gulped. How many times did he intend to do it?

He dropped the condoms on the bed and unbuttoned his

shirt, dropping it off his shoulders. She forgot her tattoo and her concern over being screwed a half dozen times as he revealed a physique as lean and toned as any she'd seen. And so bronzed; he must spend more time outside shirtless than she'd realized. And while she took in every inch of his smooth, nearly hairless chest, he sat on the edge of the bed to remove his shoes and socks then stood and stripped off his slacks.

Wearing only boxer-briefs, he returned to her side, propping himself on an elbow and smiling down at her. "Now we're even."

She declined to argue, although she doubted any equanimity held between them. Lukas cupped her cheek and turned her to face him. She shivered at the feral gleam in his eyes as they darkened to a blue deeper than the deepest ocean. "Can I...?" She didn't know why it mattered to her but.... "I want to take the band out of your hair."

"Now you can." He held still while she reached behind his head and freed his hair, which fell past his shoulders in heavy waves. She buried her fingers in them, reveling in their wildness. The man who stared down at her was not the urbane professor who had picked her up. Rather a god, a man of unlimited strength who could carry her through disasters and fears, who had built a fortress of safety and beauty inside the belly of the earth herself.

When he reached for her, she went to him, and put herself in his hands. She was living, for the first time.

Lukas took in the sight before him. Jane, small, delicate— compared to him—and almost naked. He'd wanted her from almost the very first moment and it had taken every bit of self-control he could muster not to finish what he'd started in the great room. But as they spoke, he'd realized she was no one-night stand, despite the terms of their arrangement.

Her humor, intelligence, her interest in his work. Madame Eve had understood what lay beneath his request for a single night's date. Had his loneliness come through in the long, somewhat tiresome questionnaire? Until he'd spent an evening pacing the corridors of his underground sanctuary, he hadn't even realized himself how empty his life—his heart, had been.

When he reached for her panties, she clutched his hand, panic firing in her eyes. A suspicion began to form. Less experienced, Madame had told him...but how much less? He fought down the anger at anyone before him who had touched her soft skin, inhaled her sweet breath.

Despite the urgency hardening him to granite, he'd planned to take his time and savor the journey anyway, but maybe he needed to move even slower, to make sure she traveled there with him. Withdrawing from her panties, he started at the top, stroking her hair and nuzzling her cheek. Turning her so they lay facing one another, he kissed her eyelids. "I'm going to go slow and get to know you."

"Okay."

Lukas kissed her, hands in her silken hair, lips moving over hers. She responded with sweet eagerness, resting her palms on his chest. Could she hear the thunder of his heart? Following the line of her smooth locks, he rested his hand on the outside curve of one breast. He stroked, smiling against her lips when she trembled. Deepening the kiss, he plundered her mouth with teeth and tongue. She squirmed against him, murmuring, and he broke the contact to nip at her neck. The urge to mark her became strong—she inspired a possessiveness he'd never known to be part of his makeup before—and he sucked at her neck then bent to her breast.

Every part of her fascinated him, to taste, to see, to touch. He opened his mouth wide and took her whole breast in, inspiring a rush of lust through his veins that almost undid all his plans and good intentions.

Not a woman to be rushed.

How could he convince her to stay longer? *One night...one night only....* He nipped and she squeaked.

"Sorry."

"Oh, no...not sorry...it's wonderful." She latched her fingers at the back of his head, holding him in place. "You just surprised me."

Nothing wrong with that. "Oh, I have lots of surprises, stick around."

She giggled then gasped when he bit down on the other nipple. "Intriguing, Doctor Gerard."

"I hope so, Doctor Summers." He flipped her onto her back and sat up. "But, sweetie, I can only hold out so long and those panties have to go."

The happy, relaxed smile disappeared, the flare of panic in her eyes again. "What's wrong?"

She grimaced. "Nothing's wrong."

"Am I moving too fast? Do you want to stop?" He stroked her hip, fingers tingling at the nearness to her pussy. *Please don't say stop*. Still, her nervousness fed his suspicions. "Jane, can I ask you a question?"

She swallowed. "Yes."

"Are you nervous because this is the first time with me or...." He paused, unsure how she would take his question

She met his gaze, eyes narrowed. "Or...?"

"Or," he went for broke, " is it because this is the first time...ever?"

"No." Only a small falsehood—her nerves were not, strictly, due to her virginity.

He frowned and her heart sank. "Then what's wrong?"

How could she explain? The painful ritual she'd undergone, the impetus for her mother to send her an ocean away from home? A picture was worth a thousand words, though. "Take off my panties."

"What?" The air between them, so full of heat a moment before, cooled.

"Don't ask any more questions, just...do it."

He did as she asked, but his eyes never left hers. "So, now what?"

"Look." She held her breath. What would he think?

"Shiiit."

What did that *mean?*

"You don't like it?"

He scooted down her body and nudged her legs wider to kneel between them. "You can't be serious." Tracing the outlines of brightly-colored leaves and vines with gentle fingers, he followed the tattoo's natural progression until his touches reached the naked, un-inked parts of her womanly places. "It's amazing. When did you have this done...and why?"

"Where I come from, it's a rite of passage. All the tribal girls had them, and the wise women were kind enough to allow me a ritual as well, although I was an outsider."

"Okay, but you haven't told me why."

"For my friends, the tattooing was for their future husbands. A special gift. There's more to it, spiritual aspects, but they were so busy giggling about boys you'd never guess it."

Lukas rested his palm on her mound, pressing down with the heel of his hand. She trembled under his touch. "And you? A gift for someone? Was there a boy...a man?"

"Yes...no. I did have a crush at one time, but I didn't undergo this for him."

"Did he see it?"

She blinked. "No, my mother caught me walking funny and shipped me off. She wanted to make sure I understood my own cultures before adopting any more of someone else's."

His hand slipped between her legs and rested, not moving. "It's in such a private place, I imagine few people have been able to admire the artistry."

Jane's hips rocked of their own accord, the heat of his hand sending flames licking through her core. "Besides the tribeswomen? No, not many."

He rubbed back and forth, bringing nerve endings flaring to life. "Jane, are you a virgin?"

"Yes." She gasped.

"When were you going to tell me?"

"I don't know. I wasn't even sure how things would go between us."

"I want to ask you why, and talk to you for a long time...about where we are and where we might be going, but right now, I need to know if you want me to make love to you." He circled her clit with his thumb and she panted. "Because if you don't, we have to stop now."

"I do...I want you." She'd never wanted anyone as much. His touch sent her near the edge.

"Okay, but rest assured, we'll talk about this in the morning."

She let her eyes drift closed, not caring about the morning or the next day or ever.

"Look at me." She fisted her hands in the soft blanket. "I want to see your expressions when I touch you, when I taste you."

Dear God had anyone ever been so sexy? His deep blue eyes held her captive as he lowered his head and buried it between her legs. His mouth closed on her pussy, licking and sucking until she wanted to scream. He pushed a long, callused finger into her channel, gliding in the moisture, but the alien presence reminded her in a moment or a few moments he would be replacing it with something larger, longer, and harder.

A second digit joined the first, stretching her, and his tongue swept over her tingling clit. Soon, too soon, he lifted his head gazed at her, his lips shiny with her juices. "I can't wait anymore."

"Don't." She let go of the cover and reached for him. "Don't wait. I want you inside me."

Lukas crept up to lie atop her, reaching for the strip of foil packets he'd dropped next to them. Opening one, he took her hand. "Touch me first. I want you to know me."

Jane closed her fingers over his cock, stroking it, learning its length. A drop of precum on the head melted under her touch. She'd never thought a man's penis would be so smooth, like silk over steel.

After a moment he stopped her. "If you keep it up, we won't go any further."

She preened, pleased he'd liked her caress, but as he rolled the condom over his penis, a niggling fear crept over the heat, her limbs tightening.

Looking up, he caught her expression and smiled. "Don't worry, it might hurt a little at first, but I will make it good for you, promise."

The trust she'd felt in him earlier returned to bolster her. "I know you will."

When Lukas urged her legs wider apart and knelt between them again, she breathed long and slow. He reached for a pillow and propped it under her hips. "Ready?"

At her murmured agreement, he leaned forward, pushing the head of his dick inside her then stopped. Rocking, he entered and retreated, a little deeper each time until a sharp sting of pain made her gasp. "You okay?

"Compared to the tattoo?" She laughed, joy at their union sending her flying. "Do me, Doctor Gerard."

He shook his head. "You're a nut, Doctor Summers." He thrust forward and she trembled, wrapping her arms around his shoulders and hanging on for dear life.

No, it didn't hurt anymore, but the raw power in his muscular frame shook her to her core. She'd never dreamed it could be like this, the desire for him inside her. "Deeper." As deep as he could get, his balls bouncing against her ass with every thrust, his cock filling her until she didn't think she could stretch anymore.

She clung, riding the storm of emotions and sensations, a ball of energy building in her core, and shooting her over the edge into a cavern brighter than the one in the prepper professor's gold mine. "Lukas!"

He slammed into her one more time and held still, then shuddered before joining her in the amazing place she'd flown, for a moment and forever until he dropped to her side, shaking.

Jane pulled the extra blanket over them both and curled against him. Exhaustion stole her consciousness, and she fell toward sleep, happy and secure for the first time since she'd left her island home.

Home. Oh no, what now? The thought pulled her back from the brink of slumber. Her single pointed plan had fallen to hell. She lay awake, thinking, until exhaustion took her the rest of the way down.

Chapter Six

*L*ukas woke first, as rested as he'd ever been despite the fact he couldn't have been asleep more than a couple of hours. Jane lay in his arms, her head resting against his chest, hair tangled with his on the pillows. His a little lighter than hers, but in the dim lighting, it was hard to tell whose was whose.

With a glance at the clock, he knew sunrise would approach soon. He wanted to take her outside the bunker, as they would when the quake ended. To see the world after the storm. After their storm.

"Jane?" He stroked her cheek with a finger, smiling as she squeezed her eyes tighter.

"No." She shook her head from side to side.

"Wake up. I want to show you something." He tickled her under the chin and grinned. "Come on!"

Her eyes widened. "Oh, Lukas."

"Yep, it's me."

She struggled to sit up, but he held onto her. "No rush , we have a little time."

"Time for what?"

"You'll see, but kiss me first." She pecked him on the cheek and he laughed. "That all you have for me?"

She closed her eyes and tilted her head. "Show me."

Lukas grinned and obliged her. Kissing Jane sent other thoughts flying through his mind and he allowed himself a moment or two of play, stroking her back and enjoying the heat of her soft skin under his hands. As his cock hardened against her belly, he jerked away. "Let's go."

She blinked. "Now? You don't want...I thought?"

"Oh, I want, but not quite yet. First things first."

Lukas scooped her up in his arms, blanket and all, and strode for the door. "We're going to be late."

She linked her hands behind his neck. "You don't have to carry me. I do have legs, you know."

He squeezed her tighter. "Yep, I know...pretty ones, too, but this is faster."

"Where are we going?"

"You'll see." He used his elbow to summon the elevator and they rode up to the great room. Once there, he carried her over to one of the large windows and let her slide to her feet. "Okay, you're light, but not feather light."

She tucked the coverlet around her, suddenly shy. "Yeah, thanks." To her amazement, the window slid back to reveal the opening to yet another tunnel. "So the 'desert scene' was all just images...I should have guessed. But I don't want to run down another tunnel, not naked and barefoot."

He took her hand and led her forward. "This one is short. You'll see." After a dozen steps, an elbow in the passageway brought them to a steel door and Lukas entered his code. It slid back. "I want you to see the world as we would if we'd been down in the tunnels for a long time. A fresh, new world."

Cool air rushed in to greet them as they stepped out onto a ledge. For a second, she stared at the drop off, leading who knew how far down—hundreds of feet at least. But then the horizon, with the faintest reddening, drew her eye. The low mountains of the high desert region glowed. "Oh, it's beautiful."

"You don't mind the height?"

She shook her head. "Nope."

"And down below, in the caverns, you were okay?" His worried tone touched her.

"Yes, once I realized you'd keep me safe, I was fine." Focused on the natural beauty, she welcomed his warmth at her back.

He wrapped his arms around her. "I don't want this to end, Jane. I want to see you again."

She'd prepared for this, hoped for it. In the depths of the night she'd found a possible solution, if he was willing...?

"You've told me about your research, but you didn't ask about mine."

His tone quieted. "True, I should have, too. I guess I worried you'd be uncomfortable in my world."

She patted his hand, keeping her gaze fixed on the play of reds and oranges on the horizon. A storm brewing? " Not now I'm not. So, would you like to know what I study? What's important to me as a scientist?"

"I would, very much. You are a meteorologist. What are your interests?"

Jane leaned against him, relishing his strength and watching a bank of clouds rise to the north. "I have been studying the effects of weather patterns in the Marshall Islands and the Nevada desert since the aboveground testing over fifty years ago."

"Nuclear...so that's what she meant."

"What?" She glanced over her shoulder then focused on the sky again, concern building.

"Madame Eve. She said you might be able to work with me to further my research."

"I planned to focus on the Marshall Islands side of things, but if I have a reason to spend time in Nevada, I can continue to work on both."

"I hope I'm a good reason. Do you have a geologist at the institute?"

"Doctor Lang, but he's due to retire soon." Jane squeezed his arm.

"Interesting." Lukas dropped a kiss on her head. "We should

celebrate our collaboration."

"Mmm," she said, concern giving way to outright alarm. "Can we do that later?" The wind shrieked, whirling dust and pebbles around them and droplets of rain hit the desert floor below.

"Yes, the weather is deteriorating. I'd hoped to make love to you out here, in front of God and the mountains, but I guess we'll have to take it inside."

A gust tugged at her cover and yanked it free, pulling it over the side of the ledge into space. "Ohh," she said, grabbing for it while he held her tight. "I hate to see that go."

"It's a nice blanket, but not worth your life."

She took a step back, then two. "Speaking of which, we'd better get out of this now." Rain, hail and the howling wind chased them back into the tunnel. He triggered the door closure and they leaned against the panel. "So, Mr. Earthquake Prepper, is this place any good against tornadoes?"

TWO MEN AND A VIRGIN

"Well thought out and surprisingly full of detail for such a short read."
Cocktails and Books

Chapter One

"*S*o, where ya going?" The friendly cabbie's nonstop interrogation shouted over blasting Mannheim Steamroller carols threatened to make Andie's head explode. As he cut in and out of the insane holiday traffic approaching the airport exit, she fought the urge to destroy his Christmas spirit by telling him her plans. A picture of a pretty woman and three small children propped on the dashboard and a tangle of rosaries draped over the rearview mirror led her to the conclusion he would not approve of her intent to spend the holiday losing her virginity to not one but two men to whom she was not married.

In fact, she could only lose it to one, but she planned to have sex with both of them. Many times.

If she didn't take the initiative, the three of them would end up going their own ways, a possibility she hated to entertain. And one she'd had no idea how to avoid until her friend Karin lent her an intriguing novella about two men and a woman who came together on an island for a magical—and erotic—winter's night that changed their lives forever.

Delving into the genre, she'd devoured every ménage story she could find. Could more than two people have a loving, lasting relationship? After agonizing for weeks, she took Karin's advice and contacted Madame Eve about setting up a one-night stand with the two men she desired.

But even Karin—a 1Night Stand success story—didn't know all the details. Would she be shocked? Probably not. Her choice of loaned reading matter hit too close to home.

Either way, Madame hadn't indicated any surprise at Andie's request. After asking a lot of personal questions, she agreed to set up the date….if Rex and Paul could be convinced to participate.

By the time she exchanged her seat on the wide-body jet to Anchorage for one on a puddle jumper to Castle, Alaska, Andie had reached a state of panic. *What insanity*. Was it worth the risk of losing her two best friends for a single night of pleasure? They didn't know they were meeting *her*, so she'd just stay on the plane and head back home, tail between her legs. They'd think a stranger had stood them up—and enjoy their holiday in The Last Frontier on their own.

Paul, a firefighter, and Rex, a forest ranger, loved skiing and all other outdoor pursuits. No harm, no foul, and she'd emptied her bank account to pay for everything. They would have a great time, better than if she continued on her current path.

Problem solved, she leaned back in the leather seat and closed her eyes, then opened them again when lurid images of the three of them in bed together played on the movie screen of her mind. She focused instead on the wild landscape below, hundreds of miles of open tundra and sheer mountains, herds of animals racing along. Alaska's tourism pictures didn't do it justice.

Landing and taking off a few times on runways carved from the icy plains, they dropped off locals loaded with gaily-wrapped packages and supplies for their holiday dinners until only she and the pilot—a woman bush pilot!—remained.

As the little plane lifted off, the pilot sighed. "What a crazy day. The holidays do make things busy." She clicked a few buttons on the panel in front of her. "Come up front, if you like."

Andie blinked. "What?"

"If you take the co-pilot's station, I can show you the sights. I picked up some hot chocolate at the last stop, enough to share."

She unbuckled her seatbelt and made her way up the aisle. Sinking into the seat opposite the pilot, she said, "Thanks, this is so cool. I'm Andie, and I've never been in a plane this small before."

The pilot shot her a grin. "Kathryn. And I fly this one every day, so no need to worry."

Andie settled in and stared at the bewildering array of electronics. "Wow aren't you afraid of being out here all alone? What if there was a storm?"

"I've been doing this a long time. I know how to handle bad weather." Kathryn gestured toward a thermos. "Pour us some, would you? There should be a couple of cups under your seat there."

She fished around and pulled out a short stack of Styrofoam cups. "There's a box here, too."

"Aunt Ina's famous sugar cookies. She was the lady we dropped off at the last village." Kathryn accepted the cup of hot chocolate. "Break 'em out. We'll start the celebrating early."

Sliding the ribbon off the flat gift box, she opened the lid and gasped. "Your aunt made these?"

The other woman shrugged and held out a hand. "Ina is everyone's aunt. And she's famous for her holiday goodies. Pass me a whale, would you?"

Whales, seals, walruses...polar bears. Exquisitely frosted, each wearing a red fondant bow around its neck. "Gorgeous."

"Have as many as you want, but leave a polar bear for my husband, Nick." She winked. "He'll be tickled, even though the lodge will be overflowing with holiday treats. I swear he wants to fatten me up."

Andie bit the head off a seal and groaned. "If you mean more goodies like this, it's amazing you're so trim."

Kathryn wore a bomber jacket and tight black jeans, reminding her of a young Amelia Earhart, except for the single fat braid of red-gold hair drooping over her shoulder, nearly to her lap. Slim and vivacious, she made Andie conscious of her own short stature and generous curves.

She should have gone on a diet, lost ten pounds or so before coming on her date. *Since I'm going home anyway, it's a moot point.* She popped the rest of the cookie in her mouth, savoring the sweet buttery goodness dissolving on her tongue. "Ina is a baking goddess."

"She's a sweetie, all right. No kids of her own, and her husband died a long while back, so she takes care of everyone. I think it keeps her from being lonely." Kathryn set her cup down and focused on her instrument panel. "I'm checking the weather now. Looks like you'll have a white Christmas."

In Alaska? "Aren't they all, up here?" A mountain range came into sight, its peaks frosted like the polar bear cookies, gleaming against the perpetual dusk of the winter's day.

"Yeah, more or less." She leaned back in her seat. "So, who are you meeting up with?"

Don't make me tell. "What makes you ask? I mean…how do you know…?"

Kathryn swallowed a bite of cookie. "Just a guess."

She knows I'm here on a set-up date. She must think I'm desperate. Of course, I am. "I was…but I think I'll just stay on the plane. Do you have room for me on the return trip?"

Despair overwhelmed her and she choked a little. Giving up now meant giving up forever. She couldn't afford to do this again, and if she didn't have the nerve to go through with her plan thousands of miles away, where nobody would see her, she sure wouldn't back home.

"Oh, well yes, but my next flight is after New Year's."

"What? I thought you were going to go home. To your husband?" In her panic, she tried to think what to do. "Can I at least hitch a ride wherever that is? I mean, not if you're going just to your own house, but it's in a town right? Somewhere I can stay for a few days until I get another flight out?"

Kathryn set her cup down again, hit a button on the console, and sat sideways, facing her. "Castillo Lodge is home. I'm Kathryn *Castillo* and Nick Castillo is my husband."

She fought dizziness as her escape plan melted out from under her, leaving her as suspended in air as the little plane, but with fewer instruments to guide her. "Oh no."

"The weather's good and we're on autopilot for a few." Kathryn looked at her with curiosity. "Why do you want out of your date?"

Kathryn listened to Andie's story then shared her own, explained how her doubts and fears nearly cost her the love of her life, and Andie understood. By the time they landed she was determined to go forward. Better to have loved and lost.... *God, I hope all is not lost. Paul and Rex are going to be furious with me.*

È

Paul slammed into the cabin and stomped his feet, bringing circulation back. "I've never been so cold or had so much fun. You should have come along—I'd like to take dogsledding up fulltime."

"I don't think there's a lot of dogsledding in our part of Northern California." Rex laughed. "I wouldn't have missed skiing down a glacier though. I still can't believe we won this trip from 1Night Stand." He stood and stretched, loathe to leave the armchair in front of the roaring fire. "I guess we should go to the lodge for dinner."

Stripping off his heavy outer clothing and boots, Paul moved to stand in front of the licking flames, shivering. He avoided the sheepskin rug—as they both had. Even their socks could mar its pristine whiteness. "You can go. I'm going to heat up something from the kitchen here. Looks like it's pretty well stocked, and I'm cold enough for one day. What time did you say our date is arriving?"

Rex checked his watch. "A couple of hours yet. And we still have to decorate the tree the concierge left on the porch. The decorations are in the closet under the stairs."

Paul grimaced. "Maybe we should wait and let her do it with

us—women like that kind of thing. We can get in a quick game of chess."

"The email said to do it before she got here. Something about a romantic atmosphere, you clod. And you just want to play because you won the last three matches." Rex opened the door and dragged the ten-foot fir into the warmth. The cabin filled with the scent of pine, and he sniffed in appreciation. "Smells like Christmas."

"Do you think Madame Eve thought it was odd we wanted only one girl between us?" Paul opened cabinets and drawers, and finally the fridge. "Pot roast okay?" He held up a foil-covered pan. "It comes with instructions."

"Thank God."

"Hey! I'm not such a bad cook." He read the sheet of paper and bent to turn the oven on. "It's preheating."

"I could remind you of other dinners you 'cooked,' but since we're about to eat, I won't." Rex leaned the tree against a wall and strode over to the stairs. Opening the door underneath, he chuckled. "Wow, whoever stocked this place is Yule crazy." He hauled out half a dozen boxes and rummaged through. "Okay, here's the stand."

"It's the owner's private guest cottage. The lady filling in at the front desk...I think she said her name was Mamie...told me he usually has relatives in this time of year, but Madame Eve requested it for us. I wonder how we happened to win this trip. Madame said something about an annual contest for former clients."

"Don't look a gift horse in the mouth. I think you had it right. We should move here."

"Might be a good idea at that. We'll have to come back in summer and look around, maybe make some inquiries about buying property in the area." Paul slipped the pan in the oven then continued to ransack the kitchen. "Lots of food here, but nothing else prepared."

Rex shrugged. "We can eat at the lodge when we have to. Unless our date feels like making something."

"Andie would be in heaven with all this stuff." He shut the cupboard and sighed.

"Forget her for tonight." Fastening the tree into the stand, Rex grunted. "Come and help me with this."

Paul sighed and trailed over to hold the behemoth straight. "She's hard to forget."

"That's why we're having the date. To get her out of our systems." Tree secured, he stood and stepped back. "Let's get some balls on this so we can eat."

"If we had any balls, it would be her coming here tonight instead of some stranger. We'll never get her out of our systems."

Rex took him by the shoulders and gave him a hard kiss. "She doesn't have a clue about us, lover. Nobody in that small-minded town does." He rested his forehead against the taller man's shoulder. "Until we're up front with Andie, and she can handle it, we can't have her."

Paul shrugged away and grabbed a handful of glass ornaments. "But, we have a girl coming tonight to be with us, who we can be open with and enjoy ourselves, and maybe...just maybe when we get home, we'll be able to decide once and for all whether to let Andie in on the secret that we love her and each other...or call it done."

Chapter Two

*T*he driver stopped the snow machine at a cleared lane with drifts piled several feet high on either side, and hopped out. "The party starts at nine. Your bags should arrive shortly."

Andie climbed off, awkward after the bumpy ride, and pulled her hood tighter against the icy chill. "Thanks. Is it always this cold here?"

The man laughed. "It's only about thirty below today. It's not cold." He waved and gunned the machine away, his voice floating back. "Better get inside before your nose freezes off."

She took a tentative step, the frozen gravel crunching underfoot. She may have used the last available credit on her Visa to buy warm outerwear, but was glad she had. Nothing in her Northern California upbringing had prepared her for this.

She paused to take in her accommodations. Two stories, real logs. Fragrant smoke from the chimney blew down to tickle her nose. A big front window showcased the two men inside, decorating a Christmas tree, their deep voices carrying to her.

Her heart thumped. Paul, at six foot two, with his blond hair cut short, had the broader shoulders, the deeper chest. He wore a goofy Christmas sweater, broad stripes of red and green she remembered from the year before—and the year before that. He loved that ridiculous thing. But Rex's six foot, dark-haired, dark-

189

eyed hunkiness was just as appealing in its own way. The flannel shirt and jeans he wore suited his brawny good looks. What girl wouldn't want a sexy forest ranger? No wonder she'd never been able to decide between them, or look in any other direction.

Best friends since kindergarten, the two were inseparable, and she adored them equally. Thus her problem. Each had let her know they'd be open to more than friendship....

With their heads close together, they laughed. Rex tossed a shimmering mass of something in the air and it fell over them both, catching the light. They looked so happy together, as though they didn't need anyone else in the world. Like a magazine ad for Christmas decorations. A yearning ache in her stomach bent her nearly double, and she rested her hands on her denim-covered knees and breathed through her nose. The icy blast shocked her into awareness. Could her nose freeze off?

Straightening, she hotfooted it for the wide porch and knocked on the door before changing her mind again. *This is it, girlfriend. One way or another, the cat will be out of the bag and the chips will fall where they may. Cat chips? Whatever.*

Paul stared, a clump of tinsel in his hand and a bite of candy cane in his mouth. A weakness for them both, only a few had made it to the tree. "That's her."

Having such a good time decorating the cabin, they'd forgotten all about why they were there. As if it were just the two of them celebrating the holiday like a real couple. Why did they pretend anyway? If the townspeople judged them, they could just move away.

And leave their families? Everything behind?

They'd been through it a million times. Rex didn't want to come out as gay. Neither had ever been with another man or wanted to. It had always been about loving one another. And Andie. *Andie....*

"You going to get it or should I?"

Paul shrugged off the thoughts. They'd have the rest of their lives for doubts and recriminations. "I will." He tossed the silvery stuff on the tree and wiped his sweaty hands on his jeans. Turning in a circle he took in the results of their two hours of work. They'd forgotten the pot roast in their artistic frenzy until the smell of smoke drew it to their attention. The charcoal mess rested in the sink.

But a winter wonderland waited to greet the woman willing to spend the night with the two of them. Garland strung from beam to beam and twined around the staircase spindles, candles lit every surface, the tree decorated from top to bottom. He cut off the overhead light on his way to the door.

At Rex's questioning frown, he said, "Romantic, remember?" But really the low light made him less self-conscious. Hand on the knob, he muttered a prayer to Saint Nick and tugged the heavy portal open.

Rex joined him, facing the bundled up snow angel shivering on the porch. He reached past his friend and took her arm. "Welcome, come in, you must be chilled to the bone." The hooded woman nodded and he led her to the fire. "Let us help you off with your coat and boots."

Rex, always the gracious one, even when uncomfortable or out of his element. Nobody would know when he was uneasy...except Paul, of course, and maybe Andie.

Joining the pair by the fire, Paul took the woman's coat. She sank down on the wide hearth, the fire casting her face in shadow, and bent to pull off a heavy boot. He dropped to a squat and helped her, his focus on her calves and small feet, then looked up. And fell on his ass.

Behind him, Rex made a choking noise.

She grinned. "Hi, guys. Merry Christmas."

Rex stumbled until the armchair hit the back of his knees and then dropped into it. "Andie?"

Paul scrambled to his feet. "How did you get here? Are you here for the holidays, too? Do you—oh no, you didn't win a date, too, did you?"

She looked back and forth between them, tension in her jaw

he'd never seen before. "No, I didn't." Tucking her legs up onto the ledge, she wrapped her arms around them and rested her chin on her knees. She muttered something.

"What?" Paul loomed over her like an interrogator. "I couldn't hear you."

"I said—" She dropped her stockinged feet to the floor and rose to her full height of five foot two. "I am *your* date. Both of yours." Her helpful clarification sent Rex's heart into the pit of his stomach in shock.

He moved closer. "What are you talking about? Do your folks know where you are?"

"I'm not a child, Rex, they don't need to know everything I do. But I did tell them I had plans for the holidays." She brought her gaze up to his, and he fought not to smile at her set jaw or her hands fisted on her hips.

"This is impossible...a mistake."

"I'm sorry you feel that way." The tremor in her voice belied her defiant stare, and he longed to comfort her, but was too stunned to behave like a normal person. "I thought we could spend a nice Christmas Eve together, the three of us, but I guess I can see if they have a room in the lodge available." She reached for her boots.

"Don't be silly." His mind raced, trying to assimilate her presence and determine the right way to respond. "You just surprised us."

"Big time," Paul said. "Give us a moment to absorb the...err...surprise."

They bracketed her. She was even shorter than usual without shoes, dressed in a red sweater that just met the top of her low-rise jeans. Her dark curls fell around her face, cheeks pink from the cold.

"I hoped it would be a good one, but I guess I misread the signals. I thought you both wanted me." She took a step away. "Let's just forget it, okay? But if I stay here, you might feel odd bringing girls back from the big party. After...this."

Rex reached for her hand and warmed it between his. "Why

would you think we'd do that?"

She shrugged, refusing to meet his gaze. "You were expecting a date tonight, you came all the way here for it...and you were disappointed to find me."

He stopped trying to think what to do and let his heart lead. "Never disappointed, Andie. Nothing about you could ever disappoint me...us." He tugged her against him, and she rested her head on his chest. "We just don't want to hurt you in any way. And, sweetie, you've never struck me as the two-guys-in-bed type of girl."

"It would be a first," she mumbled into his sweater.

Glancing past her to Paul's stricken face, doubt infused him one more time. Neither of them would survive a night with her unscathed. A one-night stand with the girl of both their dreams?

He needed to buy time.

Squeezing her tight, he dropped a kiss on her soft hair and set her away from him. "We haven't eaten all day."

She looked at him then at his friend's guilty expression. "All *day*?"

"Well, since lunch. Paul burned our dinner." He waved toward the kitchen and as he'd known she would, she brightened and headed in that direction. Feeding them had become an obsession with the girl, who seemed convinced they would starve if she didn't take care of them.

"What is...oh, heavens." She held the pan up and grimaced. "One of you take this outside, it's nasty." He grabbed for it. "What was it?"

"Pot roast." He moved toward the door. "And it came with reheating instructions."

She shook her head, curls bobbing, and pulled an apron off a hook, wrapping it around her twice. "I hope there's something else in here I can whip up, or we'll have to go to the lodge."

The two men grinned and sank into the chairs by the hearth. Just like at home, when she came over and cooked for them. "Do you think you might make us a few cookies? It is almost Christmas." Paul had balls...and a sweet tooth.

"Leave it to me. I swear if I hadn't come up here, you'd just be living on junk food—what would that be up here? Bear jerky?"

Staring at the fire, Rex welcomed the normalcy. If all went well, she'd make them a great meal, and they could all go the party and then to sleep, and forget the madness of the early evening. She was their friend, no matter what fantasies they entertained. And she didn't have a clue about their relationship. How the hell could they take her to bed—assuming they took that route—without her finding out?

He leaned against the high back, listening to her rattle around in the kitchen area. As always, she began to sing as soon as she started to cook. Although she wasn't a trained vocalist, her happiness came through, even when she stood at her station in the fancy restaurant where she made her living, arranging lettuce leaves topped with half a bite of lobster or mini toasts piled in creative disarray between dots of *fois gras*.

Not what she liked to cook, but it paid well enough and as long as she was doing that, the happy tunes warbled forth. He'd asked her once if she wanted her own restaurant, and she'd said no. When he pressed her, she'd smiled and clammed up. She knew them too well—they'd have bought her one and she valued her independence.

"Whatcha making?" Paul asked, craning his neck to see her.

She broke off her rendition of *Little Drummer Boy*. "This and that. The lodge stocked this place so well.... While the chicken roasts, I'm thinking of using the other oven to bake a few cookies."

Rex turned to the side. She bent double rummaging in the refrigerator, her sweet fanny swaying. He watched the girl he—they—had wanted for years, now theirs for the taking. His cock got rock hard in his pants.

He struggled to remember why they'd never made a serious move before. Two big brutes in bed with little, innocent Andie. Such a bad idea. He pictured her shock when she found out they were lovers as well. Would she be horrified at the idea or just angry they'd kept it from her?

Dancing from one counter to another, she peeled potatoes and wrapped garlic in foil to roast with the bird. Her garlic mashed potatoes were the best thing to eat on earth.

"Want biscuits, too?"

He wanted a lot of things. "Sure." But biscuits weren't tops on his list right that moment. And why hadn't they just taken her right to bed? *Oh, right, bad idea.* "We're going for a walk and bring in some wood while dinner cooks."

"What?" Paul stared at him.

"Let's go, buddy." He beckoned toward the door, widening his eyes. *Hint.*

"Sure." Paul jumped up

She waved them away. "Hurry back so dinner doesn't get ruined."

"Okay. You know we never want to miss a meal of yours." They bundled up and ducked out the door. As it slammed behind them, Rex raked his hair back from his face. "We have a problem."

Paul trudged through the drifts on the side of the cabin toward the woodpile.

"Where are you going?"

He faced Rex, exasperated. "To get the wood, remember? As you suggested?"

"There's a lean-to full of logs right off the kitchen. We don't need any more tonight."

"Then why did you say we needed to go get some?"

Rex shook his head. "We're in way over our heads here. I wanted time to figure out what we're going to do."

"Okay." He could see that. "So, any ideas?"

"Let's go to the lodge and get a present—the bottle of fancy perfume we got for our mystery date isn't good enough for our girl."

"You know you call her that all the time—our girl?" Paul stepped on the cleared path and together they headed for the lodge with its gift shop.

"Dammit, do I? Well, she is. Our girl, I mean." Rex turned onto the main road, thankful he didn't have to stumble through deep snow. "And you call her princess."

Paul laid a hand on his bicep and spoke in a quiet tone. "I guess I do." He moved in closer and wrapped his arms around Rex's shoulders, hugging him. "She just offered to be our girl and we shoved her away so fast she nearly fell on that cute ass of hers."

"We didn't mean to hurt her."

Standing so close together, Paul could almost forget the worries they had about her. He and Rex had a good thing going, but the issue of their feelings for the third in their happy trio hung over their heads. Inseparable since kindergarten, was it really possible to take their friendship to the next level?

"Of course we didn't. But it worked out the same." With a quick squeeze he released Rex and started toward Castillo Hotels' northernmost US location. Built a century before by a gold mining king from ancient trees of immense girth, it had been in danger of collapse when Nick Castillo snapped it up at auction. The multinational corporation used its enormous bankroll to restore the lodge to its former glory. A wilderness treasure. Rex's version of heaven.

"Paul, are you listening?"

Shoot, what did I miss? "What, oh sorry, woolgathering."

"Look at the tree in the front window—must be twenty feet high."

Paul blinked. "What were you saying? Before the part about the tree."

"This evening could affect the rest of our lives."

He swallowed hard. "I thought we were just looking for a present."

Andie put the pot of potatoes on the burner and switched on the gas. The biscuits browned and a pan of shortbread cookies decorated with some of the silver dragees she'd found in the cupboard waited for room in the oven. All alone in the cabin, with dinner under control, she dropped onto a stool at the counter and buried her hands in her face.

Could they have been clearer? *Andie wants sex? Oh no! Quick, get her to cook something and distract her from such an unthinkable idea.*

Done. *Finito.* She'd given it her best shot and her last dollar, but it looked like another platonic weekend with her buddies. They had been kind, but clear. Two of the hottest guys on earth had no desire for their old friend in their bed.

They'd been willing to take a woman there, but not her.

Okay. Fair enough. She had a party to go to, even if Paul and Rex weren't interested in her the way she'd hoped. The grandfather clock chimed. Five times. Plenty of time to finish cooking, get all dolled up in the pretty red velvet dress she'd intended to wow the boys with, and head over to the lodge for the big celebration. *I can't let them see how much it hurts when they turn me down.*

Christmas Eve—her favorite night of the year. She thought of the gifts in her bag and shrugged. *What a dreamer I am.* The timer buzzed, and she hurried to pull the golden biscuits out and replace them with the cookies. She made quick work of preparing the other dishes and stopped. Her suitcases. Hadn't the hotel guy said they'd be delivered by now?

At a knock, she trotted to the door, relieved to find a hotel employee bundled in a parka, holding her luggage.

"Just put it in the second guest bedroom."

He stomped the snow off his boots and came inside. "Ma'am? There's only one bedroom in this cabin. I can call the front desk if there's a problem."

"Oh, no."

"When the gentlemen checked in yesterday, they didn't say anything was wrong. They commented on how well they liked the place." The man pushed his hood back, hat hair making a bird's nest of his red locks. In his early twenties, he had freckles across his nose and an anxious expression.

"Umm, no. We'll be fine." She couldn't afford to get another room or a bigger cabin even if one was available. But—she looked around the room—where had they slept? Maybe they could order a rollaway bed or something? Someone was going to get stuck on the floor or in an armchair by the fireplace. Why hadn't she thought of what might happen if the guys rejected her offer?

Because the idea was almost as devastating as the reality.

You can't show it, though. It's your chance to give the guys the best Christmas ever. Then it's time to head home and move on. Or better yet, move away, where you won't see Rex and Paul every day of your life. Won't have to watch them meet and court their future wives, have babies, while you work at that pretentious excuse of a yuppie restaurant and yearn for a life. Maybe far away you can make your own.

In Houston or Toronto, or maybe the North Pole.

Chapter Three

*T*he cabin might have had a single bedroom, but it took up the entire loft, with plenty of space for a huge bed with room for three and a tub the size of a small swimming pool. Tempted beyond measure, she filled it and, tossing aside her clothes, sank into an ocean of bubbles.

She imagined Paul and Rex's long legs tangling with hers under the water, like summers past at the lake, when each boy took one of her hands and they leapt together off the dock into the water's chill.

Football stars, both of them, excellent students, outgoing, friendly, and popular. She'd been shy and introverted, but they chose her over the cool kids to be their constant companion. Protecting her from bullies, cheering her on when she'd been coerced into a saxophone solo at the band concert. Girls fluttered around them like bright butterflies, but they'd taken her to the prom. Both of them. As friends. The two most popular guys in school took a *friend* to the prom.

But were they ready to take their friendship to the next level—all three of them together?

They'd gone for wood...an hour ago...but she knew why they left. They'd gone off to decide. Would they take her to bed? Or try to let her down easy?

With her eyes drifting closed, and the water cooling around her, she allowed herself one more fantasy before giving it up forever.

"I've never taken a bath with two hot guys before."

"Don't worry." Rex, always protective. "We'll do everything, make it good for you."

"Good for all of us." Paul, fun, intelligent, and inventive. "I have some ideas."

She gasped as each man took one of her feet and massaged from her toes to her heels until her muscles went limp and her worries faded away. Magic fingers stroked over her ankles to dig into her calves, then her thighs, while her blood pressure rose and her breath hitched.

"Sit on my lap." Rex again. "And tell me what you want for Christmas."

A door crashed closed and boots thumped on the hardwood floor downstairs. "Andie, something's burning."

"Oh, shit." She scrambled out of the tub. "My cookies!" A huge bath sheet hung on a hook, and she wrapped in it before hurrying down the ladder.

Pulling the oven door open, she peered inside. "They're ruined." She lifted the charred mess from the oven with a hot pad and dropped the tray in the sink with a groan. "Can you believe I burned something? Just like Paul."

She turned away from the sink. Paul and Rex stood in the middle of the room, still in outdoor clothing, dripping snow onto the clean floor. She opened her mouth to make a comment, a patented Andie smart-ass remark, but it wouldn't emerge.

Both men gaped, their eyes darkening in color. She looked from Paul's midsummer sky blue to Rex's deep gold. "What's wrong?"

Rex swallowed hard, his Adam's apple bobbing. "Not a thing."

Paul shook his head, back and forth. "It's all good."

Something had changed, the air crackling with tension. She held her breath. Hope sprang anew. Could it be...? *Don't push it, Andie!*

"Okay, then. If you'll help me get the food out of the warming drawer, we can have dinner before the party." She turned back toward the kitchen.

Paul cleared his throat. "If you want to have dinner, you'd better get dressed."

"Because otherwise, it's all going to get cold." Rex's husky tone raised goose bumps on her arms and bare legs.

Bare. The towel. Ironically, considering her plan for the night, she was overcome with modesty.

"Oh, no. Give me a minute." She headed for her suitcase in the loft. "I was just taking a swim...a bath in that huge tub." *Imagining you were with me—*

"Andie, wait." God, if Rex didn't shut up she'd throw the towel aside and fling herself at them. "We've been talking."

"Yes?" She paused, holding the folds tight around her. "And?"

Paul chimed in. "And if you're serious, we'd be very honored to be your Christmas Eve date."

Her hair piled on top of her head, the big towel wrapped around her, her bare feet and ankles still sheathed in bubbles...Rex wanted her so much he couldn't think straight. In fact, he and Paul hadn't come to a conclusion about the situation until she made her entrance with all the sex appeal of a holiday water nymph.

Paul's choking inhale, his own pulse pounding, and of course the bulges stretching the fronts of both their pants made it hard to hold back. If things went badly, they might all part and never see one another again—his heart squeezed with pain at the idea—but they couldn't stay as they were forever without being honest with one another.

She stood in the kitchen, as if unsure what to do, clutching the towel around her body. Paul smiled and approached her, taking her hands away from the terry cloth. "If you want to play, you're overdressed."

Rex held his breath until she laughed. "I'm not the only one."

Whether it was a burning building or a blushing woman, trust his buddy to know how to handle any situation. The high color in her cheeks continued down to the tops of her breasts, and Rex longed to follow it with his lips.

Paul untucked the fold of towel holding it closed.

Under Rex's eager gaze, the Christmas present of a lifetime revealed itself. From her smooth white shoulders, he took her in an inch at a time; the top curves of her breasts, baby pink nipples that peaked when the cool air hit them, the sweet indent of her waist.

"I can't stand it anymore." Rex spoke through gritted teeth. "If the two of you aren't too hungry, maybe we can have dinner after...after a while."

Paul stepped behind her, resting his hands on her hips. "I'm hungry, Rex. But not for food."

She giggled, but her legs trembled. "You, Paul? Is there something you want more than a good dinner?"

He dipped his head and nuzzled her throat. "Yes."

Her knees buckled and Rex dodged forward to help hold her up. "Honey, you don't have to do this."

She gaped at him, eyes wide. "Yes, I do. It cost every penny I had to get an evening with you two, and I'm not going to waste a minute of it."

He cringed a little. They hadn't won an all-expenses paid trip. She'd paid for everything. Andie worked so hard at the restaurant, and she didn't make as much as either of them. But she thought they were worth it. He was determined to make sure she still held that opinion at the end of the night.

"You could have had us at home, you know." Paul slipped an arm around her. "Really, we're easy."

Rex started toward the ladder to the loft. "You could have had us for a loaf of your amazing brioche...hell, for a cookie."

"Not one of those, though." Paul nodded to the scorched

mess. "I never thought our Andie would burn Christmas cookies."

"Now we won't have any dessert," she said, shaking her head. "And on Christmas Eve."

Paul slung her over his shoulder in a fireman's carry and she gasped.

"We'll have dessert first," Rex said. "And then dinner."

The big bed loomed. The one where he and Paul had made love the night before, held each other, and talked of a future. Of maybe moving somewhere less small-minded.

Now Andie entered the equation. Unless it was truly for one night. And that would break both their hearts.

Paul laid her on the soft bedding and stood to strip off his clothes.

A pair of sconces on either side of the headboard cast low light over the bed and its single occupant. How many years of dreams lay before them? The rich jewel tones of the red and green patchwork quilt enhanced every bare curve and inch of her creamy skin.

Nude save for his boxers, Paul dropped to her side, across the bed from Rex, and caught his gaze, giving him a soft smile. They'd shared the dream and the fear it would never come true. But it had. Still he lingered, dressed while the two people he loved most lay in front of him.

He could look at them all day.

Or he could act on his desires. Taking a cue from his friend, Rex left his underwear on and settled down on Andie's other side.

They lay in a row on their backs, nobody touching anybody, until she giggled. "So, doesn't anyone want to kiss me?"

They all laughed then, hard and long until they cleared the air and enough of the tension to be human again.

If he didn't act, Paul would, and he wanted the first taste. "I will." Turning on his side, he took her hand and pulled her to face him. Stroking her cheek with a single finger, he gazed into her eyes. "You know you can back out now or at any time."

She shook her head. "I don't want to back out. Why would I give up my ultimate fantasy?"

For the first time in their long friendship, he could show her *his* fantasy, what he wanted from her. And he put it all into the kiss. The longing. The passion. The love. A brush against her lips, soft, urging them to part. "Baby, it's mine too."

Paul embraced the two of them. "And mine. You caught us off guard. We never dreamed you'd want us the way we want you."

Chapter Four

Sandwiched between their muscular bodies, Andie felt small, happy, and safe from anything the world could throw at her. She didn't care if a blizzard beat against the walls or if the universe came to an end. Everything she'd done to get to this point was worth it.

Rex rubbed his bristly cheek against hers. "You can still change your mind."

The surge of pure joy dimmed. Did he want to call it quits? But then, even a virgin knew when a man's rock hard erection poked at her thighs, stopping was the last thing on his mind. And judging from the pressure against her back and the sharp intake of Paul's breath at Rex's words, he was up for it, too.

"After all I went through to get you two in bed with me?" She fought for focus as her body took over all functions.

Paul nibbled on her lobe. "But, baby, anytime...listen to me." His warm breath stirred the fine hairs around her face, tickling her nose. "You can say enough at any time."

"I get it." They confused her. Did they want her or didn't they? She didn't need a pity lay.... Determination lent steel to her wavering emotions. Scrambling out from between them, she knelt at the foot of the bed. "Let's get this straightened out now."

The two men pushed to sitting, propped up on pillows

against the headboard. Paul, blond and Nordic, his blue eyes golden lashed, the tribal tattoo around his bicep outlining the muscles he needed to do his job, saving people and property from devastating fires.

Long hours striding through the forest, supervising trail-building endeavors and dealing with the sneakiest of poachers kept Rex lean and toned. Unlike show-off Paul, he kept his shirt on most of the time, so she'd never realized he, too, sported an intricate ring of characters inked on his upper arm. She wanted to push his dark hair back from his eyes, but fisted her hands. Nobody was going to touch anybody until she was confident they were there because they wanted to be. Wanted to have sex with her. And...she hoped...cared for her as she did for him.

When she dropped her gaze to his lap, then his friend's, she lost all doubt they desired her, at least in bed. Biting her lip, she considered her next move then came to a resolution.

"We signed up for one night, and I think we're making this too hard. You want me...at least for one night of sex, right?"

They both nodded, Rex's dark eyes blazing at her words. Paul opened his mouth as if to speak then snapped it closed.

"Then let's do it. Without worries, without questions, and without recriminations in the morning. You're my friends, I love you, and I spent my last penny to have Christmas in Alaska with you. The least you can do is cooperate." When Rex's lip twitched, she pressed forward. If he came around, then easygoing, ready-to-play Paul would follow. "So... if we're going to do this, would you both mind taking off your underwear so I can see what I've gotten myself into? Please?"

She didn't bother to hide her grin as they both scrambled to obey. Two sexy men at her bidding. It was going to be a good night. As long as they didn't panic when they realized she'd set them up to make her first time special. Without their permission.

Yanking his boxer briefs off, Rex tossed them to the floor and lunged for her. He'd wasted enough time. Grabbing her arms, he dragged her to the head of the bed and lay next to her. Paul took his place on her other side.

"Okay, I guess we all know why we're here." His heart lifted although his reservations about the intelligence of their actions held. *Don't over think this. You'll blow it.* He relaxed his tense shoulders. "Since you brought us together for this holiday tryst, Andie, any special requests?"

"Just one." Her green eyes glowed and her mobile mouth uptilted in a smile. "Don't squash me."

"We'll do our best, darlin'," he drawled. "But you didn't pick lightweight playmates."

"No." She shook her head, her dark curls mussing against the pillows. "I didn't. But you're the only playmates I want—big oafs that you are."

He tugged her on top of him, savoring her sweetness, exploring her mouth with his lips and tongue. How much had she wanted them if she'd spent all of her money and flown all this way? Tangling his hands in her hair, he angled her head toward him, baring her throat.

Paul took advantage of the long, smooth line, licking and sucking his way to her shoulder, a leg tossed over his. Hyperaware of the cock digging into his side, Rex tried to ignore the slippery pre-cum at the tip. How could they get through this without revealing their secret? Why were they doing that again?

Right. Because Andie might run.

She wriggled.

"You're going to kill me, baby." Rex pinned her down with his elbows. "Hold still and let us love you."

Love me. Heat curled outward from her center, rolling to her fingertips, her toes tingling. *Love me, please love me.* "How can I hold still?"

Paul laughed. "I can help with that." He sat on her thighs. "If he gets the front, I get the back."

A frisson of panic fizzed in her veins. The ménages she'd read flashed in her mind. Did he mean...not double penetration her first time out! Not that they knew it was her first time...her muscles tightened, but she couldn't flee, held captive between them.

Paul's warm fingers dug into her tense shoulders. "What are you thinking to be so knotted up? A massage, princess. We can make you feel so good. Relax."

"I thought...well...."

"I know what you thought. One step at a time, okay? There's plenty of time for anything creative later. But first, I want to touch you, kiss you all over, and I think we'll let Rex do the same. Work for you, bro?"

She closed her eyes and let her other senses take over. His strong hands worked every kink out of her back, skipping her buttocks to massage down to her feet and back up again while Rex continued to keep her mouth occupied. So sweet, he tasted of peppermint.

"You've been into the candy canes," she murmured against his lips. "Did any even get hung on the tree? Bad boys."

"You have no idea," he said.

"But we'll show you." Paul's breath against her ear made her shiver. He dropped to the side and took her shoulder. "Lie on your back, princess, and we'll show you how bad we can be."

She opened her eyes to see them lounging on either side of her. She took in the ink armbands again. "How did you guys get matching tats without me?" They exchanged a quick glance and focused again on her.

"You want one?" Paul teased. "We didn't know you were into that, but if you like, we can take you to our artist." He bent closer, and she forgot about tattoos and anything other than another warm mouth, peppermint again, but Paul's kiss held a take-no-prisoners intensity right from the start. She welcomed his tongue into her mouth, exploring and twining with hers. Rex's fingers closed on her nipples, pinching and tugging them, sending fire to her core. A warm hand rested on her mound and Rex disappeared from her line of vision.

"Open your legs, baby." He urged them apart and inserted

two fingers in her pussy. "You're so ready for us. She's so wet."

He rubbed his thumb on her clit, and she bucked, moaning into the other man's mouth. Rex pumped his fingers into her, and Paul kissed his way down to her breasts, sucking one then the other into her mouth. A wave of heat overwhelmed her, tightening her around the fingers inside her, as she rose higher and higher.

Then he pulled them out, and she whimpered at the loss. "Just a minute. I need to get some protection." He climbed off the bed, opened a drawer, and pulled out a foil packet.

His cock bobbed against his belly, long and smooth and impossibly big. It would never fit. He rolled the condom over it and came back to her. Paul, still beside her, sat up. They both watched as Rex knelt between her legs and smiled at her. "You sure, baby?"

She nodded, beyond words, excited and terrified at the same time.

He pushed her thighs wider and rubbed the head over her sensitive folds, then =inside. An inch, two, and she tensed again. There. A sharp sting and she bit her lip, tasting blood. Rex rocked his hips and sank to the hilt, then paused. She waited with apprehension, but the pain seemed to be gone and an incredible fullness replaced it.

When he began to stroke, she clung to him, the heat and excitement back in force. He thrust harder and faster, panting into her shoulder, and when she tipped over the edge, convulsing with her orgasm, he followed her, clasping her to him and shuddering to a stop.

He rested on her, until his breathing slowed, then rolled to the side. Paul's eyes were on them, the blue almost indigo. Could she do it again? Could she not?

She held out her arms and he came into them. At some point he'd also donned a condom and he took her mouth with his and plunged inside her. Longer than Rex, he had a narrower girth and slid fast and deep. Over and over while she—to her amazement—climbed to the peak again and fell, spiraling down into darkness. Paul tightened and emptied inside her.

The entire process, with both of them, was over so fast she didn't know what to think. What did it mean? Rex reached for her and tucked her against his side, murmuring nonsense into her hair.

She didn't care what it meant. Paul left for a moment and returned to curl up on her other side. Bliss was hers.

The two people dearest to Paul drowsed in one another's arms He'd fallen for her at age six. A princess, always and foremost, she'd finally noticed the two guys dogging her every step and welcomed them into her world. Smart and beautiful, he'd never known what she saw in them.

Three best friends.

Then of course, he and Rex crossed the line last summer, with each other. They'd both been afraid to tell her...and now what? He'd almost kissed Paul twice when they were making love to Andie. Would it have been okay?

Their princess in their arms and their bed—like a gift from Father Christmas. Paul climbed out of bed and bent to pull a blanket over them then paused. A dark streak marred the pale skin of her inner thigh. Blood? When she'd flinched as Rex entered her, he'd assumed it was due to the other man's size.

"Oh, Andie, why didn't you tell us?"

She stirred and frowned in her sleep and he backed away. Returning with a damp washcloth, he wiped away the evidence. He'd hold his peace until he had a chance to ask her why she'd kept such a secret. As pretty as she was, he'd never imagined she'd still been a virgin. Although they didn't talk about it much, he knew she dated from time to time—and assumed...it didn't matter what he'd assumed. She had come to them an innocent. Had they been too rough? *I hope we didn't hurt her.*

He lay next to her, reached down, and drew the soft cover over all three of them. Andie shifted and rolled toward him, resting her head on his chest. To his dismay, his cock took her sleepy embrace as an invitation and hardened against his belly.

He tried counting backward from one hundred by sevens then began thinking through his and Rex's last chess game. She snuggled closer, rubbing her cheek against his nipple, and he swallowed hard.

Stroking her back, he remembered she'd just had two larger than average cocks inside her newbie pussy. She'd need a break before any more actions. Still...he knew other ways to pleasure her.

She slept on, and so did Rex, sleeping angels while the devil on Paul's shoulder devised a plan. The scent of their lovemaking clung to the blanket, enhancing his arousal. If he could wake her up, accidentally ....

He jostled her, but she only murmured and relaxed again. He caressed her back, her sides. When he brushed her breast, her eyes opened, wide and startled.

He shook his head and nodded to the man behind her. "Shhh, Rex is asleep."

"So was I." She blinked. "You woke me up on purpose, didn't you?"

"Guilty." He palmed her breast gratified when her nipple rose against his hand. "I wanted to play."

Andie's cheeks flushed. "I don't think I—"

"Shhh, princess, I know."

She shoved his hand away and moved to sit up, but he tugged her back against him.

"Rex, sleeping, remember? He skied a glacier this afternoon. Let's let him rest...."

She stopped fighting but lay rigid. "So what do you think you know? Wait...a glacier?"

"Shhh. I know this was your first time and you're probably not ready to go another round, right?"

She didn't respond so he tipped her face up to him. "Right, Andie?"

"I might be a little sensitive. Maybe in a while?" She kept her voice low, but despite his warning he wasn't worried about waking Rex. The man slept like a rock. A nuclear bomb detonating downstairs wouldn't bother him. Still....

"Let's go downstairs and have some cocoa and talk." He chided himself for his deception. Sure they'd have the hot chocolate—she made the best—but he wanted to taste her at leisure, to spend more time between her thighs. To taste her *there*.

If Rex objected, he'd give him equal time when he woke up.

"Okay," she whispered, crawling to the foot of the bed, giving him a mouthwatering view of the moist paradise between her legs. He considered just staying where they were.

But his friend needed his rest, and Paul congratulated himself for his consideration and offered Andie Rex's T-shirt. She grabbed her panties from the floor and pulled them on under the shirt. He tugged on boxers and preceded her down the ladder, standing at the bottom to admire the view of silky calves and help her to the floor.

"You really want cocoa?" She eyed him, lifting one straight, dark brow.

"Do you mind making it?" He headed toward the kitchen. "I will, if you want."

She beat him to the refrigerator. "Oh, God, no. Rex would be sure to wake up when the smoke alarm went off."

He pouted. "I can handle a small kitchen fire."

"You know that from experience." Andie drew out a quart of milk and a can of whipped cream then bumped the fridge door closed with her hip. "I've always wondered if you became a firefighter to learn to put out the fires when you attempt to cook."

"That's not very nice." He fought the grin tugging at the corners of his mouth. She had him dead to rights, as usual. Nothing had changed.

She dropped the dairy products on the counter and reached for him, wrapping her arms around his waist and tipping her head up for his kiss. Lust surged in his belly. *Okay, maybe some things have changed.*

After a long, dick-hardening kiss, she broke away, brought

out the cocoa and sugar, set them down, and went for the vanilla extract. He sat on one of the counter stools and watched her as he had a thousand times. Except this time, something was missing. He waited and it came to him. "Andie, why aren't you singing?"

Standing at the stove, she expertly whisked the cocoa and sugar with a little water and shrugged. "I don't know." Reaching for the glass bottle of milk, she paused. "You aren't sorry, are you?"

She'd given them the most precious gift she had to give—the one they'd never dreamed of being worthy of receiving. *She* wasn't sorry, was she? She'd just kissed him....

Please don't let her regret it—us. He steeled his nerves to keep his voice steady. "Never. Do you?"

She took two mugs from the row hanging below the cabinets and filled them with steaming hot chocolate, topping them with a flurry of whipped cream. "No, but I was so pushy. I thought you might have just gone along with it. You know, so you wouldn't hurt my feelings."

She had to be insane. Paul was on his feet and at her side in a split second. "Did I come in an embarrassing two minutes to avoid hurting your feelings?" He turned her to face him, appalled at her pale cheeks and the single tear clinging to her lashes. "And when Rex was hard again the minute we were done...also to be considerate? What are you thinking?"

She stared and he loosened his grasp on her shoulders. How the hell would she know how these things worked? He took a deep breath. Rex was the sensitive one; he on the other hand, handled comic relief. How had he ended up trying to fix a broken virgin?

He had snuck her downstairs for hot chocolate and whatever other goodies he could get. And now, with Sleeping Ranger upstairs no help whatsoever, he'd have to deal.

"Princess, let's go sit and have our cocoa and talk."

Holding her Santa mug in both hands, she trailed after him

toward the fire. The crackling flames and the multicolored bulbs on the Christmas tree lit the room; the darkness outside reflecting and enhancing the intimacy, as if the three of them were alone in the world. Paul hit a button on the CD player and *White Christmas* began to play.

"Let's sit on the rug and have our drinks, okay?"

She nodded and dropped to sit cross-legged on the deep sheepskin, its soft fibers caressing her bare legs. She stared into the fire and a moment later Paul joined her.

"Look what Santa left us." He waved a bottle of brandy at her. "I think we could both use some of this in our cocoa."

She held up her mug. "Without a doubt."

When she was sipping her drink, he drew a deep breath, glanced up toward the loft where Rex slept, and began. "There are some things you should know."

Rex sat on the loft floor and leaned on the railing. Their words floated up to him, soft but clear. Paul had stepped up to the plate, and he didn't regret pretending to nap. He'd heard every word. *A virgin*. His chagrin fought with pleasure that she'd waited for them. Had they been gentle enough? She'd been shy at first, but never seemed in pain.

Hi goofball friend, lover...explaining with great patience how they'd fallen for her when they were all too young to even know what it meant. He didn't know Paul had it in him. Usually he stuck with making jokes, uncomfortable with expressing emotions even in their own relationship.

"And I never made a move because I always thought Rex was better for you. With him always getting us out of scrapes, I thought he'd take better care of you. You deserve the best."

You're the best...you both are. Yes, he was protective, but only because Paul could be careless in his enthusiasm, and with Andie sometimes lost in her own world, they needed someone to watch over them.

She laughed, a deep, sensuous sound that went right to his cock. Ready, again. "But you came up with all the best games, the wild ideas. Why, without you we'd never even have played midnight freeze tag."

Paul shifted away. "You fell in the pond and nearly froze to death."

"True, it might have been a better summer game." She moved closer and laid her head on his shoulder, the dark against the light. Paul's blond hair glowed in the firelight, a misplaced halo.

"And Rex saved you." He stayed put, but the straightness of his posture gave away his discomfort.

She got up on her knees and stared into his eyes. She murmured something and Paul nodded. Rex fought a quick pang observing the two of them without him. A trio would have a hard time—maybe he should step aside and....

"Rex." Andie said, her sweet dimples denting her cheeks. "Are you going to join us? Or were you planning to watch all night?"

"That's right, partner." Paul leaned against the recliner, pulling her onto his lap, facing the fire. "Because if you want a show, I think we can accommodate you. I enjoyed watching you two earlier." He reached for the hem of the shirt she wore and lifted it, revealing her ivory body outlined by the firelight. "I'll owe you for these." With a sharp tug, he tore away her panties. "Remember when we put on those shows when we were kids? I have a different kind in mind this time."

All the blood and good intentions left Rex's head and went to his lap. He stumbled to his feet and down the ladder. "We always put on those shows together. As I recall, you were the producer and Andie and I were the talent."

Paul lowered her to the floor and lay half on top of her, kissing his way past her collarbones and toward her breasts. "I think this time we can all be stars. What do you say, princess?"

She reached for Rex. "I want you both. Now."

So assertive. Hard to believe she was the same shy maiden of a few hours before. Still when she threw a leg over Paul's torso and sat astride him, Rex had to step in.

With her perched atop his groin, Paul didn't look capable of stopping anything.

"Slow the boat down, honey." Rex settled beside them. "I am not sure you're ready for another session with the two of us quite yet. Aren't you at all sore?"

She wriggled and Paul groaned. "I don't think so." Then she paused. "Wait...why should I be sore?"

"Honey, I heard it all."

Her mouth gaped and she flushed, but allowed him to lift her away from Paul and settle her on the soft rug between them. "I think I'm fine."

"You probably are, but no point in rushing things. Then we have something to share."

Her eyes gleamed. "Is it a Christmas present?"

"More like a Christmas surprise." He winked at her, although his stomach turned at the thought their secret could, if she was shocked by it, ruin the tentative new bond they'd formed. But he couldn't keep their relationship from her anymore. Still, just in case, he wanted a few more moments of Andie time first. "Now, lie back and let us take care of you."

She dropped back, chewing on her lip. She hated being kept in the dark about anything, which made it fun to do—usually. Very unlike her to give up so easily. But her graceful limbs glowed in the flickering firelight, and he refused to miss any time with her or ask questions that might end their night prematurely.

She looked like an offering to the Yule gods, hands open at her sides, knees parted. So sexy with her rounded thighs and full breasts. Rex wanted to give her pleasure the best way knew how. Patting her legs, he urged them farther apart, stroking the soft skin of her calves then kissing the insides of her thighs. Soft and warm, she drew him, stoked his hunger to taste her.

"Wider, honey." He draped her legs over his shoulders and surveyed the feast before him. Tracing her lips with a finger, he gave thanks for the current fashion that had even a virgin getting waxed.

Paul took over the upper half of her body, playing with her breasts and kissing her sweet lips. Rex wanted those too...wanted all of her at once. And forever. His cock rubbed against her calf, and he slipped a finger inside her, just one, not wanting to hurt her. She'd already had the two of them pounding away. A miracle they hadn't damaged her. She rocked against him, pressing her softness into the heel of his hand. Her gasp didn't sound like pain.

God, is it always this good? She gasped and rested her back against Paul's warm chest, arching her hips as Rex inserted another finger and curled them inside her, sending jolts of pleasure rocketing through her.

She shuddered and her eyelids fluttered closed. Paul's hands were everywhere, leaving a trail of goose bumps, his cock separated from her ass by the thin fabric of his boxers. He was ready for more. If Rex's fingers slipping through the wetness between her legs were any indication, she was ready to take anything they cared to give her.

Paul nuzzled and nipped at her throat, pinching and rolling her nipples, sending electricity right down to where Rex...she jerked.

"You bit me!" She shivered, looking down the line of her body at his heavy-lidded eyes and lazy smile.

"Mmm, you're like a Christmas cookie. I needed a nibble."

Despite the teeth marks marring her thigh, she laughed. "Maybe you need some cocoa with that."

"Good idea," Paul said, handing him one of the mugs.

Rex's smile grew and he took a sip and swallowed. "Not warm anymore, but perfect with this." As she watched, fascinated and uneasy, he dipped his head between her legs and nuzzled her slit. Another first for her, but one she could get used to. His dark head bobbed as he did things to her that sent a hot spiral from her core to the nipple Paul tugged and back again.

"Oh, I think, I don't know, I—" There were no words. Just the endless rise and fall of pleasure, warm lips on her neck and her pussy, nibbling, licking. When Rex's third finger joined the first two, stretching her, she grabbed him by the ears and dragged him up her body.

"Rex." Paul's clipped tones startled them both, but he just tossed him a foil square, and Rex nodded, resting back on his heels. Before she thought it possible, he was back, easing inside her. She waited, but none of the discomfort of the last time occurred; his fingers had prepared her. Only an amazing friction that pushed her to the edge without any warning.

She bucked and rocked into the orgasm, riding its peaks and valleys until she lay still again. Rex shuddered and dropped to her side.

"Andie, what do you do to me? What was that, barely two minutes?"

He rested his head on her chest and she stroked his hair, utterly content to be between the two men. Maybe they did have a future. Paul said he...they...loved her, and she believed it, but did he mean they wanted a relationship with her? Both of them? The town they lived in would crucify them all.

A chef could work anywhere, but Paul's job with County Fire and Rescue, and Rex's position with the Forestry Department might not be as easy to change.

Crazy thoughts. Why would they consider giving up their jobs, their families just to run away with me? Sure they love me...but....

"If I am not getting another turn to play...can I at least have dinner?"

"Typical Paul." Rex pulled away with a groan. "No sooner is the sex over than the other urges come to the forefront." He reached down and pulled her to her feet, then headed for the ladder. "I'm going to get dressed."

Paul hopped up and followed him. "Me, too. Want us to bring your clothes down, Andie?"

She didn't answer, just watched them scramble up the ladder, two big, handsome men with... *matching tattoos. Oh crap.* How long had they been lovers? And kept it from her while she worried about which of them she should pick? They'd already picked each other.

She tried to recall—how could she have missed it? With all the time she spent, practically living at their house. They'd always been so welcoming. The one night with the crazy bad rainstorm when she'd stayed over—and Paul offered to double up with Rex so she wouldn't have to sleep on the "uncomfortable couch."

Had they done it then? While she stayed in Paul's oddly impersonal bedroom? God she was so stupid.

Now that the idea occurred to her, she could remember many shared glances, and once they'd jumped up when she wandered unannounced into their place...what had she interrupted?

And here I am, stepping in where they'd already made a choice. Sure, they loved her. They loved their sisters and mothers, too. But they were each other's partner. Ink was a mighty permanent statement.

God, I want to die.

How could her best friends not tell her something so important? The heat in her cheeks deepened. How...could they?

"Why don't you take a few minutes and get each other off before you come back down?" she called up the ladder. Something in the loft crashed to the floor and two shocked faces peered down at her through the railing. "Because I still have to reheat the veggies and get all the food out. No hurry here." If she hadn't been so upset, it would have been funny. She grabbed for Rex's shirt and put it back on. And even if she was mad and scared, his scent on the shirt still made her sigh.

Chapter Five

*T*wo quiet men sat across the table from her, eating with less appetite than she could remember. But still eating. Feeding them had been her biggest pleasure for a long time. She'd even dreamed of making a home for them. What a fool she'd been.

Bing Crosby still crooned from the CD player, one sweet, happy Christmas song after another while Andie's world crumbled into the worst holiday of her life. And the best. While she pushed potatoes around on her plate, she tried to take stock, to assess the situation in a less emotional way.

One, they loved her. Two, they loved each other. But how did those things stack up? And why had they kept that from her? Every day, not just while in bed with her. The tension rose until she blurted out what she'd tried to hold in.

"If you didn't want to make love with me, why didn't you just say so?"

They gaped.

"I told you, we love you," Paul finally managed.

"Why would you think that?" Rex asked.

Her lower lip trembled and she brushed at the tears that dared to fall when she needed to be strong. She had nowhere to go, and she had to get through tonight. Then the rest of the week. She winced. No plane leaving, no ground transportation, and no way to pay for another room. And she'd be damned if she'd ask them for any money.

"Because you two are a couple." Simple enough.

"We are together, true."

"And you never trusted me enough to tell me. You have each other, you don't need me. Then I show up here and expect you to hop in bed with me."

They stared at her as if she might explode. She supposed she looked like she might.

Finally, Rex licked his lips. "We weren't sure how you'd react."

"After all our years together? You thought I'd judge you because you're gay?"

"It's more complicated than that, prin—" She glared and Paul changed direction. "Andie, we thought we'd lose you because we wanted each other, but wanted you as well."

"And even though you're lovers, naked and having sex, you didn't even so much as kiss in front of me? I can only think that's because this was a one-time thing, for whatever reason. Pity for the wallflower? Have sex with her but not with each other, and she'll never know the difference." Pressing her palms on the table, she stood. "Dammit, I'm confused." She faced the fire, the maddening tears streaking down her face. "And I'm stuck with the two of you for the entire rest of the week."

They leapt to their feet and thudded to her side. Rex grabbed her shoulders and shook her.

"I'll admit we were stupid not to share our relationship with you, but, baby, we thought it was a one-time thing, and we weren't going to do anything to mess up our ultimate fantasy."

Paul spun her to face him. "How many times do we have to say we love you before you believe us?" She sniffled and he softened. "I love you. We love you. Hell, we want to keep you forever, if you're okay that we love each other, too."

"Are you kidding me?" She shook her head in amazement then narrowed her eyes. "Kiss."

His eyes widened. "What?"

"The two of you, kiss. Right now." She crossed her arms and tapped her foot while they moved together and, with a nervous glance in her direction, kissed. In a moment their chaste peck moved into a deep soul kiss that made Andie's heart pound hard. The two most beautiful, amazing men she'd ever met loved each other. And her.

Rex reached out and dragged her into their embrace. *They love me, too. They really do.*

Chapter Six

*T*hey made it to the Christmas party. How, Andie didn't know. But after a while they stopped kissing and hugging and got into their glad rags. Paul wanted to celebrate, and the party was at the lodge. Along with her gift, he pointed out. She'd tucked hers for them in her evening bag.

At the lodge, the men disappeared to fetch her present, and Kathryn appeared at her side. "Looks like it all worked out?"

"I'm so glad you weren't flying out again."

The other woman shrugged. She wore her red-gold hair down, and her green velvet gown clung to her figure, enhancing her slender curves. "I'm glad, too. It's our anniversary, did I tell you? I want you to meet my husband."

A tall, dark-haired man joined them, and Kathryn fairly glowed with happiness. "This is my husband, Nick Castillo. Nick, this is the passenger I told you about."

Nick took her hand. "I hope your date is going well?"

He knew all about her, and for a moment her cheeks heated. Then she pushed any doubts aside. No shame in being well loved.

"How did you like your polar bear?" she asked.

He looked puzzled and Kathryn giggled. "I'm afraid I finished the cookies before he got to them. I'm sorry, dear."

"Ina's cookies, were they?" Nick shrugged. "I guess I'll have to get used to things like that."

Kathryn patted her flatbelly. "My Christmas/anniversary gift to Nick. We just found out."

"Congratulations!" She hugged them both, basking in their happiness, but as they wandered off to dance, she wondered if she'd have that joy. Back home, if she got pregnant the gossip would be horrible and mean. She couldn't do that to a baby.

She found herself in a corner near the glittering Christmas tree. Couples danced and shared selections from the decadent dessert buffet. *I guess the guys will get dessert after all.* The guys.... They'd kept their relationship from her for how long? She didn't know. A year? Two?

All those evenings at their apartment where she'd sat—God, she'd sat in between them, watching TV on their sofa. She'd cooked dinner for them and stayed late into the evening.

While she'd been hoping they'd make a pass at her—both of them—they'd been waiting for her to leave, so they could get down to business. How could she not have noticed?

On her own, even for a few minutes, her doubts returned in force.

Then she remembered. Rex called their evening together their ultimate fantasy. And Paul's words: *how many times do we have to say we love you?*

Maybe a baby would be out of the question, but she had enough happiness for a lifetime and to want more would be greedy.

Her men returned and Paul handed her an envelope. She tore it open and drew out a single page.

Andie,

When we went out for wood, we really headed over to the lodge to buy you a present. We looked at every gift in the shop, but no fancy Christmas ornament or pair of earrings expressed what we wanted it to say. So, we decided if the evening went as we hoped, we would give you...us. Will you be our girl, our princess, forever?

She blinked back tears, bidding good-bye to babies. Her two best friends were enough for her. "Of course. Do I get a tattoo?"

"There's a Castillo employee here this week who can do it for you, if you like. The same one who did ours." Rex's smile brightened his dark face, his eyes nearly gold with happiness.

Her presents seemed small now. *A month of dinners each.* She hadn't had any money left, but they both beamed at her gift.

Paul looked away and then back. "There's one more thing. I don't—we don't—want to stay in California. If you're up for it, we shouldn't have any problem getting work in Alaska. Rex can transfer, and Nick Castillo told me firefighters are at a premium here."

Rex nodded. "We want to be a family, and here in Castle, love comes first."

"Really?" she asked, amazed at the turn of events. "Where did you hear that?"

"Nick Castillo himself. We can even rent the cabin until we build our own," he said. "And if you want to work, he said the lodge would hire you in a minute. They can always use a skilled chef."

"Unless you just want to feed us." Paul beamed with happiness. "But first, I'm going to look into a team of sled dogs."

Two Men

"I adore Kate's stories. She has this way of really getting the importance of friendship when building relationships and it makes her stories so much deeper and, in turn, makes me more invested in the relationships she writes about than I do with many authors. I loved Rex and Paul before this story even began."

Delphina's Reviews

Chapter One

Dear Rex,

I understand your dilemma and believe I can help. I have arranged a trip to the Caribbean, to the Castillo Resort and Hotel Grand Turk, where you will have the opportunity to press your suit. Your accommodations on the romantic "Little Island" will give you the complete privacy you requested. Don't worry so much.

Best of luck,
Madame Eve

Rex stared at the tablet in his lap, reading the email for at least the hundredth time. Madame Eve's 1Night Stand service had been a desperate move on his part. Friends since kindergarten, he and Paul had gone to school together, played football, baseball, and run track. Double dated even.

In the years since college graduation, their friendship had grown. They shared a two-bedroom condo in an upscale complex—the only one built since 1955 in their small, conservative town.

As a backcountry ranger in the High Sierras, Rex spent weeks away from home, and Paul's job as a firefighter kept him at the station for twenty-four hours at a time. Why would they need separate homes? In time, they would each meet someone special and get married. Until then, the place remained somewhere to hang their hats, have barbeques when their paths crossed, and rest up between shifts.

But recently, the steady stream of pretty women in and out of their place had slowed to a trickle, which might be part of the problem. At least for Rex, meaningless hook-ups had become tiresome.

Because the vague, uncomfortable, firmly dismissed feelings he'd experienced since high school had come home to roost.

Rex had a crush on Paul. *A man crush. God.* Not that he didn't admire a lovely lady on the street, but Rex's focus seemed to have narrowed. And one day when he woke with morning wood, the image that flitted into his mind as he grabbed hold was Paul's naked chest, broad shoulders tapering to a narrow waist, and firm, high ass. In the few strokes that catapulted him to orgasm, his arousal flew off the charts.

A sense of horror and shame filled him. He'd lurked in his bedroom until Paul rapped on the door to say good-bye on the way to work, then called in to volunteer for an extra trip into the backcountry. Riding the tall, rangy horse over the mountain trails, leading his mule laden with supplies, he sought to come to terms with his unacceptable emotions and lust. He drove himself harder than ever before, handing out a record number of citations to fisherman who "forgot to bring" their licenses and an out-of-season hunter who insisted he didn't kill the deer whose antlers poked out of his pack. After three weeks, he returned to base camp convinced he'd suppressed his urges. Paul's friendship mattered too much to risk losing it for a quick roll in the hay.

Or rather, he felt that way until he opened the front door and dropped his duffel at his side to find that bastard lounging on the couch, his cock tenting the pajama bottoms low on his hips. The man never wore a shirt around the house, no matter the season. *What an exhibitionist.*

He swallowed hard and opened his mouth to announce his

arrival then noticed Paul's eyes were closed and one hand dipped below his waistband. Rex stepped back into the shadows of the foyer, unable to look away.

Paul arched his back, his wrist moving, forearm muscles flexing. There could be no doubt what he was up to. What to do? Try to slip out the door without making any noise? Rex couldn't get to his room without walking past the couch and its occupant. When his friend brought his hand out of his pants and grasped the elastic waistband, tugging it down to reveal the long, smooth length of his cock, Rex nearly came in his pants.

They'd showered together a hundred times—along with the rest of their teammates in high school—but he'd averted his eyes. This time...they were focused on the forbidden. Paul spat in his hand then gripped his dick and stroked. Squeezing and releasing, up and down, a hypnotic rhythm that Rex's throbbing cock echoed. He rubbed the front of his jeans and his member lurched toward his palm.

Paul groaned and lifted his hips off the couch, massaging faster as fluid spurted from the head of his dick. It went on and on, decorating his six-pack abs with strings of thick cum. With a shudder, he slumped back, eyes still closed.

Rex froze, hand still flat against his pants, afraid to move for fear of attracting attention to himself. But after a moment, the other man's breathing evened out, and Rex risked reaching behind him to open the door and slip outside.

His knees buckled and he slid to the hard concrete of the front steps. No way could he go back in until he had his emotions and his body back under control. He'd never seen anything as beautiful as the man pleasuring himself on their couch. How could he ever sit there and eat popcorn and chug beer again? He couldn't without remembering.

Eventually the evening's chill overcame his reluctance to face his roommate and he rose to his feet, straightened his back, and turned the knob. "Hey, I'm back."

"In the kitchen." Paul poked his head through the doorway. "I was just going to make something to eat. You hungry?"

Rex choked back a laugh. "You have no idea."

The roar of the small jet slowing interrupted his thoughts. Of course, he hadn't been able to forget what he'd seen. Or to avoid waking up rock hard with the image fixed in his mind. And over the past several weeks, he'd begun to avoid Paul, tried to be out when he was home because the friendship of nearly two decades had changed. And he didn't know how to explain.

One day he'd sat down at the PC they kept in the kitchen and found it open to a website for a 1Night Stand company. A dating service. Had Paul contacted it to set something up? To meet some girl for a night? Once Rex would have asked, but now? Now, he could barely request his best friend, and object of fantasies, pass the salt without stammering and blushing.

To his horror, the idea of Paul with some stranger tightened his neck muscles until he feared moving his head. They'd both had a crush on Andie, best female friend for years, and had dated plenty of other women, but something had changed the day he watched Paul jack off. Emotions he didn't understand tripped him up at every step.

He had to clear the air.

Scanning the website, he found a link to an application and began to fill it in. When he came to the section marked "Additional Notes," he paused then sent his fingers flying until he ran out of room to enter data. Rex lifted his forefinger and hit send. He didn't know whether his request for a date with his roommate would be granted, but he'd given it his best shot.

Two weeks later, he was on the way to Grand Turk to make his fantasies or maybe his nightmares come true.

The jet taxied to a stop and the passengers around him rose and began to retrieve their carry-ons from the overhead compartments. After a moment, he joined them, filing down the narrow aisle to the exit. The others chattered, clad in their tropical finery, ready for vacations to remember. He wished he shared their optimism.

He'd be heading home to pack his stuff and move to a place

of his own once he opened his heart and admitted his lustful fantasies. And it wasn't fair he'd hijacked his friend's date. But as long as the image of Paul laid out on the couch stroking himself, his face tensed with the intensity of his climax, filled Rex's imagination, he couldn't act as if nothing had happened. Even if Paul didn't know it had.

ന

Paul flipped onto his stomach on the cushioned lounge. Music from the poolside bar filtered to where he sunned himself on the private terrace outside his room. Another hour remained before he was due at the end of the dock for transport to his 1Night Stand date. Arriving a day early had given him a chance to relax so he wouldn't be exhausted, but the time had dragged.

Who would the famous matchmaker, Madame Eve, send him for his wonderful night? He'd indicated a preference for dark hair, dark eyes, and a muscular stature. His growing attraction for Rex made it impossible to deny he could find a man attractive. Fuck-worthy even.

He'd arranged a date with a Rex look-alike in hopes he could get him out of his system. See if he even liked being with a man. But the pressure around the house had grown until he needed to do something to blow off steam.

Even Andie, their other best friend from forever, didn't hang around as often. She came over, cooked for them, and bailed. Which kind of sucked because he lusted after her, too. *I'm a really fucked up friend.* One day the two people he cared for most in the world would realize they should be together. Honorable, protective Rex would take care of Andie and they would be a family.

He would be the guy who came over for Thanksgiving. Uncle Paul to their kids. Hiding his feelings forever, behind his patented clowning. *God.* He pushed up on his forearms and sat on the edge of the lounge, head in his hands. *Great pity party.* But he knew he was right. So there he was, on the date of a lifetime.

About to have sex with some strange guy. The fact that the date had been set up on some offshore island, where they wouldn't have any contact with the outside world for a full twenty-four hours, made it that much worse.

Would he even be able to get it up? The only man who'd ever made him hard was his best friend. Forcing back the despair that turned his limbs to lead, he headed for the shower. If he couldn't expunge Rex from his system, he'd have to go home and admit his feelings. Then move. Far away. Maybe he could get a transfer to Alaska.

And leave the door open for Rex and Andie to finally get together. As it should be. As they would have by now if he wasn't such a selfish bastard. Rex would never make a move as long as Paul hung around.

Chapter Two

*T*he small motorboat waiting at the dock didn't inspire confidence. Rex strode to the rental booth on shore and peered into the darkness. A speaker mounted under the pink and turquoise awning blasted a Jimmy Buffet tune, the cheerful music serving to tense his shoulders further.

"Excuse me," he called, over the steel drums and acoustic guitar. "Is anyone here?"

A young blonde woman in a floral-patterned halter-top and khaki shorts appeared from behind a collection of suspended, multi-colored beach balls and smiled. "Hello. What can I do for you, Mr. Forsythe?"

The personal attention he received at the resort continued to amaze him. *Does everyone here know me by name?* "I would like to speak to someone regarding my arrangements for the afternoon."

"Oh, just give me a minute and I'll be right out." She reached under the counter and a shade dropped over the front of the stand.

Rex chafed, anxious to resolve the misunderstanding. He'd expected full service every step of the way, not to be responsible for his own transportation. Heaven knew where they'd end up with him or Paul driving.

The employee—Jeanne, according to her nametag—led him back to the bobbing deathtrap. Far too small for the open ocean.

"Are you ready to go?"

"No, my date…friend isn't here yet. I was under the impression we would be driven to the Little Island by resort personnel," he said, examining the two-seater with dismay. "I don't have a lot of boating experience."

She looked around and spotted his overnight bag. Tossing it in first, she hopped down into the boat with the litheness of a gazelle. Holding up her hand, she smiled at him. "Of course, Mr. Forsythe. I'll be driving you to the island. If you're ready?"

He frowned, edginess creeping up. "What about my friend?"

"I am going to take you, then a water taxi will drop your…ummm…friend off and pick me up. It's very romantic over there, but you'll have no cell phone reception, and the boat radio is the only way you can reach us. Also, if your plans should change and you wanted to come back early, you would have a way to accomplish that."

Still uneasy, he waved her hand away and clambered onto the deck with all the grace of a water buffalo. "Neither of us is skilled at driving one of these things."

Jeanne pressed a button and the motor roared to life. "It's so easy! I'll show you how to do it." She forestalled his next question. "It has GPS so you won't have any trouble finding your way back tomorrow. If you prefer, you can radio and the resort will send someone to fetch the boat and pick you up." Reaching up onto the dock, she pulled a loop of rope off a peg and they began to drift into the harbor. "Hold onto your hat. This baby can fly."

Rex dropped into the cushioned seat just in time. Despite the crowded moorings, his driver slammed it into gear and the front of the small craft lifted from the water. Jeanne hadn't been kidding. He clutched the dashboard in alarm. "Is this thing safe? It seems awfully small for traveling among the islands."

Spinning the wheel, she guided the boat between two moored yachts. "It's perfect. We'd never let anything happen to one of our special guests."

The radio crackled to life. "Jeanne!"

She winced and lifted the microphone. "Jeanne here."

"I thought it was you. Slow the heck down until you get outside the breakwater. You know better."

"No problem, Daniel." Returning the mic to its hook, she sighed. "Sometimes I get carried away." She shifted the gears down again and they putt-putted past a number of other boats, heading toward the opening to the sea. Now that his teeth weren't rattling, Rex noticed how many people were laid out on decks, sunbathing or enjoying afternoon cocktails.

A deeply tanned man about Jeanne's age lifted a glass, but she shook her head. "Later, Eddie. I have a customer for the Little Island."

Eddie laughed, his shoulders shaking. "Take care, man. That place is pure magic."

They cruised along and reached the harbor opening. "What did he mean, 'magic'?"

Jeanne shrugged. "It's local legend. Anyone who hooks up out there is destined for a long and happy marriage. All I can say for sure is the guests come back looking happy and relaxed."

There won't be a marriage here. But maybe we can at least clear the air and stay friends. An image of Paul laid out on their couch, his hard cock bobbing against his belly, filled Rex's mind...again, but he shoved it away. No way to predict what would happen once he confessed his lust, his crush...his desire for his best friend. But for the moment, the azure bowl of the sky—the same color as Paul's eyes—curved to meet the crystal turquoise waters and a soft sea breeze caressed his cheek.

"Here we go!" Jeanne gunned the engine and he learned their previous speed had been a fraction of what "this baby" was capable of. They flew over the ocean, and with nothing around them to hit, Grand Turk disappearing behind them and a cruise ship in the far distance, he stood up and let the wind hit him full in the face. His exhilaration shocked him. A careful driver, he preferred horses to sports cars, but suddenly his daredevil actions in arranging the date, in taking a step forward in what his heart and mind demanded led him to a wanton, carefree attitude. Even if his life exploded into a million depressing pieces, at the moment he zoomed over crystal clear water on a beautiful tropical afternoon.

"Let me drive!"

☙

The slowest water taxi in the Caribbean chugged up to the island and stopped. "Here we are, man." The dreadlocked pilot waved to a pretty blonde sitting on the back of a motorboat pulled up on shore.

Paul lifted his duffel then stared at the pink sand beach before him. "So I just wade on in?"

"Yes," the blonde said, sliding into the water and sloshing in their direction. When she arrived at their side, the water hit her lower thighs. At his height it wouldn't even hit his knees. "If Donny beaches the taxi, it's a lot harder to get going again than just letting you off here. Is that okay?" She reached for the hand the pilot offered and hopped onto the deck.

"Sure, no problem." He kicked off his deck shoes, set his bag down, and dropped in, then grabbed his things and faced shore. "But where do I go when I get on land?"

"Just head straight up the beach to the path. You can't miss it...there's one building on the whole island."

He returned their waves and started toward the date that would change his life. *I can't believe I've committed to having sex with a man.* He would find out whether that was possible. Whether he could approach Rex when he got home rather than just hint. *I've had a crush on you for years. Want to fool around?* Couldn't sound lamer. But if this one-night stand didn't get him out of his system, he would do it. Rex would either be horrified and throw him out on his ass or assume he made another one of his jokes.

But he'd have to be as clear as the sea around the island. Provided he could follow through. And since all his previous experiences were with women, he didn't know for sure.

He had one reason to believe Rex might be interested, and it wasn't much to go on. How long had he watched him jack off on the couch? *Hopefully all the way to the end.*

Chapter Three

The house extended over the lagoon on stilts. Rex leaned on the deck railing and watched small fish dart past, the tiny silvery schools and larger singles moving slower in the sunlit water. Ringed by trees and foliage, the secluded spot provided all the privacy he could want for their encounter. Would Paul swim with him? Return to the wide mattress on the deck or maybe the king-size bed inside?

Or would he demand to leave? Or punch him in the eye....

Rex forced his attention back to the soothing depths. A fish lingered, every detail of its orange and yellow striping visible before it shot away, to be replaced by a half dozen others of a deep indigo.

So lovely, the most romantic spot he could have imagined—*please don't let him hate me*. The emotional roller coaster wore him down. Of course, that was why he'd made such a desperate move.

"Hello, in the house," a familiar voice called from outside the front door, and Rex considered leaping into the water and clinging to a support pole until Paul went away. But he hadn't faced bears and mountain lions, poachers and illegal mining operations without developing a certain amount of steel in his spine. Although not enough to keep his legs stable when he turned and forced each one to move forward. Past the bedroom and into the main area of their thatched paradise.

He grasped the knob and pulled the door open, taking comfort in the cheery strains of *Margaritaville* coming from the stereo behind him. "Hi."

Holy shit. Paul staggered back two steps and nearly landed on his ass. Madame Eve hadn't sent a Rex lookalike. She'd sent...Rex. Unprepared for the confrontation, he didn't know what to say. Or do. So he stood on the doorstep, mouth gaping, legs mired in quicksand.

Rex gaped back. *Must have been as big a surprise for him, poor guy. He would have been expecting a woman.*

Scrambling for a way to retrieve the situation before things took a terminal dump, he said the first thing that came into his head. "Oops, looks like someone made a mistake. What are you doing here?"

He breezed past his friend, who stood frozen in the doorway, and into the shady coolness of the little house. He'd only gotten a glimpse of Rex's face but it had been enough to tell him a mistake had indeed been made. By him. Naked pain at the man's panicked expression shattered his own heart. And he had no idea how to fix what he'd broken.

Shit and double shit.

Before he came up with any brilliant ideas for getting his size-thirteen foot out of his mouth, the door clicked closed and Rex came up beside him. He slapped Paul on the back.

"Oh, it was a last minute thing. And I hadn't seen you since my last trip into the mountains to let you know. I'm gone so much, I thought you'd never know the difference." He waved him out onto an open deck. "We can straighten it out tomorrow, but there are worse people I could be stuck with than my best buddy."

"Yeah, right." He followed Rex out and stood next to him looking over the lagoon. "Great spot, though." His mind flipped through ideas, examining and discarding them. He'd been handed his dream and been so shocked, he'd flung it aside. With a bulldozer bucket. Before he came up with anything, Rex left and headed back inside.

"Swim?"

Paul swallowed hard past the lump in his throat. "Sure, sounds great. Ocean or lagoon?"

"Ocean."

Monosyllabic answers. Although Rex had never been as gregarious as he was, this was bad. He would have to go along until an opening presented itself. If it did.

Rex didn't just change to his suit. He took it into the bathroom and closed the door.

Rex sank into a crouch against the bathroom wall, the ache in his chest echoing in the dull throb in his temples. Paul didn't think he'd made a mistake, did he? Or at least he knew the mistake was Rex's. He'd been kind enough to give him a way to save face by saying someone had made a mistake, but he'd also slammed the door to any possibility of a relationship between the two of them.

He knew Paul had a thing for Andie, they both always had. She was "their girl," their mutual prom date once, and one day one of them would have to make a move and make it official. It would be Paul. His kindness and sense of humor made him excellent husband and father material.

A parade of women had visited their dorm room and, at first, their apartment. As often as Rex traveled, he didn't know if they still did. What a foolish dreamer he'd been. Shoving to his feet, he unbuttoned his shorts and slid them to his feet, then followed them with his briefs. He donned the tropical print board shorts he'd bought at the resort and faced himself in the mirror.

It is what it is, and I have to go along with the game. We're friends. There was a mistake. It's only for one night.

A knock disturbed his self-therapy session. "You about ready? The waves are calling."

He cleared his throat. "You bet. On my way." A stern glare at the sad face reflected back at him served to remind him to school his features—as best as he could.

He jerked the door open. "Can't wait, let's hit it."

"Our dates probably would have been dogs anyway."

"Right." Rex had no choice but to go along, but couldn't stop looking at Paul's golden torso. His camo trunks hung on his hipbones like the pajamas of memory, like most of his pants. He'd been in the sun already. The man tanned almost instantly, despite his fair complexion, while Rex's olive skin would redden first. He paused to grab the bottle of sunscreen from his pack and smear it over his exposed skin before following Paul out the door and down the path through trees and low brush.

They walked side by side, but neither spoke until they emerged onto the beach. "Let's head around that bluff and see if there are any waves."

Rex nodded. "No boards, but we can body surf at least."

"Sure, that'll work. Let's get there!" Paul broke into a run, his long legs kicking up sand as he raced along the shoreline. He always had great ideas and had dragged Rex along, sometimes against his will, for years.

Paul kept him from being a wallflower in college and had taught him to surf on long weekends and summer breaks. So Rex was happy to find him waiting on the next stretch of beach, holding a pair of short boards under his arms.

"Look what I found. They thought of everything. Well, almost everything." Paul grinned, his blue eyes alight with pleasure. "Let's hit the waves."

Rex shrugged off his disappointment and grabbed a board. "Let's do it." They were friends, and he realized now how close he'd come to losing that. As he raced toward the water, his heart lifted a little. Paul in his life in any capacity was far better than Paul out of his life.

Sunlight glinted off the shimmering waves, long rays of late afternoon light casting a magical glow to the surface. The breakers weren't big, but they were long and smooth and the two of them rode one after another in, the familiar activity helping to return them to normalcy.

Buddies. Friends for life. Not everything he wanted, but he stuffed his lingering disappointment down and paddled out to duck under another foaming wave. "We'll catch a big one soon."

Paul laughed. "Here? I don't think so. But I'll take what I can get."

Rex licked his lips, tasting salt. "Me, too."

Rex's behavior didn't leave Paul any openings to undo the damage he'd done. To find a way to make things right. Yes, he wanted friendship. Surfing and dinners at home and movies with Andie. But as the afternoon wore on, he wanted more. He thought he'd known what he needed, but watching his shaggy-haired friend fall off a surfboard and come up laughing and covered with sand, his desire grew.

Rex's broad shoulders and barrel chest tapered to a narrow waist, and his legs bore the muscles gained from his work in the forest. Walking, horseback riding, trail building. But he brought more than physical strength to their friendship. Dependable, always there when someone needed him. He exuded a controlled power that women recognized and, even though he didn't acknowledge it, had them staring from across crowded rooms.

While Paul, with his laughing and jokes, brought so many women home, Rex was choosier. Paul admired that, but couldn't have told him why.

After a couple of hours, Paul couldn't paddle out one more time. He rode a final, foaming breaker to the shore and hopped off, dragging his board behind him past the water line. Dropping on his back, he propped himself on his elbows and watched Rex lie on his stomach a ways out, bobbing on the lifting tide. The tide.

He leapt to his feet and waved. When Rex noticed him and lifted a hand in return, Paul pointed to the tumble of rocks they'd passed to get to the beach with the waves. They were half covered. The cliffs around the cove weren't too high, maybe twenty feet, but they were sheer, with no obvious handholds, and if the two of them didn't head back soon, they'd be spending the night on this stretch of sand with nothing to eat or drink. And in wet bathing suits, they'd be chilly by morning.

Fortunately, Rex began to paddle toward shore. He caught a wave the rest of the way in, then hopped off and joined him on the sand.

"See that?"

Rex laughed. "Yep. Should we take the boards?"

Paul shrugged, more interested in his friend's mood and reactions than what happened to some resort equipment. "I guess. Not sure if the tide comes up high enough to be a problem, but we may as well."

Their time in the ocean seemed to have restored equanimity between them. They clambered over the rocks—the strip of sand they'd used long since covered—and took the path back to the house.

"What time do you think it is?" Rex asked, dropping his board on the porch and stomping sand off his bare feet. "I could use some dinner."

"I don't know. Does it matter?" Paul followed him inside. "Here on our deserted island, I think we can do anything we like."

Rex laughed. "Even eat dinner at any hour? Wild men, huh?"

"Uh, sure." Paul could imagine a few wilder things but he'd shut himself out of those—at least so far. "I want to take a shower though. Get the sand off."

"You go first and I'll go see what we have to eat." Rex wandered toward the kitchen, his wet board shorts clinging to his toned ass.

What would it feel like, digging his fingers into those muscles while he sucked on the other man's cock. *Radical thinking from a male/male virgin*. That led to other ideas. Anal...he could give it, at least he had to a girl or two...but could he take it?

He tried to imagine being on hands and knees while Rex's big fingers prodded his hole, stretching—

"You gonna shower or what?" Rex's voice broke his fantasy. "Because if you're not, the sand is creeping up my ass, and I'll take one."

Up his ass. The vision switched to him doing the stretching preparatory to....

"Well?" Rex poked his head out of the kitchen. "Which is it?"

Paul jumped. *Which indeed?* "Yeah. I'm going."

He tugged off his trunks in the bathroom, wincing as a shower of sand fell to the floor. Half the beach in there, Rex must have the other half. The shower adjusted, he stepped inside and lathered up, stroking soap over his cropped hair and body, but when he got to his dick, he hesitated. The dang thing was stiff as one of the boards they'd ridden, and he feared if he didn't do something about it, he'd have a hard time—hard time, yeah—making it through dinner much less the rest of the evening. Gripping it in his fist he gave a stroke, then two...then remembered Rex waiting to use the shower. He'd already done enough damage. No sense in making his friend get chafed.

With a sigh he rinsed away the suds and stepped out onto the cool, wood floor. Wrapping a towel around his waist, he grabbed his shorts and headed into the bedroom to dress.

"Your turn, I'm done."

Rex padded in, wiping his hands on a towel. "Great." Holding his waistband out, he winced. "Is it me, or is the sand sharper here?" He disappeared into the bathroom and then returned. "Did it never occur to you to take off your suit in the shower?"

Paul frowned. "No, why?"

"Get a broom and clean this up, would you? No maid service until after we leave."

Rex left the door open—no doubt so he could sweep up the sand—and stepped into the shower, pulling the clear glass door closed. Paul shrugged and went for the broom as instructed, used to being told to straighten up his messes by his neater housemate. But instead of dealing with the gritty mess on the floor, he rested his hands on the handle, his chin on his hands, and watched the show.

Although steam made the image indistinct, the silhouette moving behind the glass fascinated him. Painful, since he'd managed to screw up his one chance to cross the boundary between them, to take their friendship to the next level.

Rex's strong arms lifted as he rubbed shampoo into his locks. He needed a haircut, as usual. Paul kept his short for ease of care, but Rex's always fell into his eyes. He went to the stylist when nagged, far more particular about the state of their house than his appearance. But his careless style made him look younger, although they were both twenty-four.

His hands moved over his shoulders, one of Paul's favorite features. So broad and straight. He had no trouble picturing him rescuing an injured animal. The poachers Rex encountered surrendered at his command.

Paul rather liked the idea of surrendering to him as well. If only he would ask.

Chapter Four

A hot shower brought Rex back a degree of self-possession. He washed his hopes for the night down the drain with the sand and lather, and emerged ready to treat the evening like any other with Paul. They had taken many vacations together. Backcountry rangers always knew the best places to camp, and they went out whenever their time off coincided. He just needed to slip back into normal.

How hard could it be?

Dressed in clean shorts and shirt, he slipped his feet into deck shoes and followed the scent of burning charcoal outside.

"Hey, finally." Paul grinned at him, wielding a spatula with aplomb. "I thought I'd get a head start on dinner. There was some fish in the fridge."

Awesome. Normal. Well, almost. When they cooked out, Rex did the grilling and he didn't focus on his best friend's shorts clinging to his hips. And the sprinkling of crisp, golden hair on his chest. Usually shirtless, the man managed to look even sexier with the tropical print number hanging open. The afternoon in the sun had deepened his tan to golden bronze and the long rays of the setting sun gilded him...a Viking. Abandoned as an infant at a firehouse, Paul had no idea who his biological parents were, but at least one of them must have come from somewhere

Scandinavian...or their ancestors had. Rex could picture him plundering a village and hauling away treasure and maidens over his shoulder.

In Rex's mind, the maiden bore Andie's face, but the growing arousal tenting his shorts didn't allow him to keep that thought. An idea to deal with another time. Because normal was not going to happen.

Not now, at least.

Paul returned his attention to the grill, and Rex turned his to his nape and the fine hairs there. He moved closer, a step at a time, until he stood close enough that the other man's shirt, flapping in a slight gust, brushed his forearm. He flexed his fingers in response, lifted his hand, reached....dropped it to his side.

He'd begun to turn away, when his wrist was grabbed in a firm grip.

"Rex, don't you think this has gone on long enough?"

Rex's deep brown eyes flicked up to meet his, and he jerked his arm and nodded at the hibachi. "The fish will burn."

"I don't care. I always burn everything I cook anyway." *Why did I decide to make dinner again?* But he shoved the filets to the edge of the grill, away from the coals so a fire wouldn't distract them. A five o'clock shadow darkened Rex's tight jaw line, framing his full lips and the errant lock of hair fell over his eyes. "We've been friends too long to be dishonest with one another. Who did you expect to find here tonight? A woman?"

Rex shook his head. "No."

"Then who?"

"You." He pulled away and strode to the balcony railing, staring over the lagoon. "I knew it would be you."

Paul wouldn't let him get away that easily. He came up behind him and rested a hand on the rail on either side of him. "Then why didn't you say so when I showed up?"

Rex leaned on the rail, but Paul leaned too, his hips pressing into the firm ass in front of him.

"I didn't say so because you looked so surprised to see me." He spun around. "Who did you expect?"

Paul cupped his chin, savoring the rough stubble against his palm. "I expected someone to help me get you out of my thoughts."

A soft smile lit Rex's face. "I was in your thoughts?"

"Long time now." He stroked the whiskered cheek as the last of the daylight faded around them. Unwilling to wait any longer, unable to think of anything funny to lighten the mood, he followed his heart and did the smart thing, for once. With an arm around Rex's waist, Paul yanked him closer, fearing and liking the erection bumping his. He gave his best friend the kind of kiss that held nothing back. Urging Rex's lips open, he followed with his tongue, exploring, stroking, encouraged when they twined. Their hips ground together, and he dropped a hand to touch Rex's cock, rubbing it through his shorts, breath coming in short pants.

Now that it had begun, Paul wanted to hurry, to make a connection they would never forget. He still didn't know how it would go. Lust surged through him, tightening his balls, but when they got down to it, how would he react to another man ...sucking, fucking? In a panic, he yanked free, shuddering, and stared at his friend.

They both looked away. *Not good.* Paul struggled to think of a joke, something to lighten the mood, then realized he didn't want to. He wanted to blow on the flame they'd lit, keep it burning, because there wouldn't be another chance. Rex's heaving chest and trembling, muscled thighs turned him on more than anything he'd ever experienced. But they were still clothed, and he feared what might happen when the swordplay began.

"Let's go inside." Rex headed for the patio doors and he followed, driven on by lust and affection. Whatever happened, nothing would ever be the same between them and that fear nearly overwhelmed the desire—but they couldn't go back. They'd never be able to look one another in the eye if they didn't resolve things then and there.

And he would start with dropping to his knees and sucking Rex's cock.

℃

The best-laid plans...the bed was a divide as wide as the ocean and almost as uncrossable. Rex's arms hung at his sides, limp. But, the bulge in his pants didn't abate and Paul took hope from that. With a deep breath, he flopped across the mattress and grabbed the other man's waistband, dragging him to the mattress.

Rex barked out a laugh, which choked off when Paul unbuttoned his shorts and dragged them and his briefs over his hips. Rex's cock popped out and lay, long and smooth, against his belly. His eyes widened, but he reclined on the pillows while Paul rested his head on his stomach and took a moment to examine what he'd gotten himself into.

He touched the broad, florid head with a finger, smearing a drop of precum around. Grasping the base, he slid up and down, getting a feel. Considering how many times he'd had his hand around his own, the angle took some getting used to. Rex's testicles nestled between his thighs, the dark hair springy. Sucking in a deep breath, he opened wide and took the tip into his mouth. Rex shoved him back down and held him in place, his hips lifting to fuck Paul's mouth. He was surprised to like the salty, musky taste and even more surprised at the rush of fire in his veins at Rex's domination. Opening wider, he took the hard length into his throat, fighting his gag reflex, relishing the strength behind the thrusts. He bobbed his head, sucking and tonguing the cock that threatened to choke him until Rex muttered a curse and arched his back, his ab muscles tightening under Paul's cheek.

"I'm going to come. Only warning to...get off."

He wanted to, he thought he did, but he sucked harder, and reached between Rex's legs to palm his balls, squeezing in time with his suction. In. Out. Squeeze. *God. There's nothing like this.*

With a shout, Rex filled his mouth with salty cum, and Paul struggled to pull away, but firm hands on the top of his head held him there, offering no quarter. The creamy fluid flowed down his throat, and he had no choice but to swallow or choke on it. The moment he could, he leapt from the bed, panting.

No woman had ever overpowered him. He always set the pace, took control in lovemaking. He'd been the one to tangle his fingers in their hair, while his cock was sucked, his balls licked, his body worshipped.

He tried to slow his breaths, standing beside the bed while his friend lay shivering with the aftereffects of the blowjob. As the panic left his veins, and his heart pounded a little less fiercely in his chest, Paul took in the sight again.

He had done that, made a strong man tremble, made him come with his mouth. And...he'd liked it.

Rex's eyes fluttered open and his brow furrowed. "That was amazing."

How to explain, to express his pleasure? The women he fucked were much less complicated. He'd reached a whole new level of understanding. In triumph, he fell back on the mattress and dragged his friend—his lover—against him. "Yes."

"Was I too rough?" Rex struggled to get a look at Paul's face, tipped his chin up, and examined him. His voice broke. "God, I'm sorry."

"Don't you ever say that." Paul wrapped a hand around his neck and pulled him in for a long, soul-searching kiss. "Does that feel like I hated it? Like I hate you?" He pressed kisses all over Rex's face, his cheeks and nose, and sucked on the side of his neck. "My friend, all I can say is don't leave me hanging. Which will it be?"

Rex stammered. "Which...what?"

Joy at having broken the ice, at having been the one to make the first move—even though his love had made sure he followed through—carried Paul along. "Are you going to suck my cock or shall we just move on to the next event?" Reaching for his own dick, he stroked it from base to tip. "I'm thinking condoms and lube might be in the night table drawer."

Rex blanched. "I don't think...that is, I...."

"I can just jerk off while you watch, if you like." He squeezed the tip and rubbed down again, then up. "Just like at home."

Eyes on his actions, Rex's quiet voice gave nothing away. "Did you hear me come in? Why didn't you say something?"

Paul slid up next to him, but kept on stroking. "No, I didn't know until later. When your duffel got home before you did."

The bag...he'd left it in the foyer when he went out to make his second entrance. *Smooth.* "Oh."

"Why didn't you say something?" Paul rubbed his palm over the head.

Embarrassment fading somewhat with his voyeurism out in the open, Rex reached over and Paul showed him how to touch him, moved his hand until he had the idea.

Distracted, he almost forgot to answer. "Oh, what should I have said?" Stroke, rub, squeeze. "Hi, honey, I'm home. Nice cock."

Paul laughed. "Why not?" He trailed a finger down Rex's chest and to the start of the dark happy trail below his navel. "We could have saved a lot of time."

"True." He tightened his hand where Paul's had been. "I want to."

Paul groaned. "Want to what?"

"I want to suck your cock." Bravery surged through him. It felt great to admit his desires after holding them in for so long. "Then I want to fuck you."

Paul tensed. His hands clenched at his sides. "Maybe. Let's see how you do with my dick in your mouth then maybe."

Rex smiled, confidence growing by the moment. "No maybes at all." He winked. "You wanted a night with someone like me...I like to fuck. That okay with you?" He pointed Paul's cock toward the ceiling and licked the head. "Not bad...a little salty, but overall I like it." A garbled sound greeted his announcement. But no denial.

Resting his elbows on the bed, he bent to his task. He tried to remember what he liked and what the other man had done, but all he could think of was the elation at living his fantasy. He took as much of the dick in his mouth as he could, sucking his cheeks tight around it. Licking under the head and down the big vein, he learned the texture of another man.

Satin skin stretched over steel, heat and musk and a throbbing pulse. Life. He'd never felt so close to any of the women in his bed, never felt such a desire to please.

Paul moaned, and the sound rolled down Rex's spine. He continued his exploration of new territory, lifting and weighing the testicles in his hand then letting his fingers drift behind them to the perineum and, when fingers dug into his shoulders, he abandoned his quest and focused on the throbbing cock in his mouth.

The thrill and heat. The delight at the rumbles and groans when he sucked harder, trying to draw the semen from the man's balls. What a sense of power.... *I guess my expectations were low.*

"Ohhh." Paul's legs tensed. "I'm going to come."

Rex buried his face in his groin, taking him as deeply into his throat as he could. Hot fluid shot into his mouth. He swallowed what he could, but some dribbled from between his lips. Once it stopped gushing, he relaxed, still holding the distended flesh in his mouth as it softened.

Paul tugged him away and pulled him to his side. They wrapped their arms around each other and held on as if they feared they would be pulled apart by an outside force. Rex chuckled.

"What?" Paul stroked his hair and Rex melted under his touch.

"Your mother already thinks I'm a bad influence. She's going to hate me if she ever finds out about this."

They both laughed, too hard for the light joke, but it tapered off, leaving them in silence. Rex flipped over and Paul spooned him, tucking him against his muscled chest. They lay for awhile as the room darkened around them. Paul's whole family would hate him—if they were to carry the relationship home.

"What are you thinking?" Warm breath brushed his shoulder.

"I'm thinking, what if someone finds out?"

Paul sat up and dragged Rex across his lap. Clear blue eyes pierced him. "I don't know what to think, what to say."

No kidding. His own mother and sister were more supportive, and he still didn't believe they would accept the two of them as a couple. "I don't either, but we have all the rest of tonight here in this tropical paradise. Let's enjoy that and let tomorrow and the day after take care of themselves."

Paul nodded, toying with a lock of his hair. "I can do that. But we will have to make some hard decisions before we go home."

"Let's at least wait until morning before we worry about it. I still have a lot of plans for you and I intend to enjoy our date."

Paul brightened. "Works for me...want to share your ideas?"

Do I ever.

Chapter Five

$\mathcal{D}$espite, or perhaps because of the emotional load they'd released, a couple of hours disappeared in sleep. Paul woke to an errant ray of moonlight drifting across their bed from an uncurtained window. He stretched and glanced over his shoulder. Rex lay on his back, an arm thrown over his head.

With the covers shoved down, Paul had the opportunity to study his new lover's physique. Funny that his oldest friend could be his new anything. Tangled in the sheets, Rex's legs reflected the miles of mountains he strode in his work when not on horseback. His strong thighs, muscular calves, long feet...was there an inch of him that didn't shout "fit"?

Firemen were supposed to be strong, but Rex left him in the shadows. When they hiked together, Paul had to hustle to keep up. Something he both hated and loved about the man—his own competitive spirit was continually challenged. No other could do that. Perhaps that was one explanation for his desire for the man he'd known for so long.

Maybe his interest wasn't entirely sexual, despite the incredible rush of their earlier play.

Paul's gaze rested on Rex's cock, half-erect even in sleep. His own twitched in response and the examination ended. He leaned closer, running his tongue over his lips. They had already crossed the line to blow jobs.

How far would things go?

If they were to take the relationship all the way, could they tell their families in the most conservative town anywhere near the Bay area? If they carried their connection back home, they would either have to keep it secret or move and get new jobs. Not because they'd be fired but because their relatives would make their lives hell. Rex's father had been mayor for three terms, elected on the promise to keep old-fashioned values alive. Paul's adoptive parents attended a church so strict, they didn't even own a television.

No, their choice could affect many people beyond themselves. Paul hadn't taken any of that into consideration when making arrangements...but he suspected Rex had.

Their date took place far from home, where nobody would ever know. Rex clearly planned to make this a one-night stand. Paul had intended the night to be a preliminary, to find out if a man could do it for him and if he could get his lustful thoughts out of his system before approaching Rex. Things had sped out of control.

Paul eased from the bed, and crept to the kitchen where he poured a glass of water and gulped it, the cool liquid soothing his dry throat. The need to make a decision weighed heavy. Years of meaningless hookups faded into obscurity. Beautiful girls who wanted more but didn't get it from him. A few had insisted something was wrong with him and he'd begun to agree. Doubted he'd had a heart at all.

The moonlight streamed across the floor, a silvery pathway to the glass doors. Altogether a beautiful night, perfect to lounge around and make love.

But it wouldn't be making love, would it? It was just a one-night stand, even if the joker who never cared if the women who warmed his bed walked away learned he did have a heart—one that broke at the knowledge he'd found what he really loved—and was about to lose it again. Along with their friendship, because it wouldn't be enough anymore.

Paul headed for the bedroom and images of their night flooded his mind. None of the girls he'd ever been with could compare to the ecstasy he'd achieved in Rex's arms. And they'd only begun to explore the things they could do together. He'd been afraid his lack of experience would be a problem when the reality was much more serious.

He'd fallen in love. Not just now, although the emotion felt new. The love had grown throughout the years they'd known one another. He finally understood the depth of his feelings. Home lay where Rex spent his time, and Andie as well. In their presence, he could let the stress of his job go. The memories of a heartbroken homeowner who had lost everything after a fire. Another conflagration, leaving miles of blackened trees, or worse, the time he'd watched a house burn to the ground with someone in it because they couldn't get past a wall of flames.

They kept him sane. And they deserved one another. Rex and Andie, it kept coming back to that. His affection would have to come from afar.

Grabbing his clothes, Paul shoved his feet into his flip flops. Rex still lay asleep. On impulse, he tugged the sheet from the bottom of the bed and covered him.

Paul returned to the front door and strode down the path to the beach. Never looking back.

He could take the boat to the big island and then send someone back for Rex. Then he could hop on a small plane and be moved out before Rex caught up to him. Another session like the one earlier would make it impossible to leave. Breaking into a run, he reached the edge of the trees. *Sorry, buddy. I'll miss you.*

Rex woke in the darkness to nature's call. Returning from the bathroom, he remembered the night before and his heart surged. But the other side of the bed was empty. The side where Paul belonged.

The surety warmed him. Quelled by the need to find out where Paul went. Rex reached for his clothes and decided to shine it. Only the two of them were on the island—and they had gone beyond nakedness being a problem. The next thing to a nudist anyway, Paul would appreciate his daring.

Out on the deserted deck, unease began to creep up. Would Paul have gone swimming so early? As his confidence waned, Rex stopped in the bedroom and pulled on his shorts, then his shirt.

He'd thought their sex pretty astounding, but then he had far less to compare it with than Paul with his many conquests. All those women, few returning more than once or twice. What had he said to scare him away?

A boat motor started up in the distance. Heat flooded his cheeks. While he'd been projecting a lifetime together, Paul had never implied as much. *I came on too strong. Drove him away.* He went back inside for his things. Paul would send someone for him. Then he'd go home and pack. Request a transfer and maybe stay with Andie while he waited for it to come through.

God forbid she should ever find out what happened.

Sliding the glass door closed cut off the sound of the boat taking Paul to Grand Turk. A shower would rinse the lingering scent of their lovemaking from Rex's skin. Nearly twenty years of friendship gone in one stupid move.

Rex stood under the spray a long time before reaching for the soap, ignoring the laminated notice on the tile wall urging guests to conserve water. He couldn't wash away stupidity, but he could at least be clean.

The shower door slid open and he jumped, grabbing the showerhead before he went down.

"Want some help with that?"

Relief sagged his tense shoulders then they tightened again. "I thought you left."

Paul paused with one leg still in his shorts. "Oh, you noticed, huh?"

Rex dug his nails into the bar of soap. "Yeah, it's not that big a house. And I heard the boat."

"I left because I realized you intended this to be a one-night thing away from home where nobody knows us." Paul cleared his throat and stepped into the shower. "And I wanted more."

Rex tried to process his statement. "More? Another night?" *Don't get too excited. Remember, this is love 'em and leave 'em Paul.*

Paul pried the soap from his hands and rubbed it between his palms. "No, you idiot. I want more, *more*. And I came back to try to convince you." He worked up a lather and dropped the bar into the dish. "But if I can't, I'll take what I can get, even if it's only today."

Rex parted his lips to reply but drew in a hissing breath as Paul rubbed lather over his chest. He stood still, while each square inch of skin burst to life under Paul's touch. Blood fled from his brain to harden his dick until he feared he'd explode before anything happened.

"So what do you think? More of the same?" Paul smoothed his hands up Rex's shoulders and wrapped his arms around him, tugging him close. He nipped the side of his neck and whispered in his ear, his warm breath sending heat flaring. "Or maybe we can try something else?"

Rex's knees buckled, only Paul's strength keeping him upright. *Dear God.* "It's almost morning. They'll be picking us up in a few hours."

"I radioed and got us the island for another night." His lips descended in a searing kiss, tongue plundering for long moments before he pulled back. "I figured if this was a one-time thing, I might be able to talk you into a little longer. And if not...."

Rex choked, his throat too tight with emotion to squeeze out a word. Paul studied his face with a frown.

"But you can just call or take the boat and leave." He hugged Rex tight again and spoke low. "I don't want anything we do here to ruin our friendship. I don't want to have to go on without you."

Rex steadied his legs and stepped out of the shower, while Paul watched him go, a crease between his brows. "No chance of that, Paul. We're a team. Always have been, always will be." He winked. "And I'm taking you up on that offer."

"Offer?"

"For something else." He moved to the doorway. "Last man in bed is the bottom." Dashing down the hall, he heard cursing from behind him and laughed. His heart floated in his chest, worries drifting away like clouds.

Paul's erection dropped halfway. He'd never expected to be on the bottom the first time. Rather he'd expected to take the dominant role as he did with the women in his life. But Rex was not a girl, and Paul didn't lead him around.

Rex's voice echoed from the bedroom. "You coming or what?"

Coming.... "Not coming yet." He left the shower behind and grabbed a towel to wipe off water droplets as he walked. "But if you plan to fuck me, you'd damn well better make sure I come, or your ass is mine."

Rex knelt on the bed, a string of condom packets dangling in his grip. "I'll do whatever it takes."

Paul blinked. "How many times...?" His heart pounded but his dick hardened. Chiseled muscles and a twenty-four hour beard shadow lent his friend a wild look that somehow appealed. Reminded him of their camping trips and how he'd thought a tent would make a good place for sex.

Rex shrugged. "Like I said, I'll do whatever it takes. It's a hard job, but somebody has to accomplish it." He dropped the condoms and held out his arms and Paul joined him on the bed, kneeling as well, their torsos and groins lined up. He wrapped his arms around Rex's waist and linked his fingers behind him, holding him close. Their cocks rubbed together, a tantalizing sensation.

"Whoa, that's new."

Rex ground into him. "It's all new." He dipped his head and took Paul's lips, kissing and sucking, plundering with his tongue. A leader in their hikes, the person who made sure the house didn't fall to pieces, his command in the bedroom superseded everything else. And Paul, to his shock, liked it. A lot.

In fact, his fears about being any good with another man melted before Rex's take-charge attitude. Maybe being on the bottom wouldn't be so bad after all. Except.... He leaned back. "Try not to hurt me too much."

Rex lay on the bed and drew him down beside him. Holding Paul's face in his palms, he met his gaze. "I don't want this to be a one-time thing either." He kissed him again, deeply and tenderly. "So if you'd rather wait to explore the anal side of sex until another time, I'm fine with that." He pecked him on the nose. "But today or in a year—I go first. I won."

Paul jerked back, outraged and sizzling with passion. "You cheated!"

Rex's slow smile made his heart pound and his dick throb. "I said I'd do whatever it takes."

"To make me come."

Rex grabbed Paul's cock and used it to pull him nearer. "That, too." He closed his fist and stroked, hard and tight, the way no woman ever had. The way he did himself, but from another angle that sent him soaring.

"Where the hell did you learn to do that?"

Rex choked out a laugh and glanced at his lap. "Where do you think? You gonna watch or participate?"

Paul wrapped his hand around Rex's dick, rubbing the way he liked, gratified at the groan he earned. He rocked his hips into the enveloping touch, trying to keep his own motion up while flying high on the incredible pleasure he received.

Too soon, Rex urged him onto his back and knelt between his legs. "If you want to try it, we can take it slow.

Paul nodded and lay still, allowing him to take the lead. Again. Always? Probably not, but fine for now.

"Stay where you are."

A few drawers banged before the other man slid back in between his knees. "I found the lube. Ready?"

Paul nodded and drew his knees to his chest. Half afraid to

watch, he was scared not to. He could be aroused by a man, but he still had no idea what he was doing. Maybe Rex had a better idea.

Rex bent to take his cock in his mouth and sucked hard. Paul gasped. *So good, so incredibly good.* He arched his back, wanting more, but a chill sensation by his ass alarmed him.

Rex lifted his head. "One finger, just one, at first. I don't want to rush things." His eyes gleamed. "I don't want to hurt you. Too much."

"Comforting." But somehow, as a single digit sank past the tight ring of muscle, his fear slipped away. Desire burned fierce and hot. He wanted that cock in his ass. "More." A second finger, then the two spreading apart, stretching. Hardly any pain...some sting soon erased by a rush of pleasure.

Rex sucked his cock in again, running his tongue up and down the sides and passion tore through Paul's veins. The fingers, the tight mouth. He was going to....

"Stop!"

Rex's head lifted, his brow furrowed. "You don't like it?"

"I like it, but if you don't fuck me now, I'll come and maybe then I will change my mind about having that giant dick in my ass. Just do it."

"If you're sure." Rex moved backward, dragging Paul with him. "But tell me if I do anything wrong."

"How the hell would I know?"

Rex shrugged and reached for a condom. "Okay, then tell me if I do something that hurts more than you think it should. There's no doctor on the island if I damage you."

"The blind leading the blind," Paul muttered. "Just remember, you promised me an orgasm, too. I hear men are selfish in the bedroom."

"Maybe you are, my friend." Rex lubed his sheathed dick and scooped up more with his fingers. He rubbed it around and into Paul's hole and shrugged. "But I never leave anyone hanging. It's a policy of mine."

"Good to know." A better man than him. "Just do it, before I chicken out." Clasping his knees, he held them to his chest. The sight of that dick, glistening in the last of the moonlight, would send him into fits if Rex waited any longer. How the hell could that giant stick fit up his ass?

Rex climbed on the bed and knelt between his legs. "Wish me luck."

Paul stared. "If it's gonna take luck, maybe I've changed my mind."

"Nope, too late." And as Paul clenched, the slippery cock prodded his hole.

"Relax, or I am pretty sure I'll hurt you." Rex's breathing sharpened. "That's it, buddy."

Paul tried hard to unclench and as soon as he did, the head slipped past the ring of muscles. And it hurt. God, it hurt. Stinging, burning pain. Panic set in and he tried to lower his legs.

Rex stilled, placing his palms on the underside of his thighs, keeping them in the air. "Easy. Tell me when you're ready." Once he wasn't moving, the pain dissipated and lust returned.

"Now, do it."

Rex pulled back and pushed in farther each time, his breath harsh, whistling out through clenched teeth. After a moment it didn't hurt as much. He bucked his hips, wanting all of it, focused on the intent expression on his friend's face, the parted lips and blazing eyes.

In, out. Surging against him. Rex. The culmination of desire. The closest he could get to the other man. His friend. His lover. The ache in his ass blended into pleasure, a deeper, more intense sensation than he'd experienced before. *So good.* On instinct, Paul reached for his own junk and rubbed. The cock surged inside him. Too much, too good. "I'm going to come." Fluid spurted between his fingers and coated their bellies. He let go and grabbed Rex's shoulders, holding tight as the other man pumped once, twice, three times more and froze, a grimace of ecstasy twisting his face. He retreated one final time, all the way out. Paul sagged.

Rex let go of Paul's legs and eased them down before he disappeared into the bathroom and returned with a damp washcloth. He helped Paul clean up then fell to the bed beside him, holding him close. They lay like that while the sky outside lightened, and for a long time after that before rising to make breakfast.

Still, they hadn't said a word. But, making meals together had become second nature. When they sat down at the table on the patio with eggs and bacon and coffee, the day was well under way. Closer to lunch than breakfast time. Birds sang and the tropical breeze ruffled Rex's hair.

He struggled to think of what to say. Words seemed inadequate for what they'd experienced together. Had they lost their friendship in lovemaking? Watching Rex shovel eggs in his mouth, he didn't think so. They had added another dimension to it, but there would be no going back.

"I always thought you'd marry Andie," he finally said.

"Yeah, me too. Or rather, that you would."

Paul's mind couldn't wrap around their night, even, but still he struggled to hold onto their world as he knew it. "Well, I guess we have enough to think about now."

Rex nodded. "One step at a time, buddy."

"Yeah. One step at a time."

~ABOUT THE AUTHOR~

Kate Richards is a Southern California native who is fond of the beach, the mountains and the desert, which works very well since they are all a short drive away. She is also an incurable romantic who got married to her internet-met sweetie in Las Vegas and considers it a great city for lovers.

You can visit Kate at:
www.katerichards.wordpress.com

www.ingramcontent.com/pod-product-compliance
Lightning Source LLC
Chambersburg PA
CBHW071134170626
46809CB00002B/608